E. J. Sanborn

Dramas

E. J. Sanborn

Dramas

ISBN/EAN: 9783337341671

Printed in Europe, USA, Canada, Australia, Japan

Cover: Foto ©Andreas Hilbeck / pixelio.de

More available books at **www.hansebooks.com**

DRAMAS

BY

E. J. AND A. W. SANBORN

COMFORT IN A CORNER

THE ROGUES' MIRROR

Boston

J. G. CUPPLES COMPANY, PUBLISHERS

250 BOYLSTON STREET

COMFORT IN A CORNER.

By E. J. Sanborn.

THE ROGUES' MIRROR.

By A. W. Sanborn.

Mr. Lee. What's the noise?
Con. Like as the leaves
Were tumbled over, and with their rustle
The birds set up a twitter. The east wind
Blows morning this way, which is still their key
To wake them up to song.
Mr. Lee. No, no, I think
They have a querulous and shrill-sounding note.
Con. Yes, sure it is no song, but the harsh voice
Of their displeasure. They may be disturbed
By some one coming hither. If I call
No one will hear. No one else does to-night
Take leave his bed.
Mr. Lee. Yes, call.
Con. Hello! Hello!
Lance (*from a distance*). Ho! where are you?
Mr. Lee. Ahead here in a hollow.
Con. Right on.
Lance. Your voices go about.
Con. Here, here!

Enter LANCE.

Lance. How these sounds beat around!
Con. We spoke but softly.
A louder sound flies into echoes, which
Come from all sides at once.
Lance. This place is fit,
And far, and good for secrets.
Con. There was no need
To come here; least of bothering you,
But Martin feared some one would see, and after
Store it against us. Gossip is a hoarder
That puts to interest for a bad use.
Lance. Ay, looks out for the winter.
Con. That's her caper.
Lance. It shall be a cold day before she knows
My business, yet 'twere almost as well
To do in her face what she will unpack
If done in mildew. She does ever pry
About her feet, and like a hog, pokes up
The dung and slough of reputation. But

If there is one that's bold enough to soar
Above her trough, she cannot for her appetite
Reach such a person.   So secrecy betrays
More than it hides, and worst betrays itself.
That is of the face, but carefulness here
Is well enough.
    Mr. Lee.   I am glad you approve me ;
For a friend's praise is doubly sweet.
    Lance.   'Tis better,
I think, to hear that unfamiliar name,
A bygone tune to me.   I have been roving,
And little used to it, yet I can whistle
Snatches and bars of friendship here and there,
Like here's a golden act, done to the tune
Of generosity, or there's a quaver
Of a kind fellow, all vague as the music
Without a name.
    Mr. Lee.   This of ours shall be lasting.
    Lance. I hope so.   Call me friend and use me so ;
I will be that to every man.
    Con.   We know
Your sympathy for us, or we would not
Have put into your hands, or more your heart,
Our evil situation.   We do need
A man of judgment, but more loving friends.
We know you have the first ; seeing your face
Who could not read you?   Sagacity is such,
Dressed up in fury, no one need to miss it.
But friendship and affection, being calmer
And led to privacy, are not so open.
Here is where we need the brevity of action,
Which will most try you.
    Lance.   Oh, I have a heart
For pitiableness.   I knew your sadness,
But dared not broach it to you, because you
Kept from me.   I have heard of secret sorrows
Which take offense.   Although I watched you all,
Both you and your father, and you also, Conway,
I was an onlooker, ready to become
Judge at appeal.   How can I help you on?
Oh! what are the particulars?

Mr. Lee.   'Tis bitter
For me to tell you. If you have had dealings
Or passages of business with my father,
You know his ways.
    Lance.   I' faith I do.
    Mr. Lee.   And then you know no good of.
    Lance.   I' faith I do not.
    Mr. Lee. That's the short of it. He's become a judge,
And peers down on the traffic, or pretends
To give his time to justice, but puts me
In charge of his affairs. So he gives out
A lie, which is made public and goes round
The circle of his creditors. They with banners
Of hope come flying up to me, all mortgages,
That run to a foreclosure, or the like.
I, who would gladly grant them anything,
By make of nature, must wet their bright colors,
And flat refuse all pity. He was made
Of a harder kind from me, but worse cut out,
I think. Oh! it does break my heart to see
These folks in want, but I cannot give them
The remedy even of tears. They come and go
Around me like a post set up for runners.
And I stare at my feet, look through the window,
Or anywhere but in their humble eyes,
Which do light on me with the force of truth
Pointed with pity. Some with rugged fierceness .
Bite at me, but they fall on empty courage
And nothing to return. I am a coward
At their looks. Then come what, come will, I'll be
No longer the thin cloth of decency
Between my father and the proper world.
Those who owe him shall beg of him, not me,
And give him blame. Now if a lean-worked farmer
Asks time and time, he speaks with a bland smile
As you could paint with the fine brush of your fancy;
Tells him sweetly, he is a generous man,
But that withal, his young son has his moneys,
And looks to them. Yet he will recommend
Him to be light. Then hie to me they come,
But e'er their post, I have a sharp reproof

Of their demand, and bitterly deny them.
By this I get hate, scorn, open reproach,
So that I may not take the mellow air,
Except in the deep woods, but I am set on
With slurs and hints where two can get together;
But never one alone, as I have noted
Loneliness makes us all friends. But my father
Bears off the palm for an easy gentleman.
I cannot bear this longer and endure
The hate of all good men. I've had a mind,
Which was not half a mind, to end myself;
Then I would think better. Oh, the brook
Of youth runs muddy!
  Lance.   Oh! I feel for you.
  Mr. Lee. Is't not unnatural?
  Lance.   Yes, what is this gold?
All pelted o'er with dirt.. There's not a man
Looks at it rightly. First for independence
We yearn to get, then this obtained, pile up
For power, which got, we go on scrambling.
'Tis plain there is no definition to it.
  Con. No, the fact is reason enough.
  Lance. ·   'Twas not
Ten hours ago I saw your father draw
His silken money between his thumb and finger.
He whetted them meanwhile to get its flavor,
And found it sweet. His lips were puckered up
Into a song, as fair as birds could sing.
When I came in, said he, *What a fine day!*
Though the sun had not seen earth a week,
And clouds were gadding round. It is the heart
That makes the weather, and money the heart,
At least in him. He has more joy in grubbing
Pennies than saving souls. You would have said it
By taking a look at him.
  Con.   That's not the worst he's done by me.
  Lance. Ay, he held you in ward.
  Con. For five years, and as you know, promised me
His only daughter, Julia. He went
The way of guardians, and robbed my income;
Turns me out of the promise, now of age,

And gives her hand to our friend Harry Buel.
. But children differ where parents most agree,
And they love not each other. She does cling
To me; his fancy's touched by Jane,
So 'twould be a happy company, if we
Could bring about our love.
 Lance.   Hum, to that end
You want my helps and comfort.
 Con.   That's our case.
 Mr. Lee. What's your advice?
 Lance.   Of a positive sort.
It shall commit both you and me, for mark,
Who has my wisdom, must take it for proof
That they see no way out, but put themselves
Upon my word entire. I hold it cheap
To bandy round advice, and ne'er do I,
Unless it is bespoken.
 Mr. Lee. Go on Lance,
You are well informed about us.
 Con.   We'll abide by you.
 Lance. It hurts me to be so nice with you.
 Mr. Lee. No, that's a natural pride, but our good sense
Prohibits us from asking and refusing.
 Lance. It seems like bold discourtesy, I own it.
But how many ask my services, and leave
To follow their own bent. Such love their woes
Too well to cure them.
 Con.   Oh, be sure of us,
We are no such.
 Lance. Then first I speak from knowledge,
That should be first to every speaking, so
Depend upon my years. I have been skipper
And cargo to your father this long time;
And doubly know him. First he has a nature
Without appeal. There will no easy means
Pass with him. He did use me like a cur,
Until I got the wind of his transactions;
But mark, their sins make men uncommon fair.
Now if I ope my mouth to spit, he starts
For fear I ask a bribe. What a fine life
To lead with mutual sinners, where no one
Could gossip o'er his neighbor.

Mr. Lee.   Yes, a jail life.
Con.   Why no!   Jail birds are of different feathers,
And there is no equality in sin.
This vanity plumes her loose quills in prison,
And lives above her mates.
   Mr. Lee.   Well, but the point.
Lance.   The truth is, secrets kept are always gold,
But when let out are so much good coin spent
In that damned luxury of blabbing; I
Being in his business, know his knavery
And all his native nature.   From his harshness
I judge you can do nothing short but leave him,
And go outright.   My vessel is a refuge
For all of you at once, and soon I follow
The current on my last trip down to Memphis.
You can all bide with me a time, as 'twere
Passengers on their way.   When you are married
Matters will come to an arrangement, and
Martin will shame his father, at least he
Will let nothing out for his pride, but learn
A lesson.
   Mr. Lee.   That's comfortable advice.
   Con.   The sweetest I could hear.
   Lance.   Then you will with me?
   Con.   Yes, to th' ends of the earth.   I am no lover
Of mincing tiptoe and right merry walk,
Such as do swagger the dance beneath the moon
Of ivory April or October, when,
However rantingly the lady of the night,
Through swinging windows at the harvest home,
O'er merry huskers and gay laughter wheels.
Well, then, I'm no such fellow as does trip
The fashion of a love, but when it comes
To her possession at a tiny risk,
Grow cold as ice, or for some penny forfeit
Or breach of custom, give up a darling woman.
This custom is a whip laid on our backs,
Which we endure in selfish hope; at last
We can hit others with it.   I will neither
Use it against the world, and in that hope,
As every horse is of his master's kind,

Look for indulgence. But they shall not rot
Or rust my temper. If they gossip o'er me,
I will not mind them.
   Mr. Lee.   That's easy to say
Here in the forest's face. But if you come
To bear the scorn of fools, there is no courage,
At least in honest men to bear you out.
They run from their disgrace. Only base knaves
Can. make familiar with her. I'll away
And flee my insults.
   Con.   That is settled on,
And best for all of us.
    Lance.   Oh, wisdom!
    Mr. Lee.   What!
    Lance. I was but thinking how unapt it is
To see a pate so young, so wise.
    Con. No! No!
My wisdom's not a mention, but I cannot go wrong
While I have you and such sweet timely friends
To mix my brine of life with milk of kindness.
    Lance.   You do repay me and leave me in debt.
A friend's praise covers up a thousand faults.
Come, say no more. Your love is in arrear,
And on the morning wears. Short time ago
Some village clock beat three and even now --
Hark! hark! A rival bell like peevish men
Chides out late discontent. Shall we break up,
If there's no more, and at a future time
Fix our particulars?
    Mr. Lee.   Yes, this fog chokes me:
The river breathes it up. Such exhalations
Climb to the summit. We had best indoors
And shut our windows, e'er the morning lights.
    Lance. Good-night.
    Con.   Good-morning, that is more pleasant.
    Mr. Lee. No, good for all times. (*Exeunt Martin
Lee and Conway.*)
    Lance. Now, as I live there are some honest fellows
among mankind, right true, right independent, and right
silly in their conceits. Well, before I am done, they shall
be farther foolish, and shall not live to repent it. The

old dotard, his father, has a great sum by him, as I did count. That is plain, for I saw it with my own eyes. It would be no very hard thing to lay hold of it, and put the blame on them, as they will leave on a sudden. I can make him credit that they are not with me, but gone somewhere else. Then, if I put them out of the way, like I have better before them, all proof against me will be wiped out. If I have done this before, why can I not do it again? Those last immigrants were easy prey, but too poor. I will try them, as I live, as I live. Two such custards were never set before me, but they must go the way of all flesh. How late it is. Did I not bury a man here for company? — the very spot, and he was a rogue. I will lie here till morning. A pillow would not come amiss, but I can rest in a hollow. Ho, I must not sleep, I must say a prayer. What a godly place this is for St. Howler, the episcoper. A tree for a belfry, a stump for a clerk, a log for a bishop. Borrow a voice of the wind for your clerk and the remainder. I must rest for to-morrow. A bit of this will do it. (*Takes from a vial.*) Now my dreams will be lofty. (*Lies down.*)

SCENE II.— *In a cross-road.*

Enter JUSTICE LEE.

Justice Lee. The devil take highways. On my soul I wish he would. and lose half of his fare for doubling and twisting. This main road is every man's servant and calls at every man's door. If I had been as wise as I was stingy, I would have bribed the surveyor to run it plumb from the town to my gate. Now I must jog half a mile round or take this path. Some beggar first trod it, and all the world has since followed him; a lazy beggar and a thrifty world in its own estimate. What's to hinder me from going? The path is as straight as if the plummet bee, the yellow surveyor of nature, had lined it, and nothing very rocky. In fact sheep are better road choosers than men. Then for a brave man this has no fear, but for a coward he might turn him back. Oh, damn my hired man for a lousy knave! If he had come, I need not walk in meditation far. But bravery cares for nothing, not even its own kind. Pluck up, pluck up, there's nothing to fear! There is no robber; nor if there were, I have no cash, except a couple of eagles in my pocket, and four or five more, now methinks. Well that's no account for a brave man. If thieves were as thick as nettles, your brave man takes the alley and leaves the road to cowards. Then supposing I have three or four pieces, or on a pinch five or six more, who knows but I am a vagrant, and who would rob a beggar and get lice? This is night that dresses all men alike. Then who knows what I am? This is the way, and I will talk to myself for better company, but not a lisp of my money. Why does it clink so at every step? Is it fighting for values? 'Tis but little, one or two. If I stuff my handkerchief between them, can I go on in peace? Or had I not better sing, to drown their song? However, however — (*Sings.*)

> If I were young again
> And you were young with me,
>   We'd all so merry;
> But now old age has ta'en
> My silver tops in fee,
>   I'm still merry, merry.

That's good. Do I know another? A blind man had them for sale and I bought one out of pity. The fellow had the best of me for that I could not cheat his eyes out of his head and he could mine. Loud for an echo now, while on I tramp. (*Enter* H. BUEL.) Ho! what's that? A man, and a right tall one. Down in my pockets lucre. I'll not turn back, but speak.

> A charming lass, she is my love, —

Ah! neighbor, this is a little road for two large men.

H. Buel. (*In disguise.*) Give yourself no heed, friend. There will be one of us out of it e'er long.

Js. Lee. Nay, I beg you stand not aside, but come right on; here's the best passage for a hundred rod.

H. Buel. Nay, I will spring back these laurels and we can pass here.

Js Lee. As it like you; 'twill be foul tomorrow.

H. Buel. Not as foul as you, knave. Take that. (*Strikes him down.*)

Js. Lee. Oh, murder! I'm down.

H. Buel. In truth, and you might have said senseless, if you had sense enough to say it. Let's see. He's stiff and stark, but will come to shortly. If my stick had another foot 'twould be none too long. Now if you try your persuasion again on sweet Jane, I'll visit you in the same spot; but I must straight to my friends to prove a dozen alibis, if any show of assault is patched up against me. (*Exit.*)

SCENE III.— *On a boat.*.

Enter GRIM *and* ALLEN.

Grim. I thought the skipper was not home last night.

Allen. Neither was he, or he would have knocked our heads together for being asleep. That's proof. He could float ashore like any other empty bottle, but not back so quick the same way.

Grim. Now look you! look you! The cable has slipped a turn. If he made a whack to board us last night, he has stepped between the wharf and plank. He's an angle worm in some pike by this time.

Allen. A malt worm would suit him better; but how you will, there's more than one drunken fish in the Ohio. Let us call Stewart, if he knows anything about our skeleton. Hi, there, you bagpipes! where's skipper moonbeam all in melancholy black, as he would attend his own funeral, or was craping himself for every dead knave, for fear 'twas his father.

Enter STEWART, *from below.*

Still asleep, with your eyes shut and your mouth open. Where's the captain?

Stewart. He's off, faith.

Grim. Ay! drowned and off forever. And there's his coffin.

Stewart. God 'a mercy. I have thought of that often. Who will be master now?

Grim. None of us, mind you; but some pampered
monkey that has ne'er had the rough and tar of office, who
has sat o'er his quills and grown fat on warm meals.
But like enough he's not drowned, barring his insides,
which are so perpetual. A gin bottle is more natural in
his mouth than his tongue. But heave ho! catch up the
loop and make things tight. He'll be here presently.
Office-holders never resign, and few die.

Allen. If he were dead in good earnest, I could say a
fair word for him.

Stewart. Keep it to yourself. I would see him first in
his coffin. Such a villain deserves it to be already made
for him. If he has one good trait, 'tis freeness of his
cash, the more as I think 'tis stolen, but otherwise he
deserves to be hanged for the worst poker of mischief I
know of.

Grim. Ay, there are such fashions going about and no
good hints. What's good of a man is spoken, and what's
bad is whispered. This Lance has more said under
breath about him than all the remainder of gossip. I
cannot go into a shop but some half drunken fellow
pulls me by the coat with such things as, *Beware! Grim
hast arms,* and *Be true to thy name.* But when I strike them
for something plain, they fall to generals, for drunken
men and philosophers take the same road.

Allen. Truth, I have been jogged myself, and more of
late than ever. In most by a pilot of Louisville, who
should know the wickedness of all men, he's so bad himself. Such are up to others' crimes for no more than self-
protection. But when I would probe him to the point,
he saith the census-taker has missed the three former
hands on this vessel. Then mum, except as his liquor
talks to him.

Stewart. For that matter the captain is no saint, and
I'd not like to be on the prickly side of him. But, mind
you, these fellows tell more than they can prove. He was
half drunk, which means whole drunk for any man out of
Kentucky. 'Tis good reason you have on your coat,
united we stand, divided we fall, for there's not one of you
can stand alone, at a respectable time.

Allen. Well, so much the better.

Grim. Ay, will you slander religion? You were born out of your state in Missouri. They can make you a man here, and a citizen everywhere else.

Stewart. I'd have taken papers here, if there had been no law against honest men. You know villains will thrive where decent cattle starve.

Allen. All of us are like to starve in this condition. Where's Meg?

Grim. Ay, she can sleep, I'll not wake and want. Meg! Meg! get our breakfast!

Allen. Or we'll break thy maiden-head, virgin, and utterly spoil you with your twenty-seven lawful husbands. Get out, platter!

Stewart. Why call her platter?

Allen. For reason of her variety.

Grim. I'll throw this maul and wake her with the clatter. Now for it. (*Throws mallet.*)

Meg (from below). Let me alone, lads. Cannot let a poor body sleep? There's salt and bacon in the locker, and meal. Make mush.

Grim. Make mush of thee, old sow, unless you come a-deck.

Stewart. Let her alone; you will waste your breath and make no better.

Allen. Not I. She must have been the only daughter of a fat devil. But I have it. Let her think that the skipper, her Moses, her rod is come. Then she will out.

Grim. Ay, go ahead.

Allen. O Meg, hush and quick! We would not have called you, but the skipper is a-coming.

Meg (from below). Oh, oh, oh! Tell him I'm down here for to get his bed ready.

Allen. There's time and again, if you bestir.

Enter MEG.

Meg. Where is he? Where is master?

Grim. It's to be hoped he's in the bottom of the river; but now you have hoisted up, you can go about our mess.

Meg. Oh, you dogs! Your bellies will never be done barking. You could not let a poor woman have a nap, but you pull her out to feed your paunches. Get thy own

and be thankful for it. I'll not make porridge for your
like.

Grim. Nay, bitch. We know that cookery is not your
trade, but you can do it on a pinch.

Stewart. The skipper will tune this loose fiddle.

Allen. She'll play another, and Lance comes.

Meg. And you shall be blabbed for wishing the captain
in the mud. He would make you ache for't, if he served
you like the rogues before you. (*Exit below.*)

Allen. What shall we do for our food, unless I cook it
myself? Though there is hardly nothing in the larder,
rotten potatoes, mangy bacon smoked with the door half
open, and bran which a trader would call meal. As I
live, this skipper puts our bellies into his pockets, for
I have it straight, that is from old Lee's son, that our
allowance is fair and hearty.

Grim. Belike he has gone ashore for solicitation of us
better fare, and that's what wakes him up nights. Oh!
he has our welfare in mind.

Allen. Ay, he will say it, but is it true? A question
not to be asked. Then if 'tis a lie, what's the truth of it?

Grim. Mischief, mischief! He has it always on foot.

Stewart. Well, let him walk on. I will have nothing
to do with him, nor he with me.

Grim. So has many a sparrow said, and been clawed
by the hawk. But, look you, I pounce foremost. If he
handles me as I have suspicion he has men before me, I
will on a night throw a windlass chain over his neck and
put both into the river. He has been before the law on a
charge of murder, ay, and of his boatmen, but in another
state. I have heard the juror could not agree for
sympathy. No twelve sane men can e'er unite, and I
know not why they chose that number, unless goods are
sold more often in that measure. The right for a hanging is one out of a dozen, and in common cases ten.

Stewart. What would you with his little honor, the
cock in the pit?

Grim. Oh, the money-box! I'd hang him for an ex-
ample to the jury. He's nothing but a scarecrow to
frighten the apostles with, or the bird that picks up what
the dog lawyers have left; or, save me, he's that tower that

uo poor man can build to, but is touched easy enough from the high windows of the rich. If they were turned out every year and knocked about on election day, they would be more use than a pair of tongs.

Allen. Why, mate, has any used you scurvily?

Grim. No; and may I be damned if they do. But my stomach calls me to account. Is there nothing in the pantry, that a fire can make into a man?

Allen. The fire is not a thing to do with it. Ask what sort of a cook we have and 'twould be reason, for so as the cook, so is the larder.

Grim. Who will be the spoon in the dough?

Stewart. Not I.

Allen. 'Tis I and no other. I am no pastry by hand but a cook by nature. I have had but little practice, and that not fine, but I can beat your Frenchman in and out at it.

Grim. Come, how did you come by this knack of poisoning nature?

Allen. Why, truth I got a broken leg, being a lumberman in the upper Wisconsin, and was forced of it to lie on my back and watch a lousy Chinaman cater our food. Whereby I fell a-thinking and kicked him out with my able leg, and set up in the pan for myself.

Stewart. That was hard on the Chinese.

Allen. And for a time on the choppers, but I soon got the hang —

Grim. Ay, you deserved nothing better.

Allen. Fie! fie! till I had the hand for't. Then I was counted the best cook in the region. No beggar but would come a mile to try me, and not a one but went away to my honor. I tell you what, I am no Frenchman, no dauber. I lay it down that there is meat, vegetables, and fruit. If you can get only meat, you will live; if only vegetables, you will be best off; if only fruit, you will be pleasant; but no uniting of these in one pie. As I live, a man should eat this, and that, and not this and that together. Oh! if I took to cooking, doctors would have to live on my charity.

Stewart. Stop prating. Methinks that is the skipper coming down the path. Ay, and sober. Now there's mischief afoot.

Grim. Get to work!

Stewart. Hoist! hoist! Now the big ones, lads! (*They lift at bales.*)

Grim. Troll away!

Enter LANCE.

Lance. What's this?

Stewart. All a load for three, sir. 'Tis marked *cotton*, but I think 'tis rum.

Lance. Get along! You make a load out of nothing. All of these should be on the landing before this time. What! but one! You are the three laziest sons of whores! Take that! Now rub thyself. I will kick you a dozen next time.

Grim. An' if you do it, I will empty your knave's skull with this skid. Oh, you murderer! I should save the sheriff a dirty job.

Allen. Ay, lean guts. How many have you stabbed? How many have you robbed, pirate?

Lance. What! I could kill you all if I but put my hand on my hip, and 'twould pass in the law for self-defence.

Grim. I tell you if you make a grab for't, I will break your head and your arm, and let out your gin-soaked brains.

Lance. What does this mean, Stewart? Has Grim gone mad and clean daft?

Stewart. Nay, sir. He was witty enough a while ago.

Grim. And so am not I now. I will tell you a bit of it. First you abuse us most damnably, steal our rations, threaten us with bullets, give us the thanks of kicks, and stand ready drawn if we make a voice against it. Satisfy us with better fare and finer treatment, or we tell tales of you on sworn evidences. You shall swing and waver in the wind for your pains; that's flat.

Lance. Now get this out of thy noddle, Grim. You were always a firm man, an honest man, e'er since I knew you. Why should you come with your dog-eared complaints of starvation? What I have given, I give; what I have not to give, you must ask of his honor, not of me.

Grim. We are hungry, no matter who robs our food.

That's warranted to be no mimic. If 'tis his honor, 'tis not your fault. But there's no question that you abuse us like curs, and that you can make an end of when you will.

Lance. Nay, do not say 'tis I, Grim. 'Tis not I myself, but another man, that mistreats you, under a drug, a pagan influence, as it were. You know that all of us have our fallings off, but in earnest, 'tis out of my nature, and you know it. For the food, I fare as you, but our bellies are no creatures of reason, and the judge has no reason whatsoever in his purse. 'Tis sewn up as tight as a sow's skin, and there's no getting inside, but you rip the swine open. So there's thorn against thorn.

Allen. Then you shall lay this before his honor.

Lance. That I will! and anything else that you have trouble in. Your pay is too small; your quarters are too narrow; and above all, your food is stale. Though I hired you but shortly ago, I can remember you long, for time has no power over our memory, but only things unusual. You deserve more than can here be got; that is, if you will earn it yourselves, for I reckon you have the right quantity of villainy to success. There must needs be a bit to every fortune, and most, the golden secret of silence.

Grim. Ay, we have it. That's all men's without an effort.

Lance. No; 'tis the worst effort in all men. If I were sure that you had made and overcome it, I could put you on the direct way to fortune.

Allen. We are mum.

Stewart. Ay, as still as a wink.

Lance. Keep so, and you are made. Say nothing and you lose nothing. But all your part is to wait and let affairs come to you. Now, let us eat what little we have. Where's Meg? Has the bitch not ordered our rations?

Allen. No; she is asleep.

Lance. Wake her up, the lark of the seven sleepers.

Allen. Meg! Meg! Meg! the captain is here already.

Meg (from below). Oh! boys, let me alone. Let me alone, and go to bed early.

Lance. You butter! I will churn ye. (*Descends, and*

reappears driving Meg.) Now how does that hand feel,
and this one? (*Strikes her.*)

Meg.   Oh! oh! oh! I was sick, master.

Lance.   You will need more medicine of the same kind.

SCENE IV.— *In a wood.*

Enter JULIA LEE *and* JANE DOR.

Jane Dor.   This is so sweet a morning, I could say
No sweeter e'er tuned earth.   What birds do sing
Thorough their shuttles, which anon they play
Amid their web.   Or some that's ready done
Fly to their little ones with insects fluttering
Between their lips.   From which I'd fain imagine
With rosy fancy, that they poured forth love
Instead of bragging song.   What cause is there
To prove the contrary?

Jul. Lee.   I never heard any.
And sure it is in autumn they grow shy
And leave the orchards.   Then in heavy woods
They perch on the low branches, where before,
All high exultant in the tops they sang.
So it would seem that they are made of love.
There is no better stuff to prove a man
Or bird.

Jane Dor.   Oh, yes! If one is true to love
He's true to all the world.

Jul. Lee.   No, but I think
Love is particular and of its kind,
For some are good in that who otherwise
Are false as sin.   Some that wrong all mankind
Except their wives, and very wondrous little
In sympathy, still keep their sweethearts true
As on their marriage eve.

Jane Dor.   Yes, there are such.
At least, I hear of them.   But they are mated
With women of their nature.

Jul. Lee.   But you cannot
For that say love is not a thing alone,
And not dependent e'en upon the world,

The showing, or an afterthought; the first
And grand exception in our nature.
 Jane Dor.   Yes,
In yours, my sweetest Julia. Your lover
Can see that any time. If he were not
The proper pattern of a good young man,
And fully as much loved you as you do him,
I would pity you. You are the fondest child
That father ever darkened, and best love
That e'er made a man glad. Oh! 'tis a shame
You should not wed and wear him. If I ever
Am mother of a daughter, I will tell her
What makes a man, and point out such and such
As well reputed and within my knowledge
Suited for husbandry. Then if she will
To choose another, I'll show forth the faults
And flaws in him. That he is over-prim
In cloth and manner, and appears to me
A fop without and fool within; or spends
Too much in luxury, which makes men selfish,
And thereby worth no woman's consideration.
Also robs from the household, but I count
That secondary. But if she yet would have him
Against my grain, she should, in peace and comfort,
Not given o'er with reproof.
 Jul. Lee.   Oh! if my father
Had done as reasonable by me, I would not
Now be so sad.
 Jane Dor. Well, cast it off, at least
Until you know that they have hit a plan,
As Conway and your brother promised to us.
They will be here ere long, for lovers' watches .
Are always fast, and cannot on the tick
Equal their hearts. We'll not sit here in gloom,
Like sad, unwedded mermaids on their coast,
That I've heard tell. Come, cheer up, and be pleasant.
 Jul. Lee. I will, but there's small joy in common
  pleasures.
Good health and independence are let to us
Each minute, only left, we feel their want.
I'd rather be one moment with my love
Than dreaming of him for an absent month.

Jane Dor. They will be here anon, and should have been
Before this time. Hark! was not that their voices?
We shall have hours instead of moments, love.
    Jul. Lee.   Hither they come.

Enter M. LEE, H. BUEL, *and* CONWAY.

    Con. Ho! are you here?
    Jane Dor.   Yes, before you.
    Con.   Our shame,
But not our will. We were kept late by talking
Among ourselves if you were cold or warm
Unto our plans.
    Jane Dor. Why, we will hear them first.
    H. Buel. No, I will kiss you first.
    Con.   Yes, I'll sit here
Where I can rob you, love, a thousand kisses,
And make of them sweet points unto my discourse.
    H. Buel. Wilt thou the same, Jane?
    Jane Dor.   Oh! a little stinted.
    H. Buel. No, my share is all. (*Kisses her*.)
    Jane Dor. You will leave none for to-morrow, if kisses
Were spent like purses.
    M. Lee.   The morning is going;
We must determine here what we shall do,
And not be idly dallying. We have plans,
If they shall meet with your consent, will work
To match your loves, and get me well away
From my disgraces. Tell the matter to them,
Conway. Maids hear lovers sooner than brothers.
    Con. Nay, help me out.
    M. Lee.   Two at a truth make it
A lie. Go on, and I will listen to you.
    Con. Oh! I fear you will not approve of it.
    Jul. Lee. If 'tis to prove my love, 'tis all foreproved,
Consented, and ordained. I will listen to you
Like one wrapt in your reason.
    Con.   To be short,
We met with Lance, and after full concern,
Devised no better way than the blunt method
Of leaving your father outright, to go
Upon his boat.

Jane Dor.   That's rash.
  Con.   But necessary.
We have tried every honest ways and means
And found but this one.   Then the pluck of reason
Calls us to take it.   Did I not have the promise
Of Julia a year ago or more?
And her false father sat smiling on us,
And all his words were new, and all his eyes
Followed our motions, or at least he said so;
But now, methinks, I can recall the scene,
And in't his face, on which the roads of mirth
Were travelled well, but in sooth his gray eyes
Sat grim as milestones, which you could not pass
But you must look at them, to see how far
In his good graces you had journeyed on;
Deep dens of policy, and all for what?
To break our hearts, which at that time he hoped
Were firmly locked with the key of love.
That was his very words.
  Jul. Lee.   Oh! this was once,
But he persuades me now, that 'tis no love.
But maiden fancy that possesses me,   -
And quotes a thousand cases where young girls
Have wed disaster.   Thus stands opposite
And shakes his finger at me, which does waver
As grass blown by an angry gust of wind;
And calls up like lawyers for precedents
All unknown, barbarous bygones.   It were best
To take direct, plain things to argue on,
Instead of generations I know not,
All maidens of his youth.   So I must either
Call him the liar of these made-up proofs,
Or else allow they are my own condition,
Which I will not.   But Conway, here's my hand
And pledge, that I will always be with you
In this endeavor.   I am sick of waiting,
Which ever tarries.   He's immovable
And glued to his opinions.
  Con.   What's so quick
To change men's minds as their own lookout, love?
So do not wonder at it.   There's bright time
For us ahead.

H. Buel. But not for me; wise Jane's
So circumspect to take our flight like that.
I would choose her and leave the world; be off,
Away!
   Jane Dor. Fie, Fie!
   H. Buel.   Nay, Jane, in love and truth,
If you will go along with me.
   Jane Dor.   But I
Will not. You should have taken Julia
Instead of me, for she would go with you,
Or the desire of your parents both
Gave let to you to love and live together.
   Jul. Lee. We never were together, or e'er we came
My heart was given away; but the cold closet
Of friendship, that's next mason unto love,
Is always open to you.
   H. Buel.   I enter it,
And may I never go out.
   M. Lee.   What, of friendship?
   H. Buel. Ay, the mild passion.
   M. Lee.   Mild! that's mockery
And parrot's talk. I'd rather cry for crackers
Than take my cue from maudlin auctioneers
Of sound opinion. Friendship is no dove;
And if she were, I'd swap her for an hawk,
Or change acquaintances. Who is my friend
Is none but mine, or he's a whore of friendship;
For 'tis as monitory, dear as love;
And who has more than one friend, if you note it,
Will leave all for himself.
   Jane Dor.   Your friends are scarce.
   M. Lee. So are lovers, that is of proper ways,
For lovers are attracted by the body,
And some by mind; but what does friendship dote
Save the pure, glorious mind? Love has its conquests
At glances of the eyes, but friendship probes
Clear to the bottom of a man; and look you,
He does not pass twixt man and woman, but only
Like as a godly messenger he flies
From man to man, and there's a reason for it.
At least 'tis so, and there must be a reason.

Jul. Lee. One of those more hard to prove than show.

M. Lee. Nay, something all men know but rarely speak.
But haste! I have set time with Lance to-day
To make the stroke and place of our departure,
If you are willing in the event. I know,
Sweet sister, that you are prepared and ready,
But I know not what to say for our Jane.

Jane Dor. If you know not, you know my mind.

M. Lee.   You will not?

H. Buel. Nay, I will answer for her. Oh, my love,
Think on the weary days and wearier nights
That we must lie alone, with our cold thoughts
For bedfellows. Then in each other's company
Before the world, how we must set ourselves
To hard deception, which cannot defy
The eyes of gossip; so all will come out
In secret, and my parents feel the harder
Towards both of us. Secrets are more a sin
Than crimes they cover with those that love us.
Fie on a little wealth; no man is poor
Whose heart is strong, and I doubt that my father
Would disinherit me for so small fault,
Though he has set his soul on Julia
By some connivance with his honor, which
I cannot bottom, or perhaps a whim
To have his way. A reason conquers reason,
But nothing here can beat a prejudice.
Then, love, go with me, for you see that waiting
Will rather make our case stand worse than better.

Jane Dor. No, your father is stubborn clay, and for
            your sake
More than for mine, I am positive to stay.

H. Buel. I tell you he could not disinherit me,
Being an only son, so he must forfeit
To charity, which holds no foot in court to blood,
And all arise to me, save a small pittance
To th' object of his wish, for poverty
Is a poor dog contented with small bones.
Moreover, there's no juror in this county
But would be twelve for me against the church,
Or any of his favors; for all call me Harry,
And I them the like.

Jane Dor. You are the best liked
By every man, and one poor, faithful woman;
Nevertheless, I cannot, cannot love,
For thought of being talked about, both now
And years to come. How will the tooth of gossip
Gnaw into me, and all my crowing enemies
Throw up their heads, e'en in domestic life,
When I become a matron or old dame,
For age does season malice. Then believe me
Our troubles will end joy, if you will wait
For sorrow to pass over.

   M. Lee. I'll be gone.

   H Buel. Ay, we cannot persuade her. I am sadder
Than I have been for months; but where's the captain?

   M. Lee. Oh, on some hill.

   Con. He takes the air like foxes.

   M. Lee. And I cut him off as does the hunter. Farewell. (*Exit.*)

   Jul. Lee. Let us stay longer, while the sun shines fair,
And I will make a wreath of maple leaves,
Laid one above another, with their stems
Piercing their hearts. We'll hear soft-throated birds
Make sweetest music on their tender chords;
And best of all, I'll hear your own sweet voice,
Which is more tender to me than their song.

   Con. Oh, I could stay till evening and beyond;
But that's a time to think on more than others,
For in my recollection 'tis the one
Whereon, say striking eight, I walked with you
This self-same spot, while to our backs the sun
Just disappeared. What happy hours were those!

   Jane Dor. I beg you not to leave them. Oh, remain
And try once more your father's disposition!

   Jul. Lee. 'Tis harsh, unnatural, and will not give
A jot to me.

   Jane Dor. Nay, I have known dull men
Knocked by a fancy. give up all their case,
And clean outdo their former advocate;
For stubbornness walks with the tide, now back
As far as it stepped up. Besides, your father
Hates to see trouble, like all cowardly men,

And runs at tears, but being well away
Forgets them in his comfort. We will make
Your sorrow pangs to him, and try again
The eloquence of pity.

Con. 'Twould be wasted breath.

Jane Dor. Ay, on yourself, which is cheap luxury
And a great consolation.

Con. Nay, I tell you
Who asks with whines will be received with kicks.

Jane Dor. Well, be a beggar of rights and smooth
Your steep demands with show of humbleness.
He will be putty to my fingers.

H. Buel. But I warrant you that he has not a mere
yeasty head. If you ever happened to sound it with a
knot, you would have found it solid to the touch. Ay,
it will echo half a mile and more I believe.

Jul. Lee. What's that to do with my sadness? If to ask
him again will do any good, I am the last to shirk the
hardest of all things,—kneeling. At least it will work no
harm, if there is no hope. I am of a mind to beg him
once again with your comfort, Jane.

Jane Dor. Oh, you have the beauty and the rarer wit
of an angel.

(*Exeunt omnes.*)

ACT II.

Scene I. — *A hill. Enter* M. Lee.

M. Lee. Oh! for a hand, that I might paint my
    thoughts
In image as they rise. Oh! for a hand —
Ho! here he comes. How fare you, Lance?

Lance. Why, sparely, sparely, saving your identity,
sir.

M. Lee. Now what's the matter, captain?

Lance. You are — you are — you are —

M. Lee. Martin Lee. Has the devil possession of
your senses?

Lance. Doubtless my devil has me and entertains me.

God! God! God! You are Lee, and no doubt. That's
a fine name. You have many relatives in China, and I
have known several in Hong Kong. But look you, do
not own them and enter in with them. There's no good
man but is worse off for his kin. But foolery aside,
would you like to travel, young man?

M. Lee. Ay, passing well, Lance.

Lance. So thought I once, and indeed I have wan-
dered far and wide; not, mind you, in tubs like these, but
in tall ships, and in the forecastle, till I was wanted no
more by the merchants. I had become too wise to suit
them. But I am satisfied if they are. Let them make
their balance even and I am no loser.

M. Lee. That were happy.

Lance. Very — for me. Now if you would journey,
whereto?

M. Lee. Oh! the world over.

Lance. Wrong, my kite, wrong. If you know your
own habitation, make up your circuit thus wise. Go not
to the east — to China, Hindoo, or Egypt, or Palestine —
for the people there are stocks and stones; were ever and
will always be so. They are the only people that you may
know by description, because they are so like beasts and
herbs they can be taken in with the eye, and no traveller
I e'er read had more. That is why fools that talk about
them hit them so close. They can paint a dog, but not
a man. Therefore walk not in their dust, but turn to
Europe.

M. Lee. And there shall I find naught but men?

Lance. No, a good sprinkling of dogs, but a paucity
of men here and there, and these be what you are looking
after. If you would go among them, be to the Irish
polite, and to the Scotch praise and quote their songs,
and make a mark especially of Burns. With the English
you must part your tongue. With your gentlemen, praise
nothing but across the channel, as your fine French or
Italians or Austrians, for they can abide nothing British.
But with the merchants and the like, honor naught but
that within the Isle, for they damn all foreign. Although
you may be honey in the ears of all by cursing us Ameri-
cans, for they hate us as nobody else; and now I think
that is the best and certain way.

M. Lee. That's good advice, sir.

Lance. Nothing, nothing; but mind you be cautious with the French. Mount them up as the first in everything, and they will be no more than half satisfied, but if you shall venture on the secondaries you are damned in the opinion of every man among them. As for the Germans, you must swim into their good graces. If you will not drink yourself to a hog, they will think you no man, and, like enough, want to fight you with their swords; but lay your hand on your pistol and cry, " This or nothing!" They will grow civil. They reckon that their scars cannot make them any uglier, but they are clean opposed to taking chances of death. Parley Emmanuel to the learned and they will think you as good as a pupil, but tell them off-hand that German has the easier compounds than the Greek, they will stair you up to heaven, though you know not hardly ten words of German and not a letter of Greek.

M. Lee. You are a comfortable guide, captain. How about the Dutch, both high and low, the Swiss, Russians, Turks, Spanish, and Italians?

Lance. The Italians — hum — I know little of them; but if you happen to be in Naples, and jostle them on the gravel, cry, " *Pardon, monsignors*," or you are like to get a dagger in your ribs. They always carry this furniture of death around with them. Be also not too proud. Dress not too ostentatious and look not too mighty on ill-lit streets, especially of late years. A dirty mess, withal, to the best of my judgment.

M. Lee. I am content to take it, sir, both in what things are now and what's to come. My sister easily came round to our plans. We are made up to it, save Jane, who is more prudent than passionate.

Lance. And she will stay?

M. Lee. Yes.

Lance. Then there will be one woman less, which will mean one less man. That's the way of the world. If you take one you take two.

M. Lee. Have you knowledge what day you will be freighted to start?

Lance. By Friday.

M. Lee. Now I remember, my father mentioned it.
Are the boatmen sealed?

Lance. All with the wax of my wit. (*Exeunt.*)

SCENE II. *The sick-chamber of* JUSTICE LEE.

Enter JANE DOR.

Jane Dor. I'll ope the window, so the morning air
Will blow in on your honor. There's no medicine
An equal to it. How does it affect you?

Js. Lee. Not half as sweet as kisses.

Jane Dor.   Oh, for shame!

Js. Lee. Nay, shame is public property, and we
Will be all private. If I had my legs
I would rob one of you, but this vile sickness
Is not so bad itself as it does keep
Me from your lips.

Jane Dor.   Oh! as I am your nurse —

Js. Lee. Ay, my nurse, love, and therefore 'tis your
    duty
To give me your most sovereign remedy —
A kiss — that carries nothing and takes nothing
Away by it.

Jane Dor. That's more logic than virtue.

Js. Lee. You need not call love by another name
Than love. I hardly knew him till I saw
How pretty he was in you. Maidens before
Have tempted me, but you are the first, Jane,
To make me love for many a long year;
And you are thorny.

Jane Dor.   As maidens should be.

Js. Lee. Why, not so brief. I could hear to your words
Flow o'er the banks of your sweet lips from now
Till evening.

Jane Dor. Your honor has lost your reason.

Js. Lee. I'm gone mad with love of thee, but I should
    hold
A man a fool, and in that way, out of sense
If he could be otherwise.

Jane Dor.   You are insane.

Js. Lee. Who ever heard an insane man make love?
Nay, Jane, I tell you 'tis the loss of it
That drives men mad; and if you do deny me,
I shall go crazy.
    Jane Dor. That's most sad, your honor.
    Js. Lee. And you do know how often lunatics,
If they have loves to dote on, will recover,
Like lamps set in the passages and alleys
Of their dim, wandering minds. But I ne'er knew
A man made wild with love to shake it off
And come back healthy. More often they rush
In to their weapons. I feel at this moment
As I should do the same if you refuse me.
    Jane Dor. Now you are out of tune for good. I know
Not what you rant about; why this large talk
Of consequence and arms. If 'tis a kiss,
Methinks you would load guns for fleas.
    Js. Lee.   O Jane!
    Jane Dor. What! is your honor sick?
    Js. Lee.   Do not imp me,
And piece out my sad phrases. You do know
That soul and body are a lover's fee,
And he will take no less.
    Jane Dor.   Oh! you would have
The sweets of marriage for yourself, and leave me
When you got tired; but I must cling to you
Like dirty clothes, and put aside to wash
When you want clean ones. Thereby are we spoiled,
Being but tender fabrics, but vile men pass muster
Though they do rouse their nights in brothels, ay,
And on rank, sweaty beds pollute themselves.
This is smoothed over with the palm of custom
To a mere wink. You are a wretch to tempt me,
And I should hold myself lower than you
To give the little treasure of a kiss.
    Js. Lee. Now you do me more wrong than an opponent
In politics. My total thought and care
Were of your likings, for I reasoned thus
And thus along; considering your youth,
Which moults it's fancy, like young eagles' pinions,
And goes a better pitch; and that my age,

Though middle and sturdy, is not within years
Young maidens like to linger; it would seem
You would become less fond of me, as time
Ground down your passion.   Then you could.
Leave me for another choice, and none wiser
Than your own lips betray; for I had rather
Give up your bed and heart, than hold them seconds
Without their full consent.   But for my faith
'Tis frozen, and at this late time of life
Can never thaw.   The purest water makes
The purest ice; so was my young stream cleansed,
It could not thicken muddy.
    Jane Dor.   Do you think
Not of the law, the rights, and my good name?
    Js. Lee.   Ay, all of them.   Your fair repute will lose
No color of its fairness, for you know
I am no babbler to boast to common brooks,
That fly their words against what man they meet;
Especially old men, chirping of love.
I'm none of them, but silent, secret, stern,
As you see me.   Scandal could not reach me.
How does my face, my stark propriety
And high position shed their evil rain?
And neath this roof we may enjoy each other,
And let the world blow by.   Come, come! my love.
Oh! do not look at me.   Would you accuse me?
If I do wrong or even speak an evil,
'Tis an infirmity of nature, dear;
The spring beyond my touch, beyond my birth.
We are brought into the world already formed,
Made up, complete, and naught can work us change.
There's an excuse will stand the world in plea,
And but another, how I would convince you
That wickedness is a name and sin a shadow,
Except the injury of our fellowmen.
Law, law! a deep old bag!   What's law to me?
Naught but my prop, and when I have a hold
On anything above, I spurn it out;
Even like the minds of men or love of women,
Let down from heaven; not stayed up from earth.
But come, I wander   Will you give me promise?

I see relentment that looks from your eyes
Upon the floor. My years, like roses on me,
Are weightless flowers.
    Jane Dor.   You speak fair enough.
    Js. Lee. On my faith, Jane.
    Jane Dor.   Faith is weak oaths. Did you
Not promise Julia upon your faith
To wed young Conway; and when you found
A richer groom, rake up old scraps of parlance
Like a true lawyer 'gainst him? How should I
Expect a fairer faith from you than she,
Poor girl, and only daughter Now her cheeks
Have lost all color, though they were before
A morning red. And her complaints come soon
And late a-rapping at mine ears.
    Js. Lee.   Fie, Jane,
Have you been fooled by a silly girl? You are
Too knowing of their nature to be melted
With love-sick tears; Julia will be better
For a slight discipline; for her love is only
A school-girl's fancy, vanished in an hour,
As they do say. A month hence she forgets
That she knew Conway, and will smile as pleasant
As she were in his arms.
    Jane Dor.   Shame, sir, she's sick
And near to die. Such things occur quite often
Upon the moment, and they call them suicide.
At least all but the coroner, who's paid
To plead insanity. If you had eyes
For anything but your own lust, you would
Without a second look, see she was pale
As her own winding-sheet. She has the visage
Of one about to die, a certain flowing
Backward of all her features, which I know
To mark the end of hope. Oh, sir! wake up
To bitterness upon a morning short,
And find her drowned.
    Js. Lee.   Nay, you see it through glasses,
And your love, Jane. 'Tis not as serious
As that, but I may have been casual
In spying it, and rather judged her sadness

By general, which after all fits poorly,
Like waist-coats drawn at lottery. But faith,
Who does not call young people shallow wise,
And try to wade them, where they may prove deep?
If I had looked into her and found out
She took him so to heart, I would as soon
Stabbed in my vitals, as taken her life
Away by pining; could a father think
A girl would be so silly?

    Jane Dor.   I should judge
The contrary, considering your passion,
Which has not the excuse of coltish blood.
Why, but this moment your deep-congested eyes
Did make the maddest love e'er borne through air,
And then, with all, you cannot find excuse
For a darling maid's desires.

    Js. Lee.   I am wrong
And righten it by owning up. O Jane,
Forgive me, and be my penitence!

    Jane Dor. Nay, not a bit, until you dress with promises
Each journeying word.

    Js. Lee.   My word is my oath.
But for the once, I swear they shall be married
According to your wish.

    Jane Dor.   Now you are kind.

    Js. Lee. Wilt thou not be of a kindred sweet?

    Jane Dor. Wait, wait, your honor. You do understand the hardest lesson to learn is from thyself. Mark it.

    Js. Lee. I have it in my note-book.

    Jane Dor. No, keep it in your head; for you can leave your note-book, and by God's special grace not your head. These fellows of copy have naught in their pates; and notes and entries are wasted time withal. Therefore, write this inwardly.

    Js. Lee. Hark, hark! Jane. Is not a step in the hall?

    Jane Dor. A step, but is there a man behind it?

    Js. Lee. Methinks 'tis Lance. Who raps? Come in.

Enter LANCE.

    Lance. Faith you will know me. By my visage I am an exceptional raven. Sorry I am to break in on, to break between, to uncouple, as it were, such good company; but a whisper of your mishap had come to me, and I needs must come round for the sake of old sympathy. But pardon, pardon, have I disturbed this twain philosophy?

Js. Lee. Nay, Lance. Our reflections can keep. Jane was lamenting that Julia did not come to my quarter regards wedlock, for you know she is set on that penniless mast, Conway, or a reed for his strength, but a mast for the sail he carries.

Lance. A deserving young man; a pretty young man. The right mould for any number of grandchildren your daughter can bless you with. If I owned as much good and as few heirs as your honor, I would be looking around for the very shape of a gentleman. He's the right copy to make good heirs out of.

Jane Dor. And mark you, sir, he has the graces and true affections of a lover; and above everything, the regard of Julia. If it were otherwise, or an unequal match, she would die of what the doctors call love-sickness.

Lance. Truly, I have in mind a death of that forlornness, after a long cough. The affliction was none other than my sister, but virtuous, very.

Js. Lee. That's enough, by faith. I would not kill her; I would not strain her a particle. But maiden fancies consort not with father's wisdom, now I'm persuaded. If she takes the man to heart, she will take him to bed, and the devil cannot stop her. Though I wish the cock had his neck wrung for keeping me awake. But look you, after she has him she shall keep him.

Jane Dor. There will be no trouble, your honor.

Js. Lee. Devoutly, devoutly, Jane. If Conway is not a calf, his voice is not like his mother's. But give them fair words and definite promises if you run against either of them. I will be a messenger of good news to sail over the gulf I have late made.

Jane Dor. Fare your bark well. I will go ahead to sound them. (*Exit.*)

Lance. Now what has got into your spout? Are you clean clogged with sentiment? I thought it was agreed your daughter was to wed Harry Buel, and we were to pick his bones.'

Js. Lee. So 'twas, Lance, but I thought not 'twas so sad a case. Julia is worse off for love than most women are for fashion. She has gone into paleness and such folly, which worries me like a nightmare, now Jane has called it to mind.

Lance. Tut, tut!

Js. Lee. Nay, Lance, in all truth. She is by no means in love of Harry, nor Harry of her. I'm persuaded.

Lance. Here's a pinch at both toe and heel.

Js. Lee. No, Lance, and therein is the oddity. Though Harry has no strong feeling for Julia, yet he would wed her for my sake, if I lift a finger. He's that tenderness for me, he will dance to any music I play. I am more than a father to him.

Lance. Very like a deep puzzle, your honor. What's the cause?

Js. Lee. I know not, Lance; but that he is mine I do know. There are those subtile spirits that can lay their affection where they will, and the return will come without asking. I am that resemblance, Lance. He has given to me what his own father has robbed him of. Oh! rest yourself on him. The rub comes on the other part, as it doth always. Oh! the perversity of women.

Lance. 'Tis a great pity, your honor. Why should a girl canker at an even change in mankind? It vexes me. If I spoke homely, I would say your daughter was too fine.

Js. Lee. You are a plummet, Lance.

Lance. But for all you will humor her?

Js. Lee. I cannot help myself. There are more beggars for her than every dollar I rake. I am shot through with petitions. I am accused of her death, and my peace is tormented. Then am I near dead myself, for life is comfort who says to the contrary. Here has Jane been giving me naught but pills of worry, instead of balm for my bruises.

Lance. Have you become a mocking bird to a penny whistle, to talk of death from love? I have known a dozen prim school-girls in my time, who dared death in tears, but were happy enough on their wedding night.

Js. Lee. I could tell another dozen, captain. They are as common as leaves in autumn. It is a musty saying: Give a girl her way and she will take another. This Buel is in an open field, where we may reap at our wills, and if it were not for his hobbly father, I would warrant to glean him in no time. But he must die soon; he must die. He has the crook of damnation in him already for the devil to handle him with. Let's see; he goes on eighty. Hum, another year will end him. Then this son would be as easy as a berry on a bramble. I have a great disposition to do the knot, Lance, spite of the strings.

Lance. That would be a double blessing, but a knotty question.

Js. Lee. Not as I'm persuaded, Lance. I will smooth over this daffodil, for Buel is willing, and Julia must come to it. After she has endorsed this fellow, she will love him better. That has as good outlook as a false face.

Lance. Ay, and a feature behind it. If you buy the land you addressed me on, you must put up a clean fifty thousand. If you purchase but half the timber you will make but half the profit on sale.

Js. Lee. 'Twill stand me a hundred in three years, will it not, Lance?

Lance. Twice that, now that more building is on the gain.

Js. Lee. Fifty, and I can lay my hands on no more than twenty-five. How much may a man own and how little have in medium. All my other ventures are so good I cannot rob certainty for chances. I could borrow, but interests run so high I can make more by lending out. If I can worm the tallow out of Buel as I counted on, the hog might grunt for his pains.

Lance. An easy thing.

Js. Lee. No, the saddest step in my life. If I force Julia to it, there will be no end of sobs and taking on. From a point of policy it shines well, from a point of justice to her it has a fair aspect, but to myself it means no end of discomfort, and that sort of philosophy children prattle. But I will consider. What a pleasure that things decide themselves without thinking. I will let this sit in my mind and the cream will rise to the top of its own accord. Now to our business. Will you load with flour on this trip? The boat has a leak, and a dozen of them for all I know; and the grain might mildew. Had I better not ship in a tighter bottom?

Lance. No, no; if it gets musty, I know enough merchants who never unstop the head, an easy thing. Do you not remember a like case that I took in hand and disposed of?

Js. Lee. Ay, something of a kind; but for a word.

Enter HARRY BUEL.

H. Buel. What! my excuses are all in my face. I did not think to disturb your business, but to find an utterly broken man, as people said. Oh, sir! this happiness lays over my excuses.

Js. Lee. Not so bad, Harry. The gossips always double happenings unless they be something good. A damned, long-armed pickpocket dubbed me knight over the head, but I live lighter.

H. Buel. Oh! give me the shape of the villain, father; the astronomy of his face, and I will lay my finger on this man or that man. I will do an act of love with a matter of duty, and turn deputy to account. What was the time, the spot, the speech, the act, the voice, the color of raiment and length o' the cudgel?

Js. Lee. For the last, Harry, the stick is the most plain, and its length was a good ten yard. You may take a picture of it from my skull, knob for knob and hollow for hollow; the time near ten; the spot a dark, murderous hole; the speech like the knell of death, and the act — oh, I shall not forget it! Out he steps as tall as his shadow and says not a word, but breaks a twig behind me, at which I look over my shoulder, whereat he whisks out a club and passes at my head, but I boldly hit him back and take him fearfully somewhere, for he groans deep and at me with all his might. Then the cudgel takes me from my feet, as if the whole world were on the end of it, and throws me so far to one side he could not find me in the laurel when he looked for my cash.

Lance. Why, did he not rob you?

Js. Lee. Ay, took of me what I had, which was a good sum, as much as I should have given to a thousand beggars.

H. Buel. I will take a memorandum of this. *Done for booty, an assault!* What said you was the amount, father-in-law?

Lance. A thousand pennies, sir deputy.

Js. Lee. Hum, ten plus twenty and five. Add for yourself, Harry.

H. Buel. Now I have it. I will pass it through the maw of the sheriff. We have the clue and we wind and wind. We will trace it into the belly of some fish. Such reckless money-making should have a rope around its neck, for sure it should. If we should hap to catch the rogue, had we not better hang him off-hand?

Lance. Oh, you have cause to feel proud of your son. Now, there are some that would have broken their father-in-law's head. I could name you certain that would not have stickled to do it. Oh, he is a sweet child, your honor; but go hang with such violence, say I. There's likelihood that the thief was a familiar, and knew how hard a blow an elderly man could stand under and live.

H. Buel. I plead my passion for my father and no more excuse. 'Twas love and not hardness of office that made me say such things.

Js. Lee. My poor blessings on you, Harry, which to say most of them have no high standing in heaven. I can read you without logic. You are writ in the print of nobleness. But caution: 'twould be fun for me to try my own case. A rare joke, Harry.

Lance. This is the humor of a cock judge from a chicken lawyer. Let me in you juror and I will make short work of this fellow.

Js. Lee. Nay, captain, I am no revenger now; as odd as it appears, I have no ill feeling against this highwayman. If he were stretched before me, for my soul I could not kick him. What is that longing they call revenge, a thing unknown to me? But if the scamp had robbed my good name, or backbitten my reputation, then I would have had a feeble notion of revenge.

H. Buel. That's a nobility beyond pedigree, and good proof we shall live happy as son and father. If two of a mind quarrel, who can agree?

Js. Lee. Always in peace of mind, son. If greatness has it not, greatness is no comfort. If position is on the thorns, position had best dismount. If a husband has it not, a husband had best live bachelor. I would love better to call you my son-in-law than the moon my kingdom; but if it were disposed by heaven that you were to be my son in fret, I would forego you to my grief. My sweet Julia has sour fancies, Harry. I cannot understand them; nay, they are beyond the understanding of men, but passable to women; for Jane tells me she does pine that she must wed you. Heavenly grace, not that you are not the pattern of a man, but because she is suited with such loose stuff as that Conway. Indeed, you know two garments are a hinder in warm weather. One must be thrown and one worn, whereby she is dressed in this gaudy Conway, and has no mind for fair colors like you; in short she jilts you, Harry.

H. Buel. And this for final?

Js. Lee. No, my boy; do not look so like the inside of doctors' books, where the seven deadly sins are followed by the seventy deadly diseases. I say you, she has an indisposition, but not beyond me, not beyond your own urgency. If she were put to it, she would be your pleasant love, and not a doubt of it, Harry.

H. Buel. Do not force her. I would not have her body if I could not her free will.

Lance. The deputy has it, your honor. You should note the nature of love, the degree of love, and the fitness of love. By this you may know the course of love.

Js. Lee. What is done shall be done for your good, Harry; for the good of all means the blessing of one. I will speak with your father and mother and persuade Julia to my bidding; but how it comes on, a little thing cannot break or bind us, Harry. If I need a good turn, I shall call on you, and if you e'er need the like, come to my bounty.

H. Buel. I hold your love more than that. I must away on the errand. (*Exit.*)

Lance. Our business is coming on well.

Js. Lee. Yes. What's the hurry?

Lance. To hurry up our business.

Js. Lee. Not so fast. Take time; either you or your creditor will die.

Lance. God spare the difference. Better health to you another time. (*Exit.*)

SCENE III. — *The sheriff's inn and street near by.*

Enter LANCE *and* SQUIRE BUEL *at a distance.*

Lance. Here comes a man and I'll ask him the way to the sheriff's office. Old and crooked. Well, old men should have learned politeness, if they have it not in them. By my soul, 'tis old Buel. I would look him in the eye out of curiosity. I have seen him, but he has not me. His reputation is none of the best, and mine is none of the worst. Then we should be friends. But he has a rude name among people, and report never lies. That is second report of long standing. Ha! how he hobbles! how he creeps! There were a picture to set vanity in tears. How do I remember him once. But hush! Good-morning, sir. Can you point me to the sheriff's office?

Sq. Buel. What! what!

Lance. Your good graces and the road to the sheriff.

Sq. Buel. Ahead! ahead! follow your nose.

Lance. Indeed, if 'twere as long as yours, there would be no question, but a binnacle, a straight lead. But as I am strange to this part, will you spare a word? Where abides the law?

Sq. Buel. Oh, you snuff color! I will crack thy head open with this cane.

Lance. Though I am snuff, I am nothing to sneeze at. I could blow out your brains with a good will, if 'twere not against custom.

Sq. Buel. Oh, you shall hear from me.

Lance. The very thing, sir. Let me hear where lives the sheriff.

Sq. Buel. Dog, get out of my sight, or —

Lance. Stop your barking. People are running as your old voice were the cracked bell of doom. I will remember you as long as I live, but forget you presently. Move on. There now. (*Exit* BUEL.) That's good riddance. Straight ahead, did he say? I will walk slowly and keep my eyes out. Not far, not far, I hope; for every family is looking at me behind the shutters. There's a new coon in town. But here's my man, *County Sheriff* hung over a tavern sign-board. Well, I will enter in. It seems the law is set on the shelf. I know this publican of old. (*Enters the bar.*) Gin, please you. (*The sheriff appears.*)

Sheriff. No, as it please you, sir. You may take your pick the world over.

Lance. Then gin the world over. That's a beverage out of fashion. Not brandy, nor whiskey, though they be drinks for a man, but gin for me. As for beer, 'tis vile stuff. We knew nothing of it till your Englishman and weeping German brought it over. While we take strong drinks in small doses, we will be hale and courageous; when we swill it out of hog troughs, we will be of that family. I'll drink to old acquaintances, friend.

Sheriff. Old or new, 'tis all one to me. (*They drink.*)

Lance. No; friendship, like drink, is the better for age. Methought your face was a familiar coin. Do you not recall me?

Sheriff. Hum, no, sir, though yours is a good face, a very honest face, but I think we remember villains longest; for as the world runs, honest men are thickest. Visages become mere circles to me, I see so many. There are my prisoners, my customers and my every-day acquaintances. You were never my prisoner, that's certain; nor my customer before, for I never saw a man could drink the like of gin with you in so short a minute. Then if you know me at all, you know me casually.

Lance. Yes, by an incident, a casual. That was the manner of it. 'Twas not long ago. Methinks either this month or next of last year; in a house in Cincinnati. This house is known to but few, the alley wherein it sits to still less, and the door to a purse full of us. Now, am I familiar?

Sheriff. Let me look at you, friend. Turn your eyes into mine. As yet I have not fairly met you. That's the pose. No, you can put round your back. You may know a man by his back as well as his face, and most to men of my calling. Now, now; nay. I do not remember you, though your look is not to be forgot. But what's your name?

Lance. My father called me Lance and my mother James. If you can put one and one together, you will make James Lance, who am I.

Sheriff. That's no name of my knowledge. It's more than like you mistook me for another officer. The law is a hard file and scrapes us to a near likeness.

Lance. Nay, I can prove it to you. You remember on that day you had spoken for temperance on one of the forty platforms in the streets. At least you boasted the fact to us, and gave us a merry mock sermon over the toddy. Oh! 'twas this humor that reminds me of you. If I had seen only your face, it might have passed me quite, but we laugh away our best hours. Who can lose them? Now I remember you, stretched on three chairs and going over the letters of your harangue. Oh! 'twas the humor that is my landmark. You were a treasure, for a man of wit does not live like the rest of us dull fellows, to fill his coat and no more, but to keep us from getting dead drunk in the dumps. Who is fuddled in a merry mood wakes up in good temper.

Sheriff. Faith, it all comes to me, the whole scene, and you with it. How is it a man cannot recall one thing, but a dozen together. You were of the company and sat to my back. All the blessed night my name was ringing through the streets like a bullet to topers. A freak of mine, a way to win money on the grace of God. There's little made at following heaven through and through, but you can chop in now and then and turn an honest penny.

Lance. The humor of it. I knew that would remind you of me. Yes, I was at your feet, your disciple as 'twere. How did I then long for your wit, and think what you let go with no care, and no profit. Now if Squire Lee cries *percentum ten*, he gets the tithe due to

God; but if an honest man tries an increase on his
abilities, they will not send him one in a thousand.

Sheriff. That was my case. A penny won from honest
people and spent on honest living is an honest penny.
Then the humor of it. I cannot get over the nature bred
in me. On the whole 'twas wicked and not to be spoken
of; not to be mentioned to dull people, such as split
jokes.

Lance. Oh, certain, and other things beside. They
would not leave my lips to fly around among stupid folks.
There's a telegraph of mirth between us. That night I
near died with laughter. You owed this Lee, this
moneyed employer of mine, a round sum, and having not
the means to pay forthwith, on an evening you drove
out his sty and slaughtered them, and after sold him the
pork for the amount of your debt. I am no cart for
your humor, but my unable shortness turns it sour.
Nevertheless, I love what I cannot do, and know what I
cannot tell.

Sheriff. Let me think. I have some faintness of it.
There was some such prank played for a wager of fun,
and I was in it. But 'twas nothing to be held for, a
legal distinction.

Lance. A joke on the law, Mr. Sheriff.

Sheriff. That's all. It was not burglary, larceny or
breach of trust. I was no burglar, because I broke no
lock. I stole nothing, because I returned what I stole.
I broke no confidence, because I held none in trust.
Being sued for trespass, I defend myself that I went not
where those who forbade me not went not. In fine I
bring suit for remuneration for packing the pigs, which
his honor must allow, as he was a butcher before me.
Tell not a story but you tell a whole story. I hardly
knew my creature in your fur.

Lance. I was either too drunk to hear, or you to tell.
A gill more of your gin, that will furnish me. Does
your sweet lady — but a teaspoonful. That fits every
mouth and stomach. Man was made on the last of a tea-
spoon, or doctors have grown him to it.

Sheriff. This is rare.

Lance. The best of its kind. Here's to your lady and
six children. Have you more?

Sheriff. Two.

Lance Then here's to the other two, the shot stars. If I had as many to drink to, I would be drunk all the time.

Sheriff. I have heard Englishmen say that they rang the bells at a royal birth for joy that there was one bumper more. Another bumper born.

Lance. Save me, but that's no comparison. You put humor into your drink, which can ne'er be said they do.

Sheriff. If every man were like you, I had only to turn my wit loose in a hall and rake in the cash. Then that corking of evil deeds, poverty, would no more afflict me.

Lance. No, take my word. If you can hold one man you can a thousand, for a thousand is less than one man.

Sheriff. That's sweet advice, and makes you my friend out of hand. What is here contained is yours, and what not is yours if I had it.

Lance. That does show how generous your heart is. But I want nothing free, save your humor. Enough, enough. What! here's a customer. I will be on my way.

Sheriff. Not so fast. Only Harry; Harry with his horsewhip; Harry my deputy.

Enter H. BUEL.

Know this man, Harry? One Captain Lance, and a famous drinker.

H. Buel. We are known to each other.

Lance. Ay, I know Harry and I know his horsewhip. I would know more of him, but not of his whip. Ha! ha! here I am rammed between the walls of humor. How much would I have given to see you pat the pate of old Lee. Oh! I shall burst with laughter. Laughter has its home in the corners of the mouth, but 'tis all through me. Did he strike out? Was he valiant? I wish you had scalped him.

H. Buel. How came you by it, captain?

Lance. By your own confession; but I shall die in the

face of so much humor. Oh! you load me down with it. Adieu. (*Exit.*)

Sheriff. Now Harry, your prank will be spouted out over town and the like with mine he has hold of.

H. Buel. Why, has Tim and the sheep out? Oh! the damned hole thy brother Tim has, where other people keep a still mouth.

Sheriff. No, not that; but he knows me in Cincinnati; where I was worse off than a book for bragging. God! God! a man's evil deeds follow him home.

H. Buel. Hark you! This man I know. He is as close as a bottle, but as prudent as a cat. I ne'er heard him say a word against any man; nor look you for any man. Our secrets are as secret with him as ourselves. He is the very one I mentioned to you a time ago, that we were to depart with, French leave. If I had seen you sooner, I would have told you more. He has promised to take Conway and the company secure down the river.

Sheriff. You will go with Jane.

H. Buel. Nay, Jane will not go with me.

Sheriff. The better for you, faith.

H. Buel. I am not of that fashion, and take it to heart. Prudence has spoiled more that it has made.

Sheriff. I tell you, Harry, this Lance is not a fellow of good repute. His name is enough to hang him; and I have known it for any time.

H. Buel. Tut! tut! now you are the ear of the world.

Sheriff. That's better than to be its fool. (*Exeunt.*)

ACT III.

Scene I. — *In the yard before Lee's house.*

Enter Js. Lee.

Js. Lee. The breath of evening puts new life in me.
'Tis like the air a rescuer might blow
Into the watery lungs of drowned men.
How do they stir and gasp and rise upright,
Then fall back sleepily; I feel the same.
The wind that seems to flutter through the trees

With wings half spread and drop upon the limbs,
Shakes wide its airy fragrance to my nose.
My ears detect its motion. 'Tis a fact,
A trace of cloud, a setting sun, a breeze
Give velvet lining to a homespun thought.
I'll ponder out his slow descent. He goes
Like hearty guest met with a hearty welcome,
That says good-by, good-evening, all things good,
And when they reach the turn, wave back their kerchief.
So now his banner's foldedon the hill,
Yet I think loth to go, so am I loth.
I'll make consideration. How, what's this!
That hardly as I have begun my thought
Comes breaking in. Oh! it is always so;
Settled in privacy and anchored for a calm;
But scarce rode out a gale of care, when smack
Down on our meditations, a storm
Of harping voices, but withal they tune
My ears to happy sounds. Hark! 'tis my daughter;
And oh! such stringed music sweetened heaven
When the primeval dove, white sign of peace,
Found footing o'er the waves.

      Enter CONWAY, JANE DOR *and* JULIA LEE.

  Con.   Did you bespeak us?
  Js. Lee. No.
  Con. Well, have mercy on the question, sir.
'Twas natural for us, that coming this way
And hearing of your voice, which loudly beat
The caverns of the woods, we followed it
Up to your trumpet, and now we present
All our contritions to you.
  Js. Lee.   Contritions!
What's that to do with me?
    Con.   Nothing, your honor,
Unless you have the same as we do send
In every way. You shall meet our contritions
With no dull, sneaking parsimony, which,
Like misers to a beggar does give nothing,
But totters by; nor will we be howled off
With barking mouths and faces set to kill.

But we have come, made up and penitent,
As you do see us. If we are not met
With penitence on your part, shame to you;
Ay! double shame; all the worst killing curses.
You have killed equality, the basest murder
That e'er shamed man.
  Js. Lee.   Have you done?
  Con. For a time.
  Js. Lee. Well that's comfort, if only for a time.
Blessed be small comforts, that would turn our lives
Good half of blessedness, if we did not
Make them pay interest on our future trouble.
Now I'll be happy, while I wait for you
To bring in a spell of my woe. Let's see.
The quaint birds are dropped off. If they did sing
They would distract me. 'Tis on purpose granted
That they should close with evening, and give us
Pure silence, the best time for noble thoughts.
For then we think upon ourselves; and he
Who looks into himself, will look around
The sins of others. There he sees such spots
As will set him to cleaning and leave people
To find their blemishes. Nothing's so happy
Like changing fault for fault with a dear friend,
And showing up your sun and shadow to him
In sweet confession. Now I am alone.
Those silly fools that troubled me, that parrot
That croaked such insolence! All are gone, gone.
How do my palms here resting on my temple
Feel sweaty, but I have a tongue, a medicine,
Purge to my mind; for all that has collected
During debate, while I have sat and smiled
With inward grief, now flutters to my lips.
Oh! how unhappy, culpable in me,
To let my daughter, all my pretty parts,
Translated and made up, so full in her,
Get stuck to this vile pitch; but now 'tis done
I fear 'twill rub her skin. He shall be taken,
Daubed with some feathers —
  Jul. Lee.   Father!
  Js. Lee.   What! you here?

I thought you had departed; but my tongue
Was still on you, so rarely do I see you,
Since you grow amorous, that I fear, I fear —
What can I fear? That you take love for father,
And have no love for me.
    Jul. Lee.   Oh! father, no.
    Jane Dor. I do assure your honor, most pitifully
She has of late moaned, pined, and taken on,
That you were cold; and laid it as a fault
Against your natural dislike of her.
But I did tell her that 'twas the cram of business,
That stranger to affection, which did sour
Attention to her. And not out of your thoughts,
But from your time.
    Js. Lee.   That's right. My thoughts are good.
But I must stop, where I would go ahead
With those dear fatherly caresses, which
Call young girls home to the blessed fireside.
In future, Julia, I promise to you
Tender admixture, both of old advice
And admonition; but if these be not
Stirred and well mixed up with the yeast of love
And sympathy, then call it not my fault,
But o' the times. I'm not my own purveyor,
But lent to others, so I cannot say
My time's my own, or even my children mine.
    Jul. Lee. Nay, you may always call me yours, dear
        father,
Even if you do not see me, since I loved
And was beloved. I've not forgotten you
And put you out of mind, but you still keep
A father's love, graved even with young Conway.
Now you rebuff us, but I see your eyes
Look leniency. Oh! what a tale is there,
All of my happiness, or, indeed, yours.
    Js. Lee. No, not of mine, Julia.
    Jul. Lee.   Oh! why not?
I'll be the same to you and do my duty
As I were never wed. I would see you often,
And caress and love you.
    Js. Lee.   How fond, dear daughter.

Only the same to your vain seeming, which
Like bridal veils hide to make dear the beauty
And edge the young groom on. But not to me;
For, look you, daughter, love cannot be divided
Without it break, and gives the whole to one
And none to me. Alas! Oh! my sweet child,
This is the worse to bear.

 Jul. Lee.   I beg you, father —
 Js. Lee. Beg anything but lovers.
 Jul. Lee.   I beseech you —
 Con. No, that's idle, unless you would leave me.
He does turn me off, and by these circumspects
Hints at my riddance. Well, shall it be so?
O Julia! this is the bitterest choice
A tender girl can make. It stabs my heart
To press you to't.
 Jul. Lee. I cannot speak.
 Con.   I'll speak for you, my love.
 Js. Lee. No, no.
 Jane Dor. That's my part. Let me have a word.
I'll play your attorney, dearest Julia,
And we'll not meddle as to lawyers' fees.
For honest men are ever on the flight
Of passion as to right and property.
But no true lawyer sues his brotherhood,
Or no highwayman calls on learned judge,
Seated in castle of the legal stool,
To cut their booty for them. I advise,
Sir judge, sir wisdom, sir Jack-in-the-box,
That you give cordial judgment to my client,
Or to my client's client, which's the same,
Seeing they are one, or would be so. If you'll
But stamp their action with formality,
The seal of Heaven, you do Heaven's law,
Which never did decree on parchment roll,
Or faded letter of a printed page,
By precedent, for there no precedent
But good precedes, and good preceding on
Still needs no precedent. This code, I say,
Does not permit by breach of argument,
Or any plea, that lovers like in years

Should be thus madly disunited.
I do appeal unto your honor's practice,
And summon up the wide and whispering crowd
To be my jurors.
  Js. Lee.   Nay, I am as conscious
Without the call of jurors, as if seated
On cause of death, and all the room around
Hung on my lips. Why, even above justice
I place my daughter's welfare, more tender to her;
Because your justice is written down in scowls,
And each parched wrinkle must be carried out,
Spite of your sympathy; but here my love
Does batter down all right, and looking at you
I must consider nature's frailty.
In sooth, I do. What's more plain than you, poor girl,
Having been barred outside the company
And speech of proper men, should take this fellow
For lack of better copy. There is my fault.
I have the grace to own it, which does add
More grace unto me. My fatherly duty
Is a blessed thing, but I do abuse it
By letting you know of this smoky rascal.
Since you must love, I'll place your dear affections
Upon a right, true man, ay, such a one
As is a stem to yonder stump.
  Jul. Lee.   Oh! father,
You are too critical. I tell you fair,
I'll wed no other. I would rather live a maid
And be alone, sharpen in vinegar
Of loneliness, and bite my bitter lips
For want of kisses, than go to my bed
With one I do not love.
  Con.   Angels could say
No more.
  Js. Lee. This is capering and unwise,
My Julia. Oh! how unsorted base
Is beauty clipped of wisdom. How the mind
Illuminates plain faces! I tell you
Thou hast to get thy wit; for you have not
The judgment of a man, nor yet the years
To put you in the harness, if you had it.

Jane Dor. Nay, sir, there's naught in years. How
  many old,
Decrepit packs of eighty do we see
Get wives, that first unline their purse, then out,
Like skinless rats, drive their lean carcasses.
And wise fifty weds so fond, all men but he
Have been before him. He lives on to sixty
In ignorance, and passes off at seventy,
And leaves his faithful spouse a good round sum.
    Js. Lee. Very true, I could name —
    Jane Dor.   As for wit we women
Are well endowed, especially in love matters.
So we do ponder in circles, wherefore called
Circumspect, looking more into the nature
Than round the seeming.
    Js. Lee. That were well advised, Jane. Julia, do you
take time to peer into the nature of this man and not
round the observation. That's it; time, time. What's
time but the peck of change. Time's a name, but change
a thing positive. I hope there will be a change. Take
thy leave and ponder, think, meditate, and consider. And
may you return to me changed. That's a pretty word.
    Jul. Lee. I will do as you say, but 'tis beyond me.
    Con. Good-evening, your honor.
    Js. Lee. Make haste. Thy mother is looking for you.
(*Exeunt Conway and Julia.*) Now, Jane, I am rid of him.
I had rather endure the pleading of ten new-fledged
lawyers than one lovesick girl. I will bear it no more,
but cut things short, as the Jew quoth of his yard-stick.
    Jane Dor. Oh! you liar. Why did you give me word
that you would mate these young people, then break them
off? Now I did put them on the more. Now I lifted up
those bubbles of hope, to be broken by your vile breath.
You have deceived me, and broken all our hearts.
    Js. Lee. In simple, I have changed my mind, Jane.
    Jane Dor. And will you again?
    Js. Lee. On a chance, sweetheart.
    Jane Dor. And again?
    Js. Lee. Very like me. But please, my fair heifer, I
have taken my station here so late, to cut off old Buel and
his spouse. They cross the river before the ravens are

fairly roosted, for no other reason than to see if one of
their drove of hogs has not eaten the other. Indeed, the
poor creatures could not get food any other way. But
they are thrifty, Jane, thrifty. We will divide a bit of
their soil between us. On my soul we will.

Jane Dor. I want none of their mud, nor the baser
clay you are made of.

Js. Lee. You need not be mad with me, when I would
please you in all else beside. A ranting tongue in thy
head is as good as no head at all. Then have a quiet one.
This young Harry bears me the greatest love and rever-
ence. If he come by money from his father, it will be
mine and no question; for I can turn him round my thumb
like a ring. This is worth the toil, bonny mistress, spite
of a peevish girl. Say, Jane, is it not?

Jane Dor. If you have no conscience.

Js. Lee. A little spark, Jane, which, on my soul, I
never put powder to. Have you no years beyond girlhood?
Then have discretion beyond a minute. Our wedding
shall be a continual courtship. You shall refuse me when
you will, and take me when you desire. Ho!

(*Enter* SQUIRE BUEL, *with* WIFE *and* HARRY BUEL.)

Bless you, Harry. You are the type of a young man
to tender your mother so caringly. If you are such a
son-in-law as son, I am at the top of grace.

H. Buel. Pray you I may, if it be so determined,
father.

Js. Lee. Determined? Squire Buel, is their marriage
not already made up? The only question is, When shall
it be sent to the parson? The quicker the better for the
young people. They are lost in each other; mad for the
time.

Sq. Buel. What will the dower be, judge?

Js. Lee. A clean twenty-five thousand off-hand. As
much for you will make a pretty start in life, if the
promises of both hatch to my mind. I began with not so
many coppers. 'Twas the same with you, like enough.

Sq. Buel. Not a pinch of snuff to my name.

Js. Lee. Those were rare times for rare men. There
be no such industry now-a-day. No such ploughs, learning and delving.

Mrs. Buel. No, no, your honor.

Js. Lee. Faith, madam, your memory is younger than your years. Those who grow old as slow as you, may be ever said to be young. If my daughter take you to copy I shall be grateful to you and thankful to her, for you are the very stamp I would like to have her make. Then I have had no time and nature to educate her mornings and evenings.

Mrs. Buel. No one can say but I have done my duty.

Js. Lee. Oh! what a blessedness, madam. Now your duty is done, you shall but settle with Heaven. Then you are done for good, which is the shot of all our life; I never heard man or woman set a bad word on you, and that's more than I can say for myself, for every thief is against a judge and every cudgel on my head.

H. Buel. That reminds me, your honor, I have a clue. We wind. We wind. The thief is one Thomas Mowhawk. We have got to that knot.

Js. Lee. I will write a warrant, where'er he is.

H. Buel. The devil knows, for the sheriff does not. He was a sailor by trade and a cooper by odd jobs. Presently he has gone to sea, for he has departed his bung-holes on the very night of your ransacking. He will turn pirate for a penny.

Js. Lee. Never mind, Harry. He will be for some other justice; for there's a union of honesty the world over, but each thief is for himself. I want no revenge, only peace, which is the milk of life. But look about, or you may mistake him. To have as many beards as a highwayman is only to trick the sheriff. To light on a thief on the morn of his crime scares not his mates so much as ten years after. Therefore keep your eyes about. When I see you next, I hope I may be your father indeed. But we will go to the house and draw and certify papers, an' it please you, Squire Buel.

(*Exeunt* Justice Lee, Squire Buel *and* Mrs Buel.)

H. Buel. Has the old villain been teasing your virtue, Jane. here alone with you? Oh, if I could take your place, and light were night, he would have the warmest love of his life.

Jane Dor. Nay, you have served him once; but when we are snugly wed, hint to him the trick you have played him, for he's a quick spirit, and it would worry his meals out of his mind. Then punishment is nothing if unknown. Like a mother whipping her children for what they know not, and kissing them for the rods.

H. Buel. That would be a plague on him; but has he not some true love for me?

Jane Dor. As cheap as a penny.

II. Buel. Methought he had, but such a knave.

Jane Dor. A very band-box, made for a man, but full of all else.

H. Buel. If I had him now under my wand, what a fairy I would be.

Jane Dor. You are a lover of the law; a proper deputy.

II. Buel. Faith, I love the law for sport, and the sheriff for gains. But I get the most out of it, for I pay nothing for my sport and he pays dear for his profit. We watched all night for a sheep thief, who was none but his brother Tim, when caught. But his brother would not know him for fear. He was whiter than a fleece, and trembled like a lamb. *God*, quoth the sheriff, for mind you he never swears by Christ, for that's a lady's oath. Ay, *God*, said he.

Jane Dor. But he lacks both in his prayer. That's where all men treat the Trinity alike.

H. Buel. But he has a face of grace on him when the sessions come round. He will outlook a dozen churchmen. Then his hand is against every man.

Jane Dor. Ay, but how did you manage him?

H. Buel. For me, I nigh died keeping my mirth in. The sheriff was taken aback with ingratitude. Quoth he, *You are no brother to keep me up six out of seven for a mangy sheep. I had rather nurse the pest-house than this, Tim.* But he was that generous he would take no more than the head. If Tim had stood out for giving the tail only, the sheriff would have been satisfied. What a soup! But if he could get one every night, 'twould not be so bad.

Jane Dor. Oh, you are a mad-cap. The only good

you will ever do will to cure some lunatic. You would
make him straight. No wonder Conway and Lee should
rake off in this mad manner, being under your tutorship.
These be light young men. There will be no end of
trouble for all of us.

H Buel. I tell you, Jane, if I had my way, we would
be with them to-night.

Jane Dor. Then you would have wished to have
bragged and stay at home.

H. Buel. God save me; I am no such lover.

Jane Dor. Well, what are you?

H. Buel. No dancing fellow; no one to talk and walk
a year with a woman before I know her or my own mind.
But my heart and eyes played all at once, when they fell
on you. Now you are against the pleading of both. I
would wed you this hour, if you would so, and who will
not wed in a minute is no man, but a peeping ninny.

Jane Dor. Wed in a worry, they say, worry all your
life. We will wait till this is blown over, till your
father —

H. Buel. My father! My old box; that is what a
father becomes.

Jane Dor. I could ask no better, seeing you have the
keys to him.

H. Buel. Not I, nor no other man. Nothing but time
can ope him, and that will break him. Why do fathers
keep every copper from their sons, so their sons will
wish them dead?

Jane Dor. What! have you that hardness? Oh! you
will make a simple husband.

H. Buel. No, I would sob and take on to myself, if he
were to die; but, God save me, I could not hinder being
the lighter in heart.

Jane Dor. God condemn you if you would.

H. Buel. That needs be; that needs be! What sweet
talk for a lover. I should think you were my coffin come
to bury me all in white.

Jane Dor. For good it would be white. You are but
a child, Harry.　　　　　　　　　　　　　(*Exeunt.*)

SCENE II. — *A path.*

(*Enter* LANCE; M. LEE, CONWAY *and* JULIA *in distance.*)

Lance. Who comes?

M. Lee. Was that a voice did say who comes?

Lance. A troubled voice. I say again, who comes?

Con. Friends of the night, to meet you here to-night;
I'll give the word to light our countenance.
Do you not know us?

Lance. I now discern
Your figures on the moon and see your cloak
Fly backward from the buffet of the wind.
This gale runs with a pointed, seaward wing;
'Twill see the Atlantic e'er the peep of morn.

Jul. Lee. I wish the earth sustained such messengers,
To carry awkward mortals on their way
From what's detestable.

Con. The same express,
My love, that hastens flight, nimbles pursuit.
'Tis not a mile, or rod, or any measure
That nods to safety, but a righteous cause,
The shortest road, and wit's the longest way
Between us and our enemies.

Lance. You have
A double proof of safety, and if I
Boast not, in me a third. It must go hard
If three cannot outwit your father, who
Thinks now I am doused in his muddy plans
To bring about a marriage between you
And Harry Buel. Ah, how few are friends!
But why should he who plays the game deceit,
Expect me to be fair? Come! let's to the boat.

Jul. Lee. Is there a fire?

Lance. I smell the smoke of't.
So they have lighted one. I was so busy
Waiting here, wrapped in my cloak of care,
It passed me quite.

Jul. Lee. The night is chilly.

Lance. Ay,
The air is foul in April, but on board
There's comfort in a corner. You can prove it
Where'er the butcher wind strips earth of skin.

Con.   Yes; come on, Lance, show us the way.
Lance.   Ahead.
The road leads down, and no mistaking it.
I'll stay behind, for it may be some spy,
Or much more likely a chanced wayfarer,
Has seen you pass.   Look, how behind you black,
In truth a coffin, so deep and dark.
   M Lee.   No matter,.
No one's behind, I'm confident.
   Lance.   Not I.
Even without intent some one may be there;
Misguided to the town, or some late hunter
Lags to reach his home e'er morning.
   M. Lee.   What's the good,
If you should find him?
   Lance.   I would make excuse,
Or if he questioned who you were, say to him,
'Tis some young folks gone on a merry time,
Or frolic under way.
   M. Lee.   Oh! what a frolic
To match the night.   I would indoor
Rather than catering to the air; but go,
We'll find the way, since 'tis so short.
   Lance.   Right on,
You cannot miss it.   It were best to walk
Abreast, for yon high-steepled cloud has cut
Moonlight away from us.
   Con.   Well, be soon back.
   Lance.   A minute, till I scout all around.   (*Exeunt all*
      but LANCE.)

                              Ay, gone,
And the last time you go.   At least I think
They cannot miss the water.   The boat lies
Off from the bank, and there's a yawning hole
Under their feet.   Oh, hell! may they fall in.
Then is my plot complete, for just as sure
As the old niggard finds his money gone,
He'll yell the law on me.   But if the current
Does drive and batter them together, as
It must, they are gone; all evidence washed out,
Which will sponge me.   'Tis easily said

They had his wealth with them, and being lost,
As fast my boatman sleep and will not wake
To hear their cries. Hark! hark! 'tis almost time.
Not yet, not yet! Well, this is strange indeed.
I wonder if the wind does chill my hearing
And drive across the sound. No, 'tis not that.
I think it blows from them, but 'tis hard telling
Here in the swaying pines, whose tops do rock
Like little infants. Here I will stand stiff
To catch the jar of their dull, drowning voices.
What raps at my ears? *Help! help!* Oh! you are wel-
    come.
There 'tis again. Ah, friends, sweet friends, come in
Unto my portals! You are the jolliest callers;
But I'll go forward and be unconcerned. (*Exit.*)

SCENE III. *The river bank.*

M. Lee. A light! a light!
            Enter STEWART, GRIM *and* ALLEN.
Grim.   Here is a light.
M. Lee.   Bring here.
Grim. What's the matter?
M. Lee.   A man is drowned! A light!
Grim. Here 'tis, I tell you.
M. Lee.   No, you have none there.
The wind has blown it out.
Grim.   Ay, so it has.
I'll touch it quick. Now what's wanted of me?
Jul. Lee. Look! look! how he is stretched upon the
    mud
And strangles for the air! Leap over hither.
Your oil burns dim. What! can you speak?
Con.   ·   Where am I?
Oh! now I do perceive. I thought I died,
Or something bordering death, and you, my love,
Did take me from it, so it seemed to me;
But I suppose 'twas Martin.
Jul. Lee.   Ay, 'twas he.
He caught you providently, but if I
Had the position, power or strength, my love,
Even without them, I had done the same.

Enter LANCE.

Lance.   Ho! what is this?
Con.   Wet.
Lance.   Has there been a rain?
I did not notice it, where I was stationed,
Beneath the tented pines.   But squalls will fly,
Pent in the kettle of a small, black cloud,
And cover only rods; this was the case and true.
Each storm must have an end, so the dry edge
Did fall between us.
        Con.   Nay, Lance, have you no eyes?
I slipped from yon hollow bank, whose treachery
Was covered by the turf, and came near drowning.
In sooth I should, had Martin not been light,
And reached my arms, as I did fling them up
To grasp the clouds.   Oh! they came down unto me,
Like good and stable props.
        Lance.   'Thank Heaven for't.
The boat has slipped her cable.   That's a trick
She has often played with the current.   Ho!
Grim and Allen!   Have you not seen it before?
        Grim.   No.
Lance.   Nor you, Stewart?
Stewart.   Nay.
Lance.   Nor you?
Allen.   No, sir.
Lance.   Well, it has happed to me.   Once as I came,
Troubled in some matter that did bow my head
To the ground for an answer, I stepped o'er,
But caught the hawser.   Your best fortune favored
To have a good friend by.   The rightest-keeled man
Could not throw arm and swim in such a narrow.
        Con.   No, I did not try.   The water cut through my
          flesh,
Being so cold and at spring flood.   If you
Had not reached me, this were my last sad eve.
I do know it, and think the consequence.
        M. Lee.   No more.
Lance.   Thanks are not asked where most deserved.
Con.   Then I'll not pest you with them, brother, no.

But you have done the richest deed on earth,
Which makes man more than angel, if there be
Such perfect spirits as do wander here.
   Lance. Come, that's enough. You shiver.
   Jul. Lee.   To the fire,
And strip off your cold clothes.
   Con.   I will.
   Lance. Ay, how the poor lamb trembles. Get to bed.
The bitter and continual east could blow
No harder on the backs of unshorn sheep
Than this on you.
   Con.   Where to, captain?
   Lance.   Below,
Down to the cabin. I stay here awhile
To see things safe and proper.

    (*Exeunt* CONWAY, MARTIN LEE *and* JULIA LEE.)
                What's the time?
   Grim. Eleven, sir.
   Lance.   Hours yet. Have you ambition?
   Grim. Ay, at all hours.
   Lance.   That's encouraging.
If I behold a thorny minded man,
Pricked to ambition, I will take him up,
Encourage him, and pass promotion to him;
For he has the hatch in him which some day
Bears off a gallant brood. Dost hear?
   Stewart.   All, all!
   Grim. Are there more in the coop?
   Lance.   More what?
   Grim.   Advices.
   Lance. Short, Grim. What's your ambition?
   Grim.   To be honest.
   Lance. A most uncommon, but as your whole aim
Has chose so fair a mark, let us consider
How you may hit it.
   Grim.   I have no objection.
   Lance. Honesty, then, is first of all that quality
That plumbs our dealings, so 'tis said,
And better understood; if you be honest
Your promises are sealed, and others' dues

Respected as your own.   This makes a man
In estimation of the giddy world.
All who behold you feathered to the tips
In business honesty, think by conclusion
That outward graces shadow the inward soul,
And here misled, misjudge the internal iron,
Which in most men is lapping dross.   Mark you,
That you bide none; like ragged parsimony,
Or the dull pluck, which lets vile bullies strike
Either the moral or the bodily man.
For as the last, there be such cunning steel
That makes the bulk and sinews count for naught.
And if main courage guides a gentle hand,
All's down before him but the greatest coward,
Thy tongue.   Watch as it were a poison set
Against thy courage and thy manly part,
And hold thy stiff opinions who may laugh;
For look you, if you fall into the trap
Of currying all men, they will hold you cheap.
Rather by few and scanty want of words
Exalt their price, than battering 'gainst the sea
And froth of argument be tost and cockled.
But when you speak, with moderation trimmed
Be for a time mild and inurgent, so
To smooth their self-esteem.   If they persist,—
And fools are stubborn, — either hold thy mouth
Or decant short and sharp.   The last, I mark,
Has no effect upon these aimless pipes,
But bears you off well with the lookers-on.
You will convince a dozen, where you think
Your wit wasted on one.
    Stewart.   That's very true,
Indeed my own opinion.
    Lance.   Ay, Stewart,
'Tis common as the sun.
    Grim.   In cloudy weather.
    Stewart.   Nay, much more common.
    Lance.   So it is,
Because the weakness of mankind is seen
Both 'neath the light of day and watch of night.
But come, what's your ambition?

Stewart.   My ambition?
Lance. Your inward longings eked out with your
 talents.
Stewart. Why, to be rich!
Allen.   And I the same desire.
Lance. Yes.
Grim. And are like to have it.
Lance.   Why, I know not,
Though poverty, like dogs, comes to the poor;
But sure that in your present tracks you have
But meagre opportunity. Yet mind,
There be such bruited ways that lead to wealth,
Which will not bear the utterance. I do know
Things that would put you on the stair of fortune,
Ready to mount, and wealth within your grasp;
Than which what is more pleasant?
Grim.   Nothing, sure.
Lance. True, true, for want of it does bind the mind
Down with the body, walking a high soul
On flat and muddy sills. But if you have it,
Your soul's your own, though parsons tell you different,
And power stands within you, which is the star
Whereat men fly, like meteors at the earth.
Have you a pang for being stones for those
Above to walk on?
Grim.   God, God, I have, scores.
Lance. So have we all. Each underling must bow,
Appear obedient for his belly's sake,
And be no better than a slave, though he
Is fire within. I tell you there's a way
That you may make yourselves masters, at least
Of your own dignity. Wealth will buy that,
The greatest boon, though I could dance your fancy
With baser prospects, but that I do know
You hold this capital and to be considered.
Allen. Ay, sir, what more?
Lance.   Nothing to-night.
Grim.   I thought
You would deliver us a secret.
Allen.   Yes,
You spoke portentiously.
Lance.   Another time.

Meanwhile spur your imagination, which
I fear is growing jaded.

Enter MEG.

                           What now?   What now?
Meg. Please, they want you below.
Lance.   Me?
Meg.   So they said.
Lance. Well, I'll come shortly.

Exit MEG.

We will start this morning.
Keep your ears open, and at a future hour
I'll pour in them a project; but be quiet
In presence of these three, for they are sharp,
Keen-witted fellows; so meet them with an edge
Of calm indifference whet on your faces;
Neither condole with them nor be too much
Whispering and chattering, and for the future
I will make it plain.
    Grim.   Yes, be our lamp.
    Lance.   I will.
    Allen. We will all run in your light. (*Exeunt omnes.*)

ACT IV.

SCENE I.— In Lee's house.

Enter JUSTICE LEE.

Js. Lee. All the world's against me. Here is my box
washed dry and my moneys flooded away. If it were
not that knave Lance, then I know nothing about him.
In the past he has done fairly by me, but monstrously by
my enemies, that is my creditors. I thought he would
be true to me, because I held his mandamus over him.
But this have I learned : to trust no more villains for the
sake of their darkness. A good, silly clerk pays best in
the long run; though he lose you pennies by stupidity, he
ne'er robs you of a hoard; for dullness is but a penny
failing. The next time that I want a skipper and

supercargo and what not, I will take a short, broad man
with such a flame of honesty on his chin as would do to
light his pipe. No lean, black-headed fellow, rusted
with grey, but honest colors. Truth, I know a shore-man
that would fit me on every rib. He is red to the corners
of his eyes, and they are taking it on for looking at his
whiskers so long. I will set him in Lance's place when
I have hanged Lance, and if he make any talk of my
concerns on gallows, I will nod to the sheriff to drop him
off before the witnesses come. But who's late at a hanging. That will please the spectators, for dispatch is
business. But about this little money. 'Tis no great
matter, the subject for a tear and the remedy of a handkerchief. When I have the next occasion to cry over a
sore finger, I will put in a drop for this.

Enter SHERIFF *and* HARRY BUEL.

Well arrived, handcuffs. Can you two never part?
A prettier twain ne'er scared women or took outlaws.

Sheriff. For women, your honor, we have naught to
do with them.

Js. Lee. And for the outlaws you have naught to do
also. That is too, too cruel to the women; for look you,
they are not to be laid aside as regards man, but must be
looked into, looked after, and looked around. If you
peer not into them, you will not know what they con-
tain. If you examine not after them, they will lead you
a bad way, and if you turn them not round, you will see
but one side of them.

H. Buel. I would care to see no more than the good
side.

Js. Lee. Never think, Harry, to find that by a look.
They fold their virtue in for a rest to their own conscience, so you will see nothing but the rough of their
good wishes, whereas we men, for the sake of opinion,
lay open our fur to our friends, and rest uneasy on a
shorn skin.

H. Buel. Then, your honor —

Js. Lee. No, Harry, father by all means. This is
fatherly advice.

H. Buel. As you like it, father. Then man has no

comfort, for every man makes himself uncomfortable and every woman all beside. That is, man has two against him; himself and his wife.

Js. Lee. But he has only one for him, and she's his wife. Take that to your bosom, my son, and think that the virtues of hell are all on the surface, but of women all inward, which proves her as near heaven as able.

Sheriff. That's a mouthful, your honor.

Js. Lee. Consider it. Hath it not sense?

Sheriff. Why, a poor kind of sense, damned forever by the truth of't.

H. Buel. Tut, I thought heaven was jeweled on the outside, and women are for that matter. That should mean that women and heaven have a fair face, as well as a warm heart.

Js. Lee. Jewels are hateful to my soul, Harry. The best jewel is an open countenance. A heaven of gems is no heaven of Christians. There is a race who can tinker heaven out of a goldsmithy. I'm none of them. Solomon hath it to get wisdom, and uses his wisdom, for all I see, to get naught but wealth. His treasures travelled farther than his wit. Then they were more accounted, I take it, for our greatest parts go broadcast over our little.

H. Buel. I have heard different.

Js. Lee. No, no. That's beyond doubt. Has some one been telling evil stories of you, son? Ne'er mind them. They are clouds, and die with the first wind. Your graces will live longest.

H. Buel. I will doubt it not, if you say it. Oh! sparing the question, what was the matter, that you called us so hasty?

Js. Lee. Misfortune has me of late. But a trifle with all. It has been my custom to keep sums throwing about here and there. Ne'er in proof boxes, which are the address to thieves, but in a book on the stand, or the like. Now have I lost my pains for my wit.

Sheriff. Ha!

Js. Lee. Oh! I beg you not to laugh, not so loud.

Sheriff. I was whetting my appetite for the case.

Js. Lee. 'Tis nothing more than this is gone. There

it was yesterday. There it is not to-day; and that's the odds to me betwixt to-day and yesterday.

H. Buel. Is the deficiency any great, and bankrupt?

Js. Lee. An iota; but more than passing. Say thirty thousand.

Sheriff. Ha!

Js Lee. You are the jolliest man, Mr. Sheriff. How can a hangman get so much laughter out of his trade?

Sheriff. Not so hard for me as for an eye hangman, the witnesses. They must watch the inhumanity, but we the tackle only. We are naught but machines of death.

Js. Lee. And to come to't.

Sheriff. Ay, who's the suspect of this? Who has taken it?

Js. Lee. And how shall I retake it? That's the pain that has the charm for me.

Sheriff. Like a dung-heap, your honor, dirty but thrifty. Leave the handle to Harry and me. We are bloodhounds on the bark. Have you no clue?

Js. Lee. Dost know one Captain Lance?

Sheriff. Truly, truly, by his deeds.

Js. Lee. And no good ones.

H. Buel. Why! nothing cruel, father-in-law.

Js. Lee. Then you know him not. He's one of those monsters that lose nothing by capture, like other fry.

H. Buel. He was employed of you, and I thought that was a bill to his honor. I ne'er looked more than at the face.

Js. Lee. That's the part not worth a wink. If you had eyed him below, you would see how his velvet is laid over iron. They say that he has murdered men and robbed their corpses. Sure he is a spendthrift and not above providence. There is enough proof without evidence to hang him again and again.

H. Buel. Has he been charged?

Js. Lee. No. A citizen must either swallow his words or the captain's lead. I would laugh; no I would weep for the man that tried a prosecution.

H. Buel. Is he so tough? I suspect he has some apology of a friend that sets these things afloat. What one will cast in the streets a dozen will grab. Tattlers outdo their spite. That's the fashion.

Sheriff. Did I not tell you?

H. Buel. What?

Sheriff. Why! that this Lance was a villain.

H. Buel. And one of your friends at that.

Sheriff. His friend as I am the friend of every sinner. I am no unfeeling club, Harry. There's not a man I lodge in the pound but I wish he could sleep in his own bed.

Js. Lee. Now, Harry, you are beaten by double witness, and we are only the two ends of a long line of them. He has my money, so he must be had. To-night he sleeps on board. But I warn you go cocked, for he's a man of few words; the very shortest-spoken man I know of.

Sheriff. I will fetch him by a ruse.

Js. Lee. Ay, as you were his own mother.

Enter LANCE.

Not voyaged yet, captain? I thought by this time you would be gone for good.

Lance. So I would, but I struck a loss in the fuel, and needs stay an hour. If you had forgot anything, I call to make it right. Why, friends, is it good luck I should meet you here to say good-by, and mate business with good feeling?

Sheriff. Faith the best. This clear weather makes a fine start.

Lance. Well enough overhead, but under planks we are mouldy. The damp has crept in during the wet of lading, and the pack was none too dry of itself. 'Tis a good plan to keep fires for a time, your honor.

Js. Lee. Very pretty, Lance. I know of nothing more I can point out, unless get small-bellied men. These fellows are eating up my living; get smaller men.

Lance. I will, but send me no more of those long, lean men. They are as full of surprises as hornets' nests.

Js. Lee. What do you most fashion?

Lance. Middling men, your honor.

Js Lee. As you say again.

Lance. Good-morrow, gentlemen.

H. Buel. And the day after as well, Lance.

Lance. How happy strange for me to meet so many sweet friends all in a walk of business. As I came up I saw Julia, Conway, and your son in the town; a step further I bade Morresey adieu. Now at the last minute I plump down in the middle of more friends.

Js. Lee. My daughter?

Lance. There was no mistaking such rare beauty.

Js. Lee. And Conway?

Lance. Your fine-savored son-in-law? Yes, I would have seen more of him, but that his back was forward.

Js. Lee. Ay, my dear Conway and my son in company?

Lance. In,—that were not it quite. More to one side of their company.

Js. Lee. Well, how did they seem?

Lance. Like the fresh bride and groom they are. There is nothing better, as I know, to look at. My single life has no charm after a wink at them. I never heard sung of two doves that seemed so happy as they. Oh! an unwedded life is a bare mouthful.

Sheriff. I ne'er made but one good trade, and that when the census got in my debt.

Js. Lee. Profit comes by debt and never by credit. That is, you may profit on the credit of others and your own debts.

Lance. Then your new heir will have more than experience to profit by. A fine young man, now you have consented to the wedding. How long will the honeymoon be?

Js. Lee. Forever.

Lance. That will be good for them.

Js. Lee. And for me. Had they ta'en the car for Cincinnati?

Lance. 'Twas in that direction.

Js. Lee. Pittsburg, and after New York, then the deep sea. I hope they will keep on.

Lance. Will they so far and see Europe?

Js. Lee. No.

Lance. A custom, your honor. One would think our brides had wed Europe more than their husbands. Good-morning. (*Exit.*)

Sheriff. Shall I nab him?

Js. Lee. Nay, I am heart-broken. Have you gone blind? Why do you sit there like people who cannot speak the language? 'Tis plain, 'tis very plain. Conway has gone, so has my account. There is an inference; but mind you, say nothing of this outside your office. My daughter's name is my own, for children partake of their father. I tell you, your best coin is silence.

Sheriff. I have a mint of that stuff. Might I look for your help at the next poll?

Js. Lee. The county will stand by you without my help. Every thief will ballot for you, and that's enough to elect any man in this state of the world. I will reward you rounder. But Harry, poor Harry!

H. Buel. I am a vile coward to sit here. I will murder him, and the law will stand by me.

Js. Lee. Calm, Harry; you will not win a woman's love by killing her lover. Now they are wed, there's no undoing it. The question is, how to get over this without a smutty gossip. This pulls me down. Is it not enough that I must lose her, but you as well? That were the saddest.

H. Buel. Nay, I am your son yet. All I look for is advice, which does not flatter the fairer lookout I had of you.

Js. Lee. That's not my fault. If my ways had pleased hers, you would have been one and all before this time; but I can give you no promises. They are clean spoiled by this Conway. Oh! gratitude is a born knave, and you cannot teach it out of him. I have tended him like a father, and he has robbed me for my love. But alas! my son is no better; the worst of the two; because I would not humor him in business trifles, he has left me without a sigh. To be sure he was hard-hearted, a very stone to my poor debtors. He would ne'er pay my good nature a mark, but keep to his hard ways. But that's not all he has gone for; I think to part shield his sister's name. He has a spark of a man in him, a drop of his father.

Sheriff. I never knew a more genial young man.

Js. Lee. He had great virtues, but harsh. That was not got from me.

Sheriff. I ne'er heard him called dishonest, only snug in his dealings, which after all was only the whine of poverty.

H. Buel. He was a most good-tempered fellow with me.

Js. Lee. With you, ay; but you were not his debtor. Oh, he was a January sun to a debtor, as blue as the north wind; but spare in his diet, and I think virtuous; at least he had no bitches about him. They would earn no more than night wages out of him, he was that close.

Sheriff. What's to be done?

Js. Lee. Nothing. They shall undo what they have done. A tired dog hates his own kennel, but finds it better than none. They shall come back, and I will not whistle for them.

Sheriff. Not for them, but how for your money?

Js. Lee. It can go to the dogs. If your own cur steal your own bacon, it is not a dead loss, only costly feeding. The sorriest dog is your neighbor's.

Sheriff. Then my duty is ended.

H. Buel. And I have none to end, only my heart to break.

Js. Lee. The duty to yourself, to your parents, and to me, Harry. Get another love; that is the only way to wipe out a lost one.

H. Buel. But my memory, my memory!

Js. Lee. There is no argument for this. Get another love, Harry.

H. Buel. Oh! the disgrace.

Js. Lee. A disgrace unknown is as good as honor. Say that their marriage was managed beforehand, and you knew all about it.

Sheriff. I will freight it to my spouse; then the world shall hear. (*Exeunt omnes.*)

SCENE II.— *On the Ohio.*

Enter LANCE *and* HIS BOATMEN.

Lance. Now 'tis full day, but we can plot the same
As in the listening night. Indeed 'tis better,
Since they have no suspicion, but let stray

Their flock of senses. Do not come too close,
And seem to lay your heads together; if
They hear our voices, they will not attend
More than unto the wayward, wandering wind.
Are your minds complete?
    Grim.   We are made up to't.
    Lance.   Then all is settled, and I only have
To appoint the time and moment of the deed.
Crime grows by thinking, so I do tell you
Go about your natural works and think
Only of pleasures that will come to you
In this pursuit.
    Allen.   Of drink?
    Lance.   Of anything.
    Stewart. Shall it be on the boat?
    Lance.   No; I'm determined
To wait until we make the cave of thieves,
Which is four days ahead. There in the pit
Beneath the fair skin of the earth, no one
Can aught disturb us. Meanwhile look serene,
Like you were dallying with a cherub thought.
Be prompt, and set your eyes very politely
When they walk by.
    Grim.   We will all that.
    Lance.   Then well.
I ask no more. I am the match of them
All three, so you will but stand by and rake
The booty while I get the scars for it.
    Grim. I have a dread we will be caught.
    Lance.   No, no;
Lay aside your dread. Did I not say their father
Suspected them the theft, and thought them gone
Out of his way? For their good conscience sake
And his own reputation he'll provide
A wall of silence, mark.
    Allen.   I have it down.
Go on.
    Lance. There's an end, at least with me.
Now resolution on your souls. With you
The outcome lies, and most upon your tongue
Keep utterance of these things. Be not in drink

Until your memory, by a space between,
Has rubbed all thoughts away, and when you cease
To think of their late murder, then drink, drink,
As hardened sinners should.
    Grim.   That comes by nature, captain.
    Lance.   The gifts of nature are our soldiers, which
Bat hard for us and hard to throw. Then look,
They cannot be o'ercome like education,
But muster to our battles, or with drink
To our destruction; for if you drink once
You drink again; if twice, then thrice. So on,
Till the unruly membrage of your tongue
Gets the best of your sense. You are at mercy
Of madness in yourself.
    Grim.   Do not reprove us
For what we have not done. Is't not enough
To answer for our failings?
    Lance.   I wrong you. You are trusty.
    Grim.   As your hand.
    Lance.   But that does tremble. I need some rest and
        sleep.
Below the air is murk and foul and hot,—
Unnatural. I could not sleep in it,
But in this breezy river I'll lie down,
And do you rouse me if I wake not up
Ere afternoon.
    Stewart.   We will.
    Lance.   Ho! I forget.
Dost know that? (*Holds up a vial.*)
    Allen.   No.
    Lance.   A remedy of the best. (*Takes it and sleeps.*)
    Grim.   I think he sleeps.
    Allen.   Not like his victims sleep.
    Grim.   He soon shall be with them if I do live.
Look at the blankets of his murderous eyes;
I'll watch the river's eye, more deadly eye,
And thread it safe. Look close.
    Allen.   He sleeps for good;
No counterfeit of it, and but returns
Unto the early hours of the morning
What he did rob out of her midst. Sleep on;
We plot in comfort ere 'tis time to bed.

Stewart. I wonder if he dreams of murder. He —
Allen. If dreams are blotters of the day, no more,
And only prophets, I would prophesy
That murder is the great part of his rest.
Grim. Ay, he must die.
Allen. So must we all.
Grim. I mean
We'll kill him.
Allen. Yes. Who shall it be?
Stewart. Not I.
Grim. Here comes one of the twain, and short I'll warn
him.

Enter MARTIN LEE.

Friend, sleep you in arms?
M. Lee. No, but Conway does.
Grim. I say do you sleep on your arms?
M. Lee. Why yes,
When they are 'neath my head.
Grim. You have
No head to speak of, if you laugh at that
Which I will tell you. Levity's a trick
Of fools and cloak of cowards.
M. Lee. That's my mind
If there's anything to be serious over.
Grim. Oh, there is; something that concerns your-
self,
So twice your own. Look, how do we all seem
Like people with a joke wrapped in their face?
Are we not grimmy? Our faces more black
Than care could make them, or the calking tar?
I tell you all the fashions of the countenance
Are set in black and white. If you have knowledge
To read a primer, you can spell us out.
M. Lee. Well, to it, man.
Grim. No; are you satisfied?
M. Lee. Of what?
Grim. That we have no distrust, but speak
Most plainly.
M. Lee. Yes; whate'er it is, but short.
Why do you hang suspense?
Grim. There lies a man,

Or heaven's apology, honest to look at,
But all deep sin within.
    M. Lee.   What, Lance?   Not Lance!
    Grim.   It makes no difference what you do name him,
Although he bears a false one. The point is,
There's the man.
    M. Lee.   Oh come! less round about
And fashionable. You beat around like one
Who has a honey secret to con o'er,
And lingers sweetness out. None of these stairs
To climb my understanding. But leap down
Right fair upon it. I can stand the secret.
    Grim.   Well, fairly told, he'll murder you.
    Allen.   Yes, murder.
    M. Lee.   Oh! what play can this be?
    Grim.   One near the acting.
So near your fingers cannot stop the days
Upon a single hand.
    M. Lee.   You deceive not,
But you have been deceived. Saints have been slandered
In holy writ, and neither been the wrong one.
There's a mistake. Say what is your suspicion
That he should murder me. Say quick! Oh, say!
    Grim.   It is not long.
    M. Lee.   No tale is short to fear,
Or long to love. Come on!
    Grim.   This murderer
Has got possession of your father's money
By a means he has not told us, but he comes
Laded with it, and offers to divide
In case we put you out of the way some night,
And cover up our crime. Then to this end
He whispers to your father that you are gone,
And if you ne'er come back,—thus, thus to us
With license of his giddy, lying tongue,
Your father, though he hold him in suspicion
Like as the black northwest, will yet have a doubt
Of your fair honesty. Then to the east
And clear direction of your innocence,
This cloud does steer. And he has made it plain
By us, suborning you shall not return.

Oh! you are vapors and fogs of the morning
To such a villain, and he will murder you.
Oh! the world is a peck, and shaking brings
Great monsters to the top.
    M. Lee.   When did he speak to you?
This sadness breaks my heart, which was before
Lighter than for a month.
    Allen.   This very minute,
As you walked hither.
    M. Lee.   So short?
    Allen.   Ay, we consented
To kill you the fourth day from now, because
If we balked he would strip us dirty rags,
As he has done before, and none the wiser.
    Grim.   Even as 'tis, we stand but little chance
After your taking off. Our life no rest;
But dread that he will knife us, or with drugs
Put us to sleep forever. Instruments
Of murderers are next to wipe.
    M. Lee.   No more.
I cannot doubt you, for looking behind
Everything runs to his guilt. He's here,
And justice long delayed is better done
Than not at all. Quick! wake him up and give
Time for confession, then upon this beam
Make way with him.
    Grim.   Think he will hang?
    M. Lee.   Why yes,
If we have power. There are four to one,
And he's not strong. What danger is there from him?
I think the sudden prospect will unnerve him,
And dance his resolution up to Heaven.
There lost with God, while if 'twould combat man,
Nothing could make it even. I have it:
Unarmed he is unnerved, and his poor pluck
Lost with his steel. We will step softly forward
And turn his weapons on him.
    Grim.   Now he wakes.
    Allen. Oh, yes! his drowse is short. Those sleep the
    roughest
Who rest on evil deeds. A plank, a hide
Is soft to goodness.

M. Lee.   Now's the time.
Allen.   Wait, wait.
His bloody and instinctive hand even grabs
Into his pockets.   Some of us shall suffer
Before he dies.   Some men play with their charms,
Some with their pencils, but his constant fingers
-Are laid on implements of death.   There's time
To take him in the light of his own conscience
And end him in the heat of blood; but now
I cannot hang him.   Oh! to see him strangle
And cough and shiver in the icy loop
Would half kill me.
     Stewart.   No, no, not now.
     Allen.   His fingers
Are picking at his cloak.   He'll rise up soon.
     Grim.   Mind, say nothing to Meg.
     M. Lee.   Why not?
     Grim.   She's his,
Body and soul, and ready to his whistle
As any well-kicked cur.

(LANCE *rises.*)

     Lance.   Ho! I am sweaty.
How tall the dawning sky appears to be
In midst of summer.   I cannot attain it
By climbing with my eyes.   If winter would come
And blacken down, I think my health would mend.
But summer is an awful time to die.
If grace could choose, the winter hanging low
Would hit my preference.   How long have I slept?
     Stewart.   A quarter, sir.
     Lance.   No more?   I thought 'twas years.
How have I travelled and been all distempered;
First over my imaginary life,
From end to end, and each particular,
Which apprehended minutes.   Then quick turned
All of my seven senses into distance,
Or but one sense, of farness without end
Or measurement.   My head seemed set away
Miles from my body; not one star from star
Is quartered as the thoughtless space, which bends
Between one thing and another.

M. Lee.   That's bad.
Hum, I think your liver's wrong.
Lance.   What's good for it?
M. Lee.   No sort of drug.   But only righteous food
In convent quantities.   I have observed
How doctors thrive by overfeeding; so
Eat little, little drink, and take the sun;
That's my advice.   'Tis as impossible
That herbs should change the body as religion
Should change the mind.
    Lance.   But I care little for drink,
And hold it high absurdity for men
To be intemperate.   I am spare of food
And keep the doctor's rule better than the golden.
    M. Lee.   Well, there's the trouble.   You o'erdo the
      cure
Which you once needed, but now being well
Need it no longer.   I have often noticed
How crammed your waistcoat pockets were with vials,
That you would taste of every now and then.
These, in my weak opinion, are the cause
Of all your sickness.   If you put them by,
The pains they aggravate will go with them,
And sovran nature, her own remedy,
Patch up her dwelling.
    Lance.   Ay, that's reasonable.
I will abandon them, at least a time,
And judge their absence.   If I am no better
Within a week, or rather, if no worse,
I'll rid myself for good.
    M. Lee.   Let me smell of them.
    Lance.   Here is a dozen.   (*Hands them to Martin Lee.*)
    M Lee.   Men and medicine
Are known by odors.   Pish! what a character!   (*Sniffs
    them.*)
And these three are mates in sin.   They would hang
An honest man, for an intent to poison
All his rich relatives.   Over with them.
Now the river's sick.
    Lance.   That's quick, very quick.
    M. Lee.   So much the better.   If you had these with
    you,

The smallest pain would seem to grow, for lack
Of their relief, and you would take them spite
Of all your resolutions. I ne'er knew
A man but was more sick of fear than body;
More ready for the doctor than his dose.
Deceit's the oldest remedy, and quacks
Who can use men can cure them.
 Lance.   Ay, mere tools
Our sickness makes of us. (*Exeunt.*)

    SCENE III.— *The sheriff's tavern.*

   Enter H. BUEL *to the* SHERIFF.

Sheriff. Faith, Harry, I have been thinking.
 H. Buel. That's nothing odd, unless about something
good, like the paying of the money you owe me. If it
was out at one per cent, I would have dollar for dollar by
this time.
 Sheriff. I thought your love, more than the law, had
outlawed those things, Harry. I am clean bottomed, in
the condition of a pumpkin; my meat sacrificed to keep
up an appearance, and an ugly one at that. Bless me, I
make more money than a mint, and spend more than a
Californian. Where's the hole in my stocking?
 H. Buel. The hole in your head runs to your boots;
that's the road to bankruptcy. You cannot have a good
brand but you drink the best; nor a fat turkey but you
eat her out of jealousy of the foxes. Traders are made
to swallow the dross of their goods, or people would buy
first hand and save the per centum. Drink your stale
malt, like an economist should, and find the way to save
money.
 Sheriff. I tell you, Harry, I am concerned.
 H. Buel. And I tell you, you are not concerned in
meeting your debts. They resemble nothing as much as
the Assyrians, being as numberless as the sands. You
know well enough you have spoiled three pairs of axles
I gave you the three Christmases of last year, for lack of
grease. Every time the smoking wheels turn round

they cry out for oil, till all the thieves in the county
know who's coming. Then you forgot to feed your
horse for a fortnight, and on thinking on't, gave him a
fortnight's bait at one crib. The beast dies; not till he
has had one fair fodder. I would have shot him and
saved my grain, but you ne'er knew what was best, even
in horse-flesh.

Sheriff. Will you call up these little things, Harry?
I thought them but debts of gratitude; what comes
before or after shaking hands.

H. Buel. Ay, both after and before; but think you
seriously I would lend to you? No, I lend to honest men
and give to knaves. I expect something from one and
not a thing from the other. If you had not forty
children, that run round you like stars round the sun, it
would be a blessing to brain you outright. But come,
what's on your mind that looks through your face? A
question, but some sport.

Sheriff. That's it, sport of a serious kind.

H. Buel. What's the game?

Sheriff. Man.

H. Buel. Less than a coon and better than a partridge.
What's his name?

Sheriff. Mark you, Harry, I mean to end this Captain
Lance. If you had as much foresight as wit, you would
see the need to us and the justice to all the world. He
knows our secrets. He's a brand to our powder. That's
not all. The more I think, the more plain he has a
villainous intent on our friends.

H. Buel. Oh! not so bloody.

Sheriff. He has more blood on his hands than in his
body. I know as well as the law knows not, that his
last three boatmen were put out of the way. I had it
straight from one man and another, so I am bound to
hitch him up to a tree, and save the costs to the county.
No one has a better right than I, or a better pluck to
draw it. Mark how he flung a cap over old Lee. He has
the money and he has our friends. 'Tis easy to see what
will happen to our friends. Put to it, he can say they
left me here or there. The whole world cannot disprove
him. Now I am bound on a private dance this time; I

am made up to it, Harry. I am a clock to that tick. I will not be nayed.

H. Buel. I am mum.

Sheriff. So will Lance be by to-morrow night.

H. Buel. How is it to be done?

Sheriff. I have thought of that. His death is nothing. 'Tis the catching of the fox. Then here's his hole. It is the custom at this time of the year to take wood at Stoughton; and as he has a leaky tub and few men, he will tie for the night. He sleeps upon the deck, so it will be all the easier.

H. Buel. For God's sake no hanging. I cannot stomach it. A hangman's gravity is a hangman's special gift. It holds not in me, but if you are in for sudden work with a gun, I'm with you to the end of't.

Sheriff. The farther the better. A bullet is none too long off for him.

H. Buel. Well, then, I am in the pack with you. I can lay my numbers over any man in well doing.

Enter TIM *and* HOLLIDAY.

Sheriff. What put it into your head in the nick of time to come out here?

Tim. Our heads? Ask our stomachs and the answer is behind you. What now, brother?

Sheriff. No; what will you?

Tim. The best. That's the only I know. Have it writ on my stone : *He died of the best.*

Holliday. Odds; that's the very thing I'm fond of.

Sheriff. Now drink till you get courage. I have better work anon.

Tim. I am ready for either. Are you in it, Harry?

H. Buel. In thy mug? No; and save you the cannibalism.

Sheriff. That's Tim's own. There is nothing but that and the cask to fill his appetite. When the tester of weights and measures came to seal mine, I gave him this, and full to the handle at that. Oh! he took three breaths and tugged, but 'twas no go to the bottom. *You are a ruined man*, quoth he, and his standard looked like a gill in a peck.

Tim. To the point, brother. That's an old story.

Sheriff. Old tales are the sweetest.

Tim. As old rats have longest tails.

Holliday. Ay, to the point. What's on the line to-day? Since I was sworn deputy with my left hand, for the judge said 'twas all one for a left-handed man, I have been piped to nothing but dull executions and debtors' oaths. I will murder my wife, if nothing more than to go to a hanging.

Sheriff. Know you one skipper Lance?

Tim. Faith yes; who knows him not?

Sheriff. Then you get at my meaning. It is well known by every one save the juror; he has more murders than years. Wherefore, what are we for? That's a question without an answer, because the answer is plainer than the question. If we have not a right to hang him, I know not who has. Are you dough to that stiffness? Do your knees answer? How now?

Holliday. Like steel. He has no right to live longer. I thought of going alone by myself, but company is most pleasant where least needed.

H. Buel. Could you as easy as that?

Holliday. One to one is a fair match, but I might be put through for manslaughter, or grand larceny, or the like, if I was single. They will hang one where they will praise a dozen. The world thinks every crowd makes the country. But one honest man can spoil a dozen knaves.

Sheriff. But there are thirteen knaves to every honest man.

Tim. Come, brother, is Lance to swing or not; are you playing us a joke or no?

Sheriff. To-morrow night, by nine at least, if your horses can run to Stoughton so quick. Is that enough? Get strong girts and be ready. We start before the sun, and that rises at five, so be on hand no later than three this morning. Then we can pick our way by daylight, for I mean to take short cuts round bends. And mind you there will be less talk and more of another quality needed.

Holliday. How shall we take him?

Sheriff. He has the custom to sleep in his hammock on the deck like a grackle on the corn. We will rush in and shoot and throw his body overboard.

Holliday. Leave this and that to me. No man is better able to shoot than I, or to fling than I, or do aught than I. I was born, bred and begot in Kentucky, where all three of those things are practiced in prime. My mother said I was begotten in the eastern parts and brought to light in the western; for my father had moved meanwhile, so no one can say he has more of Kentucky in him than I.

Sheriff. Save Tim.

Tim. Now the world be done for.

H. Buel. That's like saying grace over you. Be a good dish.

Sheriff. He'll be hot in a minute. Leave him alone for eating.

H. Buel. Come, this is enough. Go home and take a nap. We have a hard ride and a bitter end.

Holliday. Where shall we meet?

Sheriff. Here before the door, and do not come galloping up the street, to spare your horses and let the neighbors sleep. If there are no questions asked, there will be none to answer. If some are put, lies must be told, and lies are sticky, even in a good cause. Be sly. Every man approves of this, but fears every other does not. There's nothing a wise man fears as his own opinions.

Tim. Now I'll believe you when you say you are afraid of nothing.

H. Buel. Take my arm, Tim. Take my left, Holliday. My road is the same as yours. Along, along! We have bad work ahead.

Tim. There was but one man made like you, Harry.

(*Exeunt.*)

SCENE IV. — *A room in Lee's house.*

Enter HARRY BUEL *and* JANE DOR.

H. Buel. Oh! I must hurry away, the more the pity,
Because as often as I set my heart
In your sweet ties, and think to spend an hour

In love with you, some one breaks in. Then soft,
We must be unsuspect. The better part
Of freeness, for that's love's own child, is whipped
And fastened in our looks, and there, poor child,
He would sob, the rods would hear. That's the first
    spasm
That after drives me to a mad vexation,
And ends in doing nothing. All this trouble
For fear it shall be known we love each other;
The gossips get the scent and drive it home
Unto my father. Then those who sell scandal
Retail us round the town. Oh, how I hate them,
These folks that set themselves up for our copy,
But gaudy stamps, so mean and flashy, so
Ill representative of what the world
Holds dearest in its unexpressed bosom;
For those who talk the least, least rate themselves;
And those who most, put a vain price upon
Their quantity. So haps it, as thyself
Art the first person to thy own success;
The parrots of the world win by esteem
And a self confidence. I tell you, Jane,
That I will wed you spite their clack and caw.
Wilt marry me to-morrow?
    Jane Dor.   If I live.
    H. Buel. And why shouldst not? How sorrowfully
    you look
Upon the ground. Art turned a Jewess, sweet?
For they are ever wont their heavy eyes
To drop upon their toes. A merrier man
Would quote your cheeks the very rate of health;
Your season May, and these your cherub lips
All dappled o'er with kisses. Give me one,
Or lend it me in debt. Then I'll begone.
    Jane Dor. What is your hurry? It cannot be yet
Five minutes since you came.
    H. Buel.   Oh! some business.
    Jane Dor. Something you will not tell me?
    H. Buel.   No, not that.
What's the use to wed and love, if mates
Keep secrets from each other?

Jane Dor. Good-by.

H. Buel. Why! not so sad.

Jane Dor. I cannot help it.

H. Buel. Fie,
To-morrow shall be our happiest day.
Kiss me and I'm off. (*Kisses her and exit.*)

Jane Dor. He's not himself.
No, there's an oddity about him; a strangeness
That lacks a definition, save in his eyes;
And those are dictionaries without words,
And so they tell him best. Hum, if I read,
They are troubled some, and indeed are drawn
Farther beneath the shelter which o'erhangs them.
So they were ready to jump out the further
Upon a wrathful errand. Sure this bodes
Something unnatural and out of sorts.
For on a hundred occasions have I seen him,
Nor once ensconced like this, but fair as Heaven.
His vision forward, and his every part
A bright confession, as young men should show,
Not frowning like a stormy angel, but
A bashful forwardness. Sure this was he,
And the same still. Only I think he bears not
The like proportion of his cheerfulness.
But that's all one; when he has reached his middle
These trifles will be no more than pelting hail;
And when his age, they'll fall like snow-flakes soft
Upon his beard. But hush, my thoughts, and live
Only within my bosom. 'Tis his honor,
Or garbed honor, but that's enough.

Enter Js. Lee.

Js. Lee. I thought I heard your voice, Jane. Were
you a-talking?

Jane Dor. Yes, to myself. I want no further and no
better company.

Js. Lee. You must have a split tongue, like a young
crow, and one side talk to the other. Listen and I will
teach you the prettiest knack of words of any bird. For
you are my little bird.

Jane Dor. You vex me. Indeed you vex me.

Js. Lee. That's nothing odd. I am vexed myself.
The cares of justice, the public well-doing, my duty, my
office are breaking me down. I am sick, but all shall say
when I die, *Now —*

Jane Dor. Now what?

Js. Lee. *Now his duty has worked him to death !*

Jane Dor. Your duty! Fie. They may say it, and
draw the price of a lie on your estate. That's quite the
fashion. If a fat senator, swilled with grease and wine,
or a tinkering cabinet member drop dead in their platters,
'tis their duty that killed them, not the lazy apoplexy.
Oh, fie, fie, fie! Such bellies, such heads, such knaves!
Such stuffing out of the common trough and grunting
from the common sow. If a farmer or coal-heaver goes
off at thirty, 'tis nature that took him. Oh! shame,
shame!

Js. Lee. Whate'er's the cause, Jane? I am sick, sick.

Jane Dor. Pity on you. I cannot help it.

Js. Lee. Pity, none of that sour quality. Spare me
from the whines of pity. What I want is thy love, thy
caresses. Now my son is gone, my daughter gone, I need
your consolation. You will deny me no longer.

Jane Dor. Why, deny you before the parson?

Js. Lee. The parson to his hobby, damnation, and we
to love.

Jane Dor. No, your honor, I am nothing of that kind.

Js. Lee. You are a silly girl, though your years betoken
you a woman. Have you not learned a bit of the world?
Have you not studied, what's unknown is unrepented?
Your conscience is your good name, no more; and good
names come by stiff faces. Now, my love, my dove —

Jane Dor. Away, away! Get to your meals. (*Exit.*)

Js. Lee. I will follow you. I will pest you. (*Exit.*)

SCENE V. *The boat and shore at Stoughton.*

Enter SHERIFF, HARRY BUEL *and* HOLLIDAY.

Sheriff. I'm sorry for the moon.

H. Buel.   Well, let her shine,
The light of villains.

Enter TIM.

Sheriff.   Are the horses baited,
So they'll not neigh and set him on the watch?
That's an unnatural sound.
    Tim.   Ay, tied and baited.
    Sheriff. That's well. Can you see Lance? From
    where I stand
The waning shadow of the moon bars off
My lookout of the deck.
    H. Buel.   'Tis plain from here.
And now already he is lain to rest.
He's early for the morning start, and soon
Will be fast locked in sleep.
    Sheriff.   He shall not wake.
Come, choose a weapon.
    Holliday.   Daggers are the surest.
    Sheriff. What's best? Now, or wait for the later
    hours,
Which are the masters of men's dreams? If now,
We may uprouse them all.
    H. Buel.   No, not so long.
That would be tedious to my soul and body,
And doubly out of the way. If his crew
Wake to his rescue, which I think they will not,
We will stand off, after we hit him once.
I will be short, and not harm innocence.
That is not our mistrust.
    Sheriff.   Yes, that were best,
Than harm a guiltless hair. But who of us
Shall be the one to end him?
    Holliday.   I've forgot
My knife.
    Sheriff. And you?
    Tim.   You know I'm in the habit
Of carrying only pistols.
    H. Buel.   Ay, if need
For nothing but daggers. But come stand by me.
There's nothing to be done but must be done.
And to shirk the inevitable is worse
Than cowardice. Yet I hate to slop my fingers
In his blood. But come on. 'Twill soon be over.

Holliday.   Ay, we are here.

H. Buel.   Well, do not show your faces.
He may cry out your names. Soft, now I'm on him.
                                        (*Advances.*)
Lance! Lance! Wake up!

Lance.   What, is it morning yet? (*Rises.*)
No; who are you? 'Tis midnight by your looks.
Say, what's your errand?

H. Buel.   We have come to kill you;
And for your murders done. Nay, do not stir.
I hold your poor, weak body in my hand
Like a dead stick. Now if you have a faith
In any providence, short be your prayer.
I do not like to murder you so darkly.

Lance You have not this hand. Die! (*Strikes with
    a knife.*)

H. Buel.   Friends, hold me up! (*Dies.*)

Sheriff. Why do you weigh so heavy? Are you dead?
Oh! he has done for you. Quick! quick! revenge!
Murder and hack the villain that has done this.
Ho, there! where are you?

Lance.   Dog, here come your cries.

            Enter BOATMEN *and* MEG.

Tim. Hurry, fly, fly!

            (*Exeunt* TIM *and* HOLLIDAY.)

Sheriff.   You cowards to the quick.
If I had one good man to take this burden,
I would strangle you this minute. Think of me
Every night, and you shall live to wish
That you were never born. (*Exit with body.*)

        Enter CONWAY, MARTIN LEE *and* JULIA LEE.

Con.   What is the noise?

Lance. Of some one running.

Con.   Whose horses do I hear?
What does it mean?

Lance.   You are question for question,
And fairly even with my ignorance.
Now that the hurry's over, I surmise
A band of robbers tried to steal in on me,

And rob the fruit of my person. But I woke
In time to hit the assassin, or one
Who bended o'er me with his knife undressed,
And hand upon my arm. But I was swifter,
And hit him in the heart. ·Least he fell back
Upon a mate, who bore him off with curses
And cries of vengeance. This is all I know.
My arm begins to pain me. Will you look?
Has it been broken?
    Meg.   Yes, oh, yes!
    Lance.   Art sure?
    Meg. The bone pricks through the skin.
    Lance.   What if my neck
Had grown upon my wrist. Ha, ha!
    Stewart.   I will set it.
    Lance. There's bandages in the cabin. Come quickly
Before it swells.

    (*Exeunt* LANCE, STEWART, ALLEN *and* MEG.)

    Grim.   This floor is washed with blood,
And I can tell you that 'tis no catiff's mire,
But the life of a man. Yet I did know him
Only by hearsay, but all folks proclaimed him
Above a hint of dross; even of one
Who passes with the world, for what it makes
Out of its idle time; what it would be
If it had not a being that could not be so.
And what every parent would set up
Before his children.
    M. Lee.   What, and a bold thief!
Well, strange graces adorn strange men. A good man ·
Often has such a crabbed knack of giving
He will make more enemies than a robber
Who is polite with humor. One tragic bow
Outshines a thousand smiles.
    Grim.   Why dost imagine
That these were thieves?
    Jul. Lee.   Were they not?
    Grim.   No, I tell you;
What I thought you suspected. These were officers
On his arrest; I o'erheard Buel say so

When he fell down. He was the topmost fellow
In many a good man's heart. 'Tis a great pity,
But cannot now be helped. One time before
In Alabama a parcel set on Lance
To hang him out of hand, but he got off
With courage of the quickest.

   Jul. Lee.   Buel ! O Buel !

   M. Lee. Art sure 'twas he?

   Grim.   None other, lady.

   Jul. Lee.   Dead?

   Grim. The captain was ne'er known to miss, but death
Follows upon his hand. It has not erred
To spare a good man.

   Con.   Now silence on me;
I take a double vengeance in his death.
Oh, I shall speak! It seems to me my tongue,
More than my steel, could do him execution.
What's that cold hand that lays us in a minute
But a great joy. He shall not die as easy
As my poor friend. Not if I have the handling
Of his last moments; but he shall pass off
Afraid of what's to come; and knowing it
So well, his lips will part, his eyes stand out,
And breath strain through his cold and chattering teeth.
Those should be the outward signs, whereof to show
How his soul is distressed. Leave him to me.

   M. Lee. Welcome.

   Jul. Lee.   His death will not bring to life
As fair a gentleman as ever lived.
He might have been my torment, and not seemed
More than a lover, whose sweet pestilence
Tickles the world, but drew my salt tears down;
Yet he did see my inclinations, and
Whate'er were his, let go his suit, and saw
Only with smiles his rival. He was all
That you say in his honor.

   Grim.   If you knew him,
To know him was to prove him, and enough
Without my praise.

Con.   Poor soul, he shall to-night
Be whole.

M. Lee.   If our vengeance could make him so.
But those that die still seem to share our spirits
After their death; so what does us inspire
Seems to please them.

Con.   We will wait some days longer
To take him in the act.

Grim.   Three days ahead
And we shall make a cavern, where he will stop
Out of pretences for your entertainment.

Con.   We understand it.

M. Lee.   But be meanwhile
Like nothing had occurred.

Grim.   I pledge you. (*Exeunt.*)

SCENE VI.— *A grave.*

Enter SHERIFF, HOLLIDAY *and* TIM.

Tim. This is sad. I would as lief see myself in the grave as poor Harry. There had not one of the deputies died for so long I thought I should be first to go, seeing I am naturally weak of body. But Providence takes without asking. If it would have laid its cold hand on me, what a blessing to my tears.

Sheriff. A great blessing, but not to be looked for.

Tim. No one knows, brother. There are certain twinges around my heart that may carry me off any day. Sadly, sadly, but I have faith, and that's better than fine summits over one. What a life in faith, Holliday! What a smile!

Holliday. Ay, the whip of death makes no mark on a good man. Upright men are as full of courage as uprightness. They never spare danger, because they fear not the end. Harry was this mould of a man. He was our copy, and to tell the truth, we had near hit his bright parts. Some would say we had passed over him, but only to my back. No man dare praise me to my face. I hate flattery worse than death.

Sheriff. I wish the funeral would pass.

Holliday. I love not to see the dead. 'Tis only duty.

Sheriff. But it would relieve the wit of you two.

Tim. Brother, this grave is of thy own digging. If you had had the proper pluck you would have stopped the villain's arm. But as 'twas you only dragged off a dead body, which is nothing to boast of to a live man.

Sheriff. And you. God gave you nothing but legs, by the way you ran. If you had as much speed in your hands as your heels, the skipper would be floating down the river before this. As for the blow, no one on earth could have managed it.

Tim. Brother, thy name is ingratitude. If poor Harry were alive, he would scatter his thanks from his bushel. Not this, oh not this!

Holliday. He spurns us, Tim.

Tim. That was always his jade's trick. From his youth up he was as much unlike our Harry as you could reckon. An ungrateful brother, a neighbor of no more grace than a hand-spike. When his next door offered to give him half of his beeve, if he would not steal the other half, he took it without thanks, but quoth, *I lose beef by it.* Drain him off, he is all mud, Holliday.

Holliday. A great pity.

Sheriff. A great lie, and told like grace. No man of any stomach would think of it more. But there are sour men that take these stories for good. Look, Tim, that you peddle them not among such. They are idiots; you know they are.

Tim. Yes, fool against fool.

Sheriff. I could say nothing against the mettle of you and Holliday, more than my own. 'Tis a bad mess and no mending. If we get well out of it, we must make one story fit three mouths.

Holliday. Agreed.

Sheriff. Then all rest easy. But hark! Can you not hear the pacing of the funeral horses? The bearers must take the burden hither from the gate. What a task they make of it! Some thought I should have been one, but I should have cringed, let go my hold and be totally cold. What a ghostly love of the dead possesses some! Now they come. Hold your eyes on the ground, though 'tis more natural to weep to heaven. But the fashion is the feet.

(*Enter bearers with coffin, also* Js. Lee, *the father and mother, and other mourners.*)

Mrs. Buel. Oh, dead, dead, dead!

Js. Lee. Ay, dead, but do not weep
And wring your hands. Gone in a little sense
And shallow meaning of the pitied word;
That is to die, and leave the outward world
To try the marvels that above await us.
Ay, dead in life. That hits the very haven
Where he does lie; but to say dead to life
Were most unholy falsehood. Rather, I
Think him more live than dead. Oh! 'tis not he
That needs the droppings of our grief, but us
Left to the flat bereavement. Now when life
Borders eternity, just reaching out
For what we'll not confess, but really is
A son to be our care, comes with a frown,
More looking unto us than to our prop,
The dismal face of death. Well, give him welcome,
And leave thy sobs for thy own bitter self.
If he were one than otherwise what he is,
The ten commandments done in living letters,
There might be cause for grief and secret mourning
Behind thy walls. But now your open tears
Run for his virtues. So when you go home
Meet calm resignment on the threshold of it,
And let her lead your life, not rough, not wet
With nightly weeping for your son's decease,
But like it was before. That were his wish.

First Mourner. How movingly his honor speaks!

Second Mourner. Oh! tender,
And full of grace.

First Mourner. He's a sweet gentleman.

Third Mourner. And so consoling.

Second Mourner. He seems like an angel
Whispering into her ear; I wonder why
She sobs so.

First Mourner. Ay, why?

Third Mourner. 'Tis a strange perverseness;
More contrary in women than in men,
This pelting of the ground with tears.

First Mourner.   If only
She would put her handkerchief before her eyes,
'Twould be more seemly.
        Second Mourner.   Hush, now he speaks.
        Js. Lee.   Come, madame, take my arm.
        Mrs. Buel.   Oh! your honor.   (*Exeunt*) *and drop.*)

ACT V.

SCENE I.—*A cavern.*

Enter LANCE *and* HIS BOATMEN, CONWAY, M. LEE, JULIA
        LEE *and* MEG.

   Lance.   Oh, it is wearing late and wearing late,
But yet I cannot sleep.   Why are you up
And shadows of my watch?   I do advise you
Straight to your beds.   This fever works in me
A heady, walking temperature to rise,
Caused by my arm, I think.   A single part
Being distracted, eats as does the rot
Into the system.   This runs through the channels
And arteries of my blood; but by the morning
It will be well; and you are younger eyes.
Feed them with sleep, if you would keep them bright.
Tomorrow will be time to sound this cavern.
I will delay.   In fact, my only reason
For letting you this visit, was to show
What a fine house it makes.
        M. Lee.   For the dead?
        Lance.   No,
But for the trade of life, eating and sweating.
        M. Lee.   I think a finer charnel.
        Lance.   It is gloomy,
If that's all that a story-teller needs
To build a dead-house.   Yet, for all I see,
'Tis a good dwelling, made by the first mason
Who roofed his house with the world.
        M. Lee.   The world our roof;
That's worth remembering, a new sentiment.
I've heard you were a preacher on a time,

But gave it up for better trade.   Yet still
You speak like one.
    Lance.   Our first lessons are last
To be forgot.
    M. Lee.   Then you were a young preacher?
    Lance.   No bishop ne'er ordained me, but I tried
A hand at it.
    M. Lee.   Truly a hand?
    Lance.   Ay, I could have said two.
    M. Lee.   But that's all one.   I was thinking of the
      world.
The world a roof; the world a leaky roof.
Who trusts to it, to this ungrateful world,
Gets rained on for his pains.   Is that not so?
    Con.   A trusty moral for bad purposes,
But true.   I thought you would say something more
To that effect.
    M. Lee.   So I would.
    Con.   Well, go on.
    M. Lee.   Lance, here Lance, here!   How would you
      like to die
And lie here in your coffin?
    Lance.   That's an odd question.
    M. Lee.   Death is at odds with all.   He is that angel
That has no worshipper.   For speculation
Where we may travel, like in unknown countries,
That's all.   The topmost apple of knowledge, captain.
    Lance.   Hum, then 'tis not worth climbing for.   Those
      are
The fairest fruits of knowledge, which do hang
Only within your reach.   The others else,
Fantastic and unsound.
    M. Lee.   No; but I pray you.
    Lance.   Well, then, death to me is like to every man,
A thing to talk about, and little thought on,
Because it is the habit to talk idly
And think in earnest.   A blessed uncertainty
That never bothers mortals.   And my grave
Can only trouble me while I do live
And have no use for it.   After my death
It makes no matter where I lie.

M. Lee.   'Twere best
Not to pore o'er our death at all.
Lance.   That's it.
M. Lee. I can see you are a philosopher,
Or else your song belies your voice. Then tell me,
As thought is music to well-tuned heads,
How a lank villain feels about to murder
His three truest friends?
   Lance.   What's that?
   M. Lee.   I say,
Can you divide the passions, as some make show,
One from another, and tell what are the feelings
Of murderers about to kill a friend.
   Lance. Unfriendly.
   Con.   Come, do not bandy with me;
You know our meaning. Why does your hand reach
Beneath your skulking cloak? It does not find
The treasure it is after; thy knife, thy knife.
Oh! 'tis not there. We are not such innocence
To take any chances with you.
   Lance.   Fie, Conway,
Your joke is tragedy.
   Con.   Oh, villain! villain!
I will act it soon. Do you not see this knife,
That looks forth from my hand into your face?
Has that the seeming of being play? You know
'Tis not, or you could see by looking round.
What's in our faces, murderer?
   Lance.   They all try
To look me down. But what's the cause for it
Is o'er my hills of memory. Perhaps
You know the cause. I hope you do, but I
Am ignorant as a dog untaught. 'Tis pity
To kill an innocent man.
   Con.   Talk not of innocence
That are about to die. We have struck hands
To be the law. The morning shall be black
Under your eyelids. Therefore prepare for death.
   Lance. Stewart! Grim!
   Grim. Do not call on us. We have told.
   Con. Yes, they have let all to me; your theft, your
     plot.

You would not this for forty years of honor,
But for a little pelf. How strange, how usual,
And usual, because 'tis strange.

Lance.   Ho, Stewart!
Help me from this madman.

Con.   I will not hurry.
You shall have time to think. Villains like you,
That hold no pity for any man or woman,
Have a great deal for themselves. Heaven ordained
They should be punished some way.

Lance.   Oh! sweet lady,
Have you a heart to see this?

Jul. Lee.   You are guilty.

Lance. Guilty of what?

Con.   You laid in to murder us.
That we do know, and we can only guess
How many immigrants have been your prey
For their lean purses. You have stabbed poor Buel,
And called him thief, to save yourself.

Lance. What! on the deck?

Con.   Yes.

Lance.   I knew not who 'twas,
As I said at the time.

Con.   But you killed him.

Lance. Yes, or he would have me.

Con.   I do not blame you
For your defence; a herald from the heart,
Like all quick acts, but for the evil deeds
That made it necessary. There's the fault.
God have mercy on you. Be short your prayer.
Some would have hanged you, but I will use
Quick, honorable steel.

Lance.   Must it be so?
Look to yourselves. No one does see you here,
But sooner or later this must come to the public.
A secret shared is secrets told; and you
Tell all you know, at least you did to me.
These drunken fellows will be among mates,
Rousing a spree, and want something to boast,
And peach you all. First a dark hint or two,
Then the whole story, and your fountain-head

Of a puddle of trouble.   The hard law
Will be the last to hear, but worst to hold you.
Their deafness makes men stubborn.   If at last
You are let off by perjured evidences,
The stain, the stigma, and the voice of men,
Is against one who kills a fellow.   Mark
The time you will be held as witnesses
In prison, oft outlasts the punishment.
That is not all.   My friends are thick as stars
And swift as meteors.   Oh, you had better
Be walled within a prison than let them know
You have done this bloody thing!   Yes, you will come
To think a stinking cell a grateful dwelling;
And the chatter of lawyers' clerks a song
Compared to their threats of vengeance.   All I beg
Is law and justice.   Here, bind my well arm,
And tie my knees, and wrack me with disgrace;
Load me on dung-carts, if their wheels will carry
My sick and feeble body to the law.
   Allen.   He speaks it well.
   Stewart.   The captain speaks it well.
   Allen.   'Tis certain who fills up his hands with ven-
     geance
Steals from the law.
   Stewart.   Ay, steals the law's right.
   Allen.   What do you say?
   Stewart.   'Tis true the law was made —
   Con.   You! you! you! —
   Lance.   Oh! do not hit me.
   Meg.   Here!   Here!
Here is your knife.   (*Hands* LANCE *a dagger.*)
   Lance.   Now I'm myself.   I'm gone.
But think of me.
   Con.   Turn back.   Die, die!   (*They exchange blows.*)
   Lance.   Oh! you have done for me.   (*Dies.*)
   Jul. Lee.   Are you wounded, love?
   Con.   A prick, that's all, but a very little closer
And I would take my journey along with him.
   Grim.   He stares at us most dreadfully.   (*Exit Meg.*)
   M. Lee.   I wonder
How old he was.

Con. His face might be a youth,
Sported with mad excess, or an old man,
Naturally gone down.
M. Lee. But close on to fifty?
Con. Yes, always lacking sleep. That cuts more
wrinkles
Than any other folly. It can cure
Them all save its own lack.
Allen. Where's Meg?
Jul. Lee. She ran away as soon as the skipper fell.
Allen. That saves us the hanging of her.
Con. She was in the deed with him, or like a child
followed his deeds. But there's not a morsel of bread
within a ten mile. Starving were as bad as hanging, any
day.
Allen. She has enough in her belly to last her any distance. She cannot want, for she was born with her
profession about her. There's a good living at it till all
the world is women.
Grim. She was a sweet cookery. All her dishes
smelled like the federal court.
Stewart. And tasted like the judge's verdict, more
pepper than salt.
Allen. What shall we do with the body? The river
would be a proper cemetery. There's not a Christian
denomination would give him burial, not a preacher that
would come a mile on a chance of saving his soul, because
the chances were against him. Take his feet, Grim, and I
his head. That's the way many a brave man has gone
before him.
M. Lee. We could as well put him in the ground.
Con. We must come to the same, one place or another.
Grim. That's wise. The same and dust. March on,
Allen, to the tune of dust, and we will start this clay on
its last road. (*Exeunt with body.*)
Con. Getting a new master makes a new man.
Stewart. It's to be hoped you will be better than the
old one.
M. Lee. That I will. You have saved our lives, what
they are worth. You shall be used decently, and that's
all I can give you now.

Stewart. The whole thing was our own lookout. First 'tis the mother and then the young ones. He has the wisdom of a serpent. It would have been our turn to follow you.

Jul. Lee. What's to be done next? Shall we here or there, hither or thither?

M. Lee. I think it best for me to return with this property. That's my part, but you shall keep on as if nothing had happened, till you hear from me.

Jul. Lee. That is an easy part for me, but a hard one on you. I could not think of you but I would be sorry I had not gone myself. When we were small, as young as first-mated birds, I was never so worked up as when I had shirked a task upon you. I must think of my ungratefulness, small endeavor, and your hardship. To dread labor is to do it thrice, and to shift it to some other is to do both theirs and your own.

M Lee. Fie! sister, a bit of repentance pays for a load of wrong. The tiding state of girlhood has its own excuse. Our father will be so glad to see his property, any one who carries it will be welcome. Then you know, sister, he has no temper against me, more than a stub that trips him up. We are a man and a missile, and so ends our battle when I stop throwing myself at him. I will be put across in the boat and start short, the quicker the better.

Con. Wait till the morning.

M. Lee. I will not let the morning wait for me.

Jul. Lee. Then go, and my love help you along.

M. Lee. Stay, and my love be with you. Blessings are as good at home as on the road. Good-by. (*Exit.*)

Con. What's the burden of your mind, sweet?

Jul. Lee. As there were happier times ahead.

Con. Because there are bad behind. Our forethought is always looking for a change.

Jul. Lee. I hope so much. This bloody crime has wrought me up bitterly. I could not bear to think; I must shudder at the time to come, as what has gone by.

Con. Nay, you shall not. There's no way to get rid of frights as to forget them. Let's wash ourselves in sleep and we will wake clean of all this. There's nothing like the light to settle evil dreams.

Jul. Lee. All that happens in the day takes a foul color, and troubles me in the night.

Con. Not if I can keep them away by kissing you.

Jul. Lee. Fie, are you not the same nettled?

Con. No, the opposite. What's evil in the day is fair in my dreams.

Stewart. I have heard of men taken that way.

Con. 'Tis as good as any, seeing life is struck even between good and bad.

Enter GRIM *and* ALLEN *with a keg.*

Stewart. What have you there?

Con. The last testament of the captain.

Jul. Lee. Hark, do not speak of him!

Con. Let us to bed, sweet. You have not the blessed gift of drinking.   (*Exeunt* CONWAY *and* JULIA.)

Stewart. Now uncradle thy secret.

Allen. Get the breeze from it, man.

Stewart. (*Smelling.*) It has the family likeness of malt, but which brother plagues me. Some foreigner, I reckon.

Grim. Beer, fool, beer.

Stewart. All hail! Where was he from?

Grim. When the late skipper could not get gin he would swig this, though they must consort like two cocks in the belly. We are his heirs. Fall to.

Stewart. Methinks the palates of criminals are as bad as their morals.

Allen. Have you no soul, man?

Stewart. (*Sings.*)

> We are three merry men,
> And we are three merry men.

Grim. That's the sweet tune of it. The more you drink the merrier you grow. Where did you learn that, Stewart?

Stewart. In my spelling-book, next to the word liquorish. There was "Drink and be Merry" on the same page, also.

Allen. It takes too much of this to get tipsy. More! more!

Stewart. Who's too lazy to drink?

Allen. The man that is sober. He is spare.

Stewart. (*Sings.*)

> The world began
> With a lazy man,
> So it goes by kind,
> I'm a lazy man.
> My father and my mother,
> My sister and my brother,
> Did all forswear me.
> But I got me a wife,
> The honey of my life.
> Oh! sweet bee! she does care me.

Grim. So. Drink, I tell you. Every day is too short for good deeds and hard drinking.

Stewart. That's the mint, sweetheart.

Allen. Here's more, twin Adam. Is there no end to you? (*All drink.*)

Stewart. (*Sings.*)

> Pretty snatches
> Go by catches.

Grim. Those were the very words of the last hangman. *Catch as catch can,* quoth he, and the poor fellow was in heaven, so the parson said.

Allen. What was his crime?

Grim. Hatred of war. He left the army for love of peace, and was furloughed up to the angels. Oh! to the war, to the war, to the war!

Stewart. (*Sings.*)

> There's war enough at home, my boys,
> There's war enough at home.
> Who takes to field or stony fort
> Turns coward back on home.

Grim. He has a wife, Allen.

Allen. After the fashion of mine. *Where have you been, whoremaster?* quoth she. *With one of my kind,* quoth I out of spite. With that she lards me with a kettle of perch that was frying on the stove.

Grim. You were good bread and butter. How did you feel?

Allen. All too cheap at ten cents a double loaf.

Grim. Was that the like of your battle, Stewart?

Stewart. (*Sings.*)

> Let Dixie fight for herself,
> She's big enough to do't;
> And if she can't get through't,
> She may go, go to Dixie.

Allen. Those were the last words of his fancy. To the same, only the next neighbor, which is hell and no further.

Stewart. No, my wife is yet to make; my sweetheart, yet and anon. (*Sings.*)

> I have gone a-wooing,
> And for my love to get.
> Her eye is like to summer,
> Her hair more like to jet;
> She is fine, she is fine, she is fine.

Hold me up a bit, Grim. I nod, I nod.

Grim. Here, niddy. Does she love you?

Stewart. Truly.

Grim. She must take to odd fish.

Allen. Methinks the odd fish must take to such bait. Drink more, Stewart. They will soon put an embargo on the joy of life. It will be all up with us for a long twelvemonth.

Stewart. They hate us merry men. But 'tis yes yet, and no doubt. This state is in a state of sense, and be blessed. Then, then — (*Sings.*)

> Tell me how the votings go,
> Be they ay or be they no?
> What has been the parson's role
> Jailing man and bailing soul?
> Who has often to us told
> Folly in young men's born old.
> Fire, fire away, old gun;
> You can't miss i' the long run
> Sins that we have knowing done.

Grim. Don't frighten me with a thought of denay. Tell me of lovely love; something with balm and rosemary in't.

Stewart.   (*Sings.*)

> Time in and out of mind, girls,
> Dance around the May, girls,
> Stand the boys behind, girls,
> For to get their pay, girls.

Grim.   Sour, sour, Stewart.   Not so dainty as should be.

Allen.   Another of these, you will be as drunk as a fiddler.

Grim.   No, there's no bottom to our ¦bliss while the keg holds out.

Allen.   I have seen men so deep they had no bottom, but I am not of that kin.   A song, Stewart, a pitiful one. I shall weep soon.

Stewart.   I know something my mammy taught me with the help o' the parson.

Grim.   There 'tis, the parson again.   Forever flinging the parson at me.   Talk not to me of parsons, doctors and lawyers, the three ministers of death.   One to look after your soul, one your will and one your health.   Each on his bed-post, and the undertaker hanging to the fourth.

Stewart.   Never mind, dear Grim, sweet Grim.   They were two poor bodies.   (*Sings.*)

> Let us greet
> When kisses are sweet.

I am hoarse, lads.   That was a vile little song.   My brother said it was.   More of the muster.   Here! here!

Allen.   Here 'tis.   (*Hands him the keg.*)

Stewart.   Thanks and thanks.   Bless the cheerful giver.

Allen.   I must needs be cheerful.   You are as endless as a German with a long name.

Stewart.   Greatest Germans have shortest names, where fortune loves them.

Allen.   And you have the longest belly, where fortune loves not the rest of us.

Stewart.   The keg is the deepest by the tape of my eye.

Grim.   Where, oh! where am I?

Allen. That's the question. Where?
Grim. (*Sings.*)

> Eyes as bright as e'er was dew,
> Or little twins dressed in blue,
> Have made all my bosom rue.
> I, alas, what could I do?

> Nothing is my remedy,
> That within my own do lie.
> They shall be my cemet'ry;
> I, alas, I think I'll die.

> When the green is daft in snow,
> And the winter winds do blow,
> Dig me deep the frost below;
> I, alas, preferred it so.

Allen. Why, man, do you weep?
Grim. Is it not sad, Allen?
Allen. Faith no, the jolliest little song of a year.
Grim. Oh, you prick me. That was my own case, my very pity case. See my tears.
Allen. As big as apples. You must take some out, where so much goes in.
Grim. She was my untrue. Oh, sad soul.
Allen. Hush thy nonsense. What's in the entrance there? Oh! oh!
Grim. A ghost, a ghost, the captain's spirit, Stewart!
Stewart. I love them all the same, ay.
Grim. Wake up, fool. See the white thing, the captain.
Stewart. What?
Grim. His ghost for murder.
Stewart. Where's the jolly old ghost?
Grim. There!
Stewart. Ay, there. The ghost is drunk. He's a tipsy ghost.
Allen. He's come back. Run! run!
Stewart. No, that's a lie. He said he was done for himself. (*Sings.*)

> Every black has its white,
> And every sweet its sour;
> Every day has its night,
> And every knave his hour.

Allen. Help me, Grim. Drag him along. Ho!
Grim. Come. (*Exeunt, carrying* STEWART.)

SCENE II. *A room in Lee's house.*

Enter JUSTICE LEE *and* JANE DOR.

Js. Lee. I have wronged you, Jane, and I will confess
My sin in hope of pardon. Pew and preacher
Of every faith agree that all us mortals
Must beg before forgiveness. 'Tis not offered,
Like dew and rain, to every one on earth,   .
But to the humble and the very wretched ;
I think you are an angel sure. Then do
As angels do ; I beg you to forgive me.
  Jane Dor. For what?
  Js. Lee.   O Jane! you are one of those tyrants
That love to see men cringe to them.
  Jane Dor.   Not I ;
But I love honesty and independence.
  Js. Lee. I am honest as gold with you. Have I not
      sought you
To be my wife?
  Jane Dor. Yes, when you had found out
I would not be your mistress. Now you grow
Like a model of virtue with a cough,
And take great airs for doing this last hour
What honest men would have done in the first.
  Js. Lee. You are hard on me. There is not a man
But has two seasons in his life. One is
The time of anger and more angry love ;
Th' other the springtide of calm-bred delight.
I've wronged you in the first, because I could not
By any means prevent it. My love was
Like that brief madness we allow in law
To lessen crime, It does not wholly clear
Of sin, which every man is born into.
If we were perfect, we would be our God ;
But what's repented is ne'er done. That's how
Heaven does look on us. Can you do less
Who cannot be unerring, but must fall

Into mistakes? Oh! 'tis presumption in us
To judge our fellow-beings by their sins.
What's broken can be mended. What is past
Has been repented, even by His grace
Who died for all of us. Think of my sin
Only as dirt that has been wiped away.
Now will you wed me?
    Jane Dor. No; what is this marriage
To make men over? 'Tis only a word
Spoken in silk and broadcloth. If your heart
Has not the true love of the marriage vow
In it before, virtue will last no longer
Than the lost newness of my body. Oh!
You will leave my fair bed for common women;
I know the ways of men like you.
    Js. Lee. Then you
Know naught but what is good.
    Jane Dor. Why, I know nothing
But your bad use of me. You may have been
A tender husband and a generous friend
In times gone by. I have not taken trouble
To ask your neighbors. Your unmanly treatment
Of me was sign enough of your cheap manhood.
    Js. Lee. I shall not hear the last of this. The slips
Of good men are more censured than the fall
Of wicked ones; more talked about and harped,
As if the jealous world was bound to get
Even with righteousness. Crime is the first
To point the finger at an erring brother.
The reason is plain. Sin makes all men equal;
But you have done none. No, 'tis all my fault.
You do not want to be even with me;
That par, that makes man and wife only happy
When they are wed. You wish to hold yourself
Above me in my household; to make me cringe
And shiver out consent. Av, on the strength
Of my love-led and idle words, you try
To humble me and play the little tyrant.
    Jane Dor. No, I hate bullies, whether they be women
Or stronger men. Only you shall confess
That you have wronged me, if not to the world,
To you, your inward world.

Js. Lee.   Have I not, love?
A dozen confessions, and each one
Worse than the last, would not make you love me,
Or better my small fault in your large eyes.
Oh! be my wife, and do not look so at me
Like a petty overseer.
    Jane Dor.   You need a lesson
In virtue.
    Js. Lee. Oh! you are a bitter teacher.
Less teacher than a master, as folks used
To call the quacks of knowledge. What a jest
On them and us! I could be very merry
At the pert strut of learning! what is past
Compared to what fleers in our faces. But
My sadness chokes me. Think of what you are,
And do not fetch me down to humbleness.
What are we all; the pensioners of an hour
All men do quote? That is the short duration
Of vaunted power. Then why should a man
Love to tramp on another? Why a woman
Cut down equality, the flower of life,
The sweet mint of the meadow among rank
And stinking mud of toil? Why do you look
Upon me like a shrike of office, which
Spurns worthy for the unworthy, who, though raised
To power by his beings, thinks that they
Can never pull him down? You have a seat
Of virtue, and cast on me insolence
For being not so high. That is the trick
Of all the world. Each one above looks down
Upon the one below; the one below
Looks up to him above, and makes his place
Most mean by his consent. It often happens
The world sees men through their own eyes,
And above all you women. If I were
A jaunty fellow, as young in the face,
As light unto my faults, you would become
The beggar and not I.
    Jane Dor.   I would not hear him
While you could whistle Dixie.
    Js. Lee.   I am much
The better of the two. The fluent blood

Of youth has no excuse, as 'tis oft pled
By the fond fancy of a parent. Now
You would choose me, love.

Jane Dor. Oh, yes! Of two evils take the least. That
is the only rule to marry by, now that French finery,
which is put on over loose morals, has the upper hand.

Js. Lee. We will be wed in a week. A day further
would drive me mad. These long months of waiting are
like codicils in old men's wills, a sign of folly. A quick
marriage shows a warm heart, and a long space between
betrothal and parson a sort of probation, like mechanic
people take o'er a bargain.

Jane Dor. So short?

Js. Lee. Would you have time to change your mind,
as the fashion?

Jane Dor. No, those who make fashions shall wear
them. That's punishment enough. I am none of the
fashion.

Js. Lee. You are a fashion of your own, and that's
the worst. Let the time be short, at least. A woman
should set her wedding day.

Jane Dor. Then in six months, if you will husband
me.

Js. Lee. At any time, love.

Jane Dor. Not so quick in your promise. Those who
mate easy, break easy, and you have cause. You shall
hear from me. When I am done we will hold the past
nothing and the future nothing, and the present time
enough to forget all in. Now you will not love me so
well in a minute.

Js. Lee. What's the matter?

Jane Dor. I will tell you what will melt your vows.
I have abused you to your back. I have helped your son
and daughter to get off with Lance. I am knowing to all
their plans and their abuse of you. I played you off like
a silly man to get your free permission to Conway and
Julia. I would not have then thought I would come to
have regard for you; but that ends in earnest I began in
play. Yet I do not repent what I have done, and would
not ask your pity for a thousand forgivenesses.

Js. Lee. No, Jane, you have not wronged me as much

as I myself. I love you the better for being candid.
Advice without envy is only a wife's office. A friend has
the pride of the sex, and an open friend is soonest lost.
I want none of the gender to disclose me to myself in
their crooked glass. They are so cracked, so flawed, so
seamed, so welted. I would not look in them, but go to a
woman's face.

Jane Dor. Now what do you think of Julia?

Js. Lee. She has a spirit above mine. An angel could
not censure her.

Jane Dor. I am glad we two are of a mind. If you
were not more tender on what you called her faults, I
would throw you off, like a roof rain. There is a conclusion foreconcluded. Am I a wife already, that I speak
with the terror of sureness? But I could not be happy
without her back with me. You will make all even where
you have done her wrong.

Js. Lee. As quick as I can get to them. You say they
are with Lance, and he is not to Louisville yet. But
what a villain! What a traitor! What a knave! How
will he make an excuse, or look me in the face?

Enter MARTIN LEE.

Ho! good morning, son.

M. Lee. It is evening.

Js. Lee. Morning is easier spoken on the breath of
surprise. Sure 'tis late. Where is your sister?

M. Lee. Yes, 'tis a sweet-sounding word, and runs
well with its yoke fellow good. I am glad to see you
Jane as a week could make me.

Jane Dor. How long is a week?

Js. Lee. Your sister?

M. Lee. She is well; so is her husband.

Js. Lee. That is happy. Marriage is a hospital, where
one should be always nurse to keep up sympathy. Never
mind. Did you come from the captain?

M. Lee. No, unless I came from the other world.

Js. Lee. Has he gone off? Dead?

M. Lee. Yes.

Js. Lee. I thought he would not live a year when I last
saw him. There was a coroner's verdict in his every

motion. He has drugged himself more than a dame of
fashion, and drank more than her man. What was his
trouble?

M. Lee. The shortest of all, a knife.

Js. Lee. He was ever moody. Suicide goes before
disease. 'Tis only an early winter, and gets a little
sooner what a later month would take.

M. Lee. No; flatly, we have murdered him.

Jane Dor. Oh!

Js. Lee. Fie, Jenny. He was deserving, no doubt.

M. Lee. Yes, truth is always short. He was made a
villain by nature, but well disguised. He robbed you,
then laid in with his boatman to murder us, but they
warned us from the first. He would throw the blame on
us, and being dead no one could say nay. That is all but
his death.

Js. Lee. What a history! He made me mistrust you
utterly, though I knew him of old. Has he left a will?

M. Lee. Nothing for lawyers, but all for honest men.
I have safe what he has taken from you, and come to
return it.

Js. Lee. A trifle, Martin. I thought not at all of it.
I blame myself ten thousand times for thinking such a
thing of you.

M. Lee. A consequence.

Js. Lee. One better understood than spoken. It
shall not happen again. But I have tragic news for you.
Young Buel has been stabbed to death in a raid to take
the thief Larkin. The church-bell does not ring, but I
count to hear it toll his years. It is the saddest thing in
a lifetime.

M. Lee. How did he come to die?

Js. Lee. Larkin rammed his knife through him.

M. Lee. Who said so?

Js. Lee. I had it from the eye of the sheriff.

M. Lee. He has a beam in his eye, like the run of his
kind. He might have told the truth, seeing his part was
brave enough, but lying is easy after thinking. No, he
fell by Lance.

Js. Lee. The bloody villain!

M. Lee. All of that. One night, when we were moored

at Stoughton, the sheriff, with Harry and the deputies, made a rush from the bank to take the captain alone. There was his end. They had, like enough, a suspicion that Lance meant us harm, for the sheriff must have known his repute.

Js. Lee All men are liars. I will run another for the county and beat the sheriff out. I cannot trust such a tongue with the juror. He would hang a man for the rope. He is so lazy he had rather sit in the steam of a court-room than open a window. How can we do God's justice without God's air.

M. Lee. A little more reason, father. He knows too much for us to offend him.

Js. Lee. He's a wedge.

M. Lee. Look out how you hit him. Let him pry others, not us.

Js. Lee. I will wait till I take him bribing the next witness.

Jane Dor. Can I speak a word among your rabble? Where is your sister, and how may she soonest get here?

Js. Lee. I am in a worry to see her, Martin.

M. Lee. And her husband?

Js. Lee. They are one. I cannot part what God has joined, as some say.

M. Lee. Well, they are on the boat, not a thousand miles from here, and waiting word from me.

Jane Dor. What's the station? I will line what shall call them home like music from fair fingers.

M. Lee. Send to Louisville explicit. They will look after it there.

Jane Dor. Good-by.   (*Exit.*)

Js. Lee. I am ruined. Send your wife to every place but a telegraph office. She will out-bargain you all but there.

M. Lee. Will you wed her?

Js. Lee. Have you a suspicion?

M. Lee. Yes, of all women.

Js. Lee. She is above it.

M. Lee. All baser sort. She will make a good mother to me.

Js. Lee. And me a good wife, boy.

M. Lee. Your way will be a bridegroom's, always strewn with roses. Oh, rosy!

Js. Lee. You do her justice, dear son. May I be blessed with many children, and you with brothers. Then will you learn the kind art of dividing, when I die. Where there are many, not one is selfish.

M. Lee. That is a maxim for black birds. But father, I doubt you have the strength to beget me relatives at your age. I have heard that you were a wild young fellow.

Js. Lee. A lie, whoe'er monged it. And I spent a small part of my virtue in creating you.

M. Lee. I fear so, indeed. But may you prosper in it. I will begone with your leave.

Js. Lee. Where so fast?

M. Lee. I have had a fancy I would like to see the world before I became one of it. How can I do this but by travel? I will go and prepare myself as soon as possible after I have said good-day to Jane.

Js. Lee. There are means enough for you.

M. Lee. I shall draw at will; and nothing on a pinch. Do not be surprised if my notes come in large. (*Exit.*)

Js. Lee. He has not lost his grudge against me for those begging fools I put on to him. Oh! the memory of children is long for evil and short for good. Now I wonder how much he will cost me. Let me reckon. No, I will not. He's as changeable as the wind. Ten to a dozen, he will get so in the habit of going to his bed he will forget there is another. (*Exit.*)

THE ROGUES' MIRROR.

THE ROGUES' MIRROR.

PERSONS OF THE PLAY.

JUDGE FORD.
RANSOM, nephew of FORD.
VERRELL, } companions of
CADE, } RANSOM.
RATSEY, }

LEVEC.
CHRISTOPHER KEEN, Clerk of Law.
STEPHEN WRY, in the hire of FORD.
CATHARINE, daughter of FORD.
DAME DURRELL, an old woman.

Also Officers, Citizens, Ladies, Host, Friends of FORD, etc.

SCENE.— *Chiefly in village near Portland.*

ACT I.

SCENE I. — *The garden of Ford's house.*

Enter JUDGE FORD.

Ford.   Soft! what a night, so calm and fit for death!
I cannot sleep upon it in my chamber,
The pinched and stifled air so strangles me;
But oh, how soft the fingers of the wind
Do smooth my haggard brow! If this be night,
Fly, troubled day, and come, oh shades of death,
Continual night.
             Enter CATHARINE.

             Hello, my fancy!
Speak, ho! who comes so fast?
    Cath.   Was it a voice?
    Ford.   Come hither, Kate.
I have much noted that of late your eyes
Run at my heels, like greyhounds, wait upon
The moments of my solitude, and peep
Warily into mine; even as the birds,

-119

That dive i' the gusts, and ever and anon.
Half spread in the falling snow, look timidly
Upon our fireside comfort through the pane.
This curiousness sorts not well with the gay season
And tripping times of youth. It is the wont,
So I have heard, and know from seeing it,
Young people run to life as to their meals
With hearty appetite; but you, forsooth,
That heretofore was ever on the prick
Of mischief, early risen as the thrush,
As early in your bed, running from darkness
As from a robber, to the arms of sleep,
Must now rush forth in the unpeopled middle,
And change-watch of the night. Are you in love,
And have I for the nonce unheeding walked
Between the sun and shadow?
    Cath.   Nay, father, speak not so.
    Ford. Indeed, 'twere strange.
I do remember, when the love o'ertook me
Of your fair mother, I did run away
Out of the sight of men, for as I thought,
My love sat like a mask upon my face,
Not to be pulled apart; and when a friend
Smiled for a morning's greeting, I did think
'Twas laughter at my plight, and all my eyes
Skulked back into my head for very shame,
Or fell upon my toes; then would I jest
On love, fie upon marriage for a bane,
And call it a rough officer to take
Into arrest our slight affections;
Make practice with my wit at the bald mark
My silliness did set up.
    Cath.   Pray, more of this.
    Ford. Fie, not to-night. These memories are like
        coals,
No sooner touched but dropped.
    Cath.   Are they not happy?
    Ford. Come, come, the night is damp; get you a-bed,
And let it be made softer with soft prayers
For them that have it not. There's many a man
That takes the hazard of the waves to-night,

Stands in gross need of them; for I do taste
A mettle in the air, such as forcruns
A gale at sea. Now are the fisher-folk
Up to their knees in surf, whereat their eyes
May gain upon the night; while we, dear Kate,
That are but tenants of the day, think not
How very blessed we are.

  Cath.   I had more thought
You had affected sadness; scarce a smile
Has tripped upon your face these many days,
But rather melancholy, and your mirth
Is heavier than your sadness. I can tell
Some sorrow runs before your every thought,
And robs it of its health. Why is't that I,
Who am the familiar of your happiness,
Not partner of your sorrow? I'm not apt
In velvet words, or I would tell to you
How there is but one cell in all my heart,
And in it you are prisoner, though you still
Put me aside with sorry smiles and bid
Me back to sleep; and what know I of sleep?
That oft, unbreathed, listen till the night
Musters her thickest hours; for then I hear
Your slow return and too unsteady feet
Halting upon the stairs, as if a groan
Were dropped at every step; and then I dream
Too deep for memory. Oh, these hidden ills
Do bark up all my terrors, which are not few,
Seeing I am a woman, and have not
The armor of hard terms to hide them in.

  Ford. Is this curiousness?
  Cath.   Nay, father, 'tis love.
  Ford. How do you know 'tis love?
  Cath.   How should I know
That I am flesh and blood, and not a dream,
Tripping my life in minutes o'er the brain
Of some love-laboring youth? Why, I have sense,
Limb, marrow, heat, — some say I have beauty;
Touch, smell, discretion, and the parts of mind;
All which make up (whether it is a dream)
At least what we call life; so is my love

A sense that has no counterface in words,
Nor in the crafty corners of discourse,
But is to the heart alone; and all I have
I give to you as you gave life to me.
   Ford. Why, my fair advocate, this is well said,
And is well answered with a confidence.
'Tis true I have a secret.
   Cath.   Tell it me.
   Ford. A secret parted is an open tale,
But never mind; it is a sin that bears
Upon your life, therefore it shall be told;
But only for this reason, that it runs
Into its fifth act, and must soon be known,
I do surmise, whether I will or no.
   Cath. A sin?
   Ford. Pray, sit you here upon this seat, while I
Give some directions; for a sudden business,
On tiptoe at my ear, calls me away
To Portland ere an hour. Stephen! Stephen!
   Cath. What! shall you ride to-night?
   Ford.   It must be so.
Stephen! Stephen!

            Enter STEPHEN.

   Steph. Who calls?
   Ford. Stephen!
   Steph. Is it you, your honor?
   Ford.   Have you seen anyone?
   Steph. Not even you, your honor.
   Ford.   Well, well, so be it.
An't please you, get the horse and wagon ready.
I ride to-night, and needs must hit the stage
Upon the Portland road. Make haste! make haste!
   Steph. Will it not rain to-night?
   Ford.   No, it will pour.
   Steph. 'Tis at your honor's liking.   (*Exit.*)
   Ford.   Now I'll drive
Into the story, though it is a tale
That cries upon my honor. When 'tis finished,
Let it be cold between us, never mentioned
Nor booked in the eyes; I am thus sensitive.

Cath. It shall be so.

Ford. Well, let it rest.
'Tis easy as the breath to tell a lie,
But truth is harder parted. Some years ago
(Out of your memory) I had much note
In the affairs of state, and as I climbed,
My eyes climbed higher still. 'Twas natural.
This is the first ambition of us all,
(The rest sit at its feet) to push our name
Into men's faces. So; all public office
Is won on wings of gold; I had it not,
But twice as rich, had I but reckoned it,
One faithful friend. He was a merry fellow,
Trimmed with a native honesty and grace
That quite upset the painted desperate ills
We Puritans so love; and when he shook
The laughter from his cheeks all nature smiled
To see so gay a creature.

Cath. All's well thus far.

Ford. So all was well till I
Became the drudge of my ambition,
And though to see, in the open door of the times,
A road to office; but I had no money,
No money; 'twas a pity; had I money,
Or courage to have ta'en it without stint,
I should have cleared the breach. Well, well, it chanced
This friend of mine sat in a place of trust
Over the federal wealth.— Your eyes, dear Kate,
Are wonder-wide, and seem to bend their lights
Backward upon me, like good torch-bearers.
You know what I would say; under his name,
Masking my hand, I somewhat freely dipped
Into the public moneys, which I thought
By thrifty use of office to repay.

Cath. You took the money?

Ford. I stole the money,
Spent it, and threw myself, with kneeling thoughts,
On my friend's mercy. He did never look
Upon me with reproach, but sorrowfully
Foretold his ruin. 'Twas a forward truth.
I know not how it chanced, the public favor

Turned me her back; it was a bitter fall
To me, for I had played a smiling game,
And lost the gambit.   But a crueller fate
Let fly at my poor friend; he was discovered
In the default, the lack-wit of his cause,
Making no face against the proof of crime.
    Cath.   And did you not confess?
    Ford.   Look, Catharine:
I had a wife that in her dizzy fondness
Made me her worship, and yourself, dear Kate,
Was in the dew of life; but I'll not scarf
My villainy in that; I was a coward,
Which is the basest confession under heaven;
And in the double standing of my doubts,
Whether to speak and suffer, or to unload
My sins upon another; if 'twere better
To rot in prisons, or 'scaping the fate,
To run into the hands of one more dread,
The rust and mildew of the conscience,
I did offend the better part, and shut
My trembling lips upon my trembling secret;
Nor did he ope his mouth, nor fasten me
Into his plight.
    Cath.   I will love this man,
Even in the dust.
    Ford.   How know you he is dead?
    Cath.   Is it not that you weep for?
    Ford.   Kate, you are dull,
Or have a bitter humor.   He fled to France,
While yet he had provision of his time,
And in the patriot wars lifted his nâme
A head above the others.   But the wars
Are over; I have note of his return;
And in the here and there of idle comment,
I fear I stand in harm's way of his tongue;
Else is he free of passion as a stone,
And lacks of gall, which once, I do remember,
He had in quantity; he was a man
Of hearty mirth, but in his sober hours
Not to be ta'en in jest.
    Cath.   Will he come hither?
    Ford.   Now you hit the adventure

That I have oft played o'er; for when my wits
Play me the runaway, I often start
Up from my pillow in a sweat to think
He raps upon the door, as his remembrance
Raps at my breast; for look you, Catharine,
'Twere wondrous strange, after this breach of years,
His love should hold the bent, and if his anger
Is in the measure that his love has been,
'Twould waft a snow in summer; and it needs,
So his mind take the color, but a word
To prick my high-blown pride, and bring my fortunes
About my feet. But soft! I hear the wheels,
A fair good-night, love; I shall straight to Portland,
And slyly put inquiry on foot,
That shall confound my fears, or at the least
Give them proportion. But for you, dear Kate,
Think not the less of me for what you know,
But rather judge by love that you know all.

Re-enter STEPHEN.

Steph. Sir, the wagon's ready.
Ford.　　　　　　　So am I.
A good-night, Kate; I have a fire within
Will fence me from the cold; let us be speedy.
　　　　　　　　　　　　　　　(*Exeunt.*)

SCENE II.— *A room in Ford's house.*

Enter CATHARINE *and* TWO LADIES.

First Lady. If anyone should say to me, I saw Apollo
riding by Newport strand, I would outface him for a
peddler of tales; for indeed we saw him as we came
hither, in the full smack of his godship. If there were
not nine graces with him there were something less than
nine, all smiling like good reflectors; and his godship's
self was smiling over his finger tips, perched fore-front
in the lap of — plenty; Lord, Lord, and left nothing but
dust. To be short, Kate, we saw your cousin playing the
runaway with a bee-hive of young women, that stung
him into laughter twenty times and again. Fie on his

courtesy, and he wagged his head at us, thus and thus, as he passed. What is this cousin of yours, Kate, that people so talk about?

Cath. An indifferent good cousin.

Second Lady. So will he say of you when I tell him how scanty your praise was. A little more would have been more cousinly.

Cath. And a little less would have been more truthful.

First Lady. You will trim him down to a vagabond in another piece-meal or two. Indeed, the townsfolk say that is his figure, a million and odd for deviltry, and a cipher for virtue. But I care not for that, save the envy of it. There is not a two-footed innocent in the town (bating the sex) since the gown (that's your father, Kate,) sentenced madcap Verrell for a peccadillo. Find me, and you cannot, a man of them all that is not a finger-mark for the community; and a great rogue is no blacker in my eyes than a little rouge; each proceeds on inclination, not capacity. But they say your cousin hath a black pitch about him that sticks all rascals into a lump, and he is the life of it. Pshaw! Kate, you shall give me a passport to his acquaintance. What was his hailing-place?

Cath. Is it possible the townspeople have not told you?

First Lady. Is he not direct from Germany?

Cath. Yes, from the academies. He studied there two years, aiming to be doctor of physic, and came away by a good chance with all he knew before. There were some sufficient properties fell to him when his father died, and he inherited much good advice by his uncle's will. The properties are in law and the advice is in parchment. If either escape their prison, heaven help my cousin that he use them well. But I know not. He would do well, I think, to stick to his pestle and gallipots.

Second Lady. Would have done well? Why?

Cath. He has the perfect parts of a good sheepskin doctor. In these days, if a goose but quack, people come running to be cured.

Second Lady. By my faith, you have as bitter humor as a Scotch bag-pipe; a very bag of sourness.

Cath. I do not pipe well to all touching.

First Lady. They say he's witty, too; much keener than plain country folk, so that he keeps the cock of his wit down out of safety to people. Well, you are in good fortune that sit so near the fire; I am sure all else here-about is only smoke.

Cath. Why, 'tis thus: his humor has some flavor to a starved wit, like dry bread to a beggar, but no relish for a full one.

First Lady. Oh! then 'tis hearty victual. But indeed I thought you had affected him, Kate; nay, I did not, but truth and falsehood go at a flight in gossip. I know you well; you will mate with a mild-mannered man, and your cousin, by all telling, was a great vaunter and challenger in the academies; calls for hilts in a quarrel, and quite outfaces the town with his boldness.

Cath. Why, for that matter, his red eye cries out in the distance, so ferocious, twenty paces and — swords.

First Lady. Well thrust — again!

Enter RANSOM.

Ran. Fair play, cousin.

Cath. What brought you hither?

Ran. An ill wind; but, i' faith, I am very lucky to fall among so many, indeed, so many —

Cath. Well, what?

Ran. Roses, by the breath.

Second Lady. You are more hurt in the thorns, sir, than you think. Your cousin and my friend here have disputed over you these two hours by the clock, but only as vultures, which should feed upon you most.

Ran. Why, then, I shall go the whole course over again. Disputes are the sweetmeats of discourse; they sicken, but purge. Now, I will call myself villain —

Cath. What, conscience-struck?

Ran. And then all the world, cousin, will be at odds with me; so if I hang myself in a halter of tough words, you shall cut me down with your good opinions. They say of the Dutch skippers that they have more wine in their lockers than wind in their sails; so that they never reach a port but they go by it; as if nature had pitched about to keep Dutchmen always at sea. 'Tis in this fashion the world weighs men, either over or under. For my part, I am underweighed. I have more worth than I ever told of; more fire in the pan —

Second Lady. This is not your cue, sir.

Cath. Why, my cousin has crammed so many wild boasts into his memory, one must needs fly out if he but ope his mouth to sneeze. Pray you, forgive him.

Ran. 'Tis sweet to be forgiven; and as I wish you nothing but sweetness, I will repay it upon you.

(*Music without.*)

First Lady. Hark! I hear music in the corridor.

Ran. 'Tis Christopher Keen. Be quiet, he will not see us.

Enter KEEN, *singing and playing.*

Keen.

> A raven all so prickle plumed
> Sat on the limb of a tree;
> And all the day changed into night,
> So funeral croaked she.

Ran. Well sung, Christopher.

Keen. Now God bless my fortune, I have not walked into the river bottom; God bless my fortune. I beg your pardon, ladies. My senses were wrapped up in sweet music. I will be gone directly.

Cath. Nay, this is no interference. We are strangely counted here, and one other neither mends nor mars, for there will still be one more to talk than to listen. I knew not you could sing.

Keen. I am something expert. Indeed, I play and sing very finely.

First Lady. I never heard a better.

Ran. Faith, you outclap the Turks. He did but tune himself. When he has well unsaddled his tones, I will wager my right hand to my left he shall sing you a song as if 'twere shaked from seventy tubes. He has a marvelous gong and a good discretion; for all his notes were gotten out of the hand of nature, all as his straying flocks he fed. And there's disaster; for he had rather lose a sheep than a stave, which was arm's-length from his father's sense of property. So is he become clerk of law, to put music into the debtor's oath. You shall sing for us, Christopher.

Cath. There shall be no excuse. How can we spend our ears better?

Keen. So be it; a passion song?

Second Lady. Yes, yes.

First Lady. Ay, that's it.

Ran. Oh, now you stick daggers in me. Did it not smell too much of arrogance and assumption I would give you much crafty advice. Nay, I care not for the smell o't. Hark you, friend Christopher, steer a free course from all these herring craft of poetry, all short-stepping verses, pit-a-patter rhymes, musty sonnets, spavined hexameters, and the like new kinds of prose. Of those great poets that sprinkle their tears over a little world, I say nothing. May God help them to better quarters. And I say nothing of those pets and kittens of fashion who so hug their verses that the lines blush for shame in the eyes of all the world. Mark you, I say nothing of these nor of other, but may heaven make you pregnant of this wisdom that you deliver us a simple household ditty, such as were sung before people became eloquent. Now, sir, stand to it.

Cath. Pray, are you done?

Ran. Not if you would have me say more.

Cath. Now God forbid. But look how I shall put you down with plain honesty. 'Tis three to one, Christopher, that you sing us a love ballad.

Ran. Faugh!

Keen. As ladies wish, Ransom. I have in my memory a song which has a clear title to your favor. It is called *The Soldier's Lament.*

Ran. Look how my flesh weeps in sympathy.

Cath. Let us have this song before any other.

Keen. So sets the wind, ha! (*Plays and sings.*)

Where is my laddie gone?
Where is my laddie gone?
Robin the rogue is in the marsh,
And with his thorns and creepers harsh
His tender flesh has torn.

> Where is my laddie gone?
> Where is my laddie gone?
> The lark and chat are whistling shrill,
> And the flag of the sun upon the hill
> Leads on another morn.
>
> Where is my laddie gone?
> Where is my laddie gone? —
> I hear her in my midmost sleep,
> And ever I wake and vigil keep,
> And wish the morrow morn.

Ran. Now for the chorus.

Keen. 'Tis complete; there is no chorus.

Ran. Oh, what a carpet song is this, to be hung in mid air without a chorus!

First Lady. A good song, and well delivered.

Ran. There are worse, there are worse; but had any other made such a pass at my discretion, I would have unsheathed my wit for my honor's sake.

First Lady. Oh, then, I warrant I should have been slaughtered. 'Tis said men fight best for what they have not.

Ran. What! no honor?

First Lady. Indeed, sir, I can see none.

Ran. Why, this is levity; as if you should say honor is to be taken in the hand, and looked at; for all the qualities are freeholders, and but one keeps open doors, as you may see; thus, admiration lives in the eyes, and is partial; love lives in the lips, and is volatile; veneration lives in the ear, and is crafty; but honor has a throne —

First Lady. Pah! this is sentiment.

Ran. But honor has a throne in the pocket, and is yellow. If that is sentiment, take it for a medicine.

Second Lady. You should have more honor, then, than the general.

Ran. Look how my hand runs through my pocket without clinking even honor's penny. (*Pulls out a paper.*) Ho! what's here? Beshrew me, I had forgot what called me hither. Here's a note, cousin, that has your name running over it at a villainous slouching gait. A vile hand, a vile hand; I found it in the garden, but the inditor alone knows where it was bred; for it had married the north wind so merry, and was setting the fashion to runaways. Here it is, cousin.

Cath. If it be not some trick or trap, I thank you.

Enter STEPHEN.

What is it, Stephen?

Steph. The ladies are waited for.

First Lady. We must be gone speedily. Good-morrow, sirs.

Keen. Your wishing shall be warranty of it.

Ran. Oh, happy Christopher!

(*Exeunt* LADIES *and* CATHARINE.)

Steph. I would tell you, too, Christopher, the bell is rung.

Keen. The bell rung? Bless me, I must straight to prayers! (*Exit.*)

Ran. Oh, the villain! He is flown after his victual.

Steph. I care not. He ordered me to warn him by the clock.

Ran. I doubt it not, I doubt it not.

Steph. Am I victual, too, that you feed your eyes on me?

Ran. I doubt it not, Stephen.

Steph. Are you gone mad, sir?

Ran. I did but look on you; I never saw the like before.

Steph. Why, I am only plain Stephen Wry.

Ran. So thou art plain, Stephen. Tell me, why did nature make so great a nose to stand sentinel over so small a mouth? If she had gone to arm's-length after the making, you had not come into the world at all, or else come better furnished. But nature's a blind bitch, and gets blind children.

Steph. Well, I cannot help it.

Ran. Was your father of this handicraft?

Steph. He was very much as I am.

Ran. This father of yours was a knave, Stephen; so were all your ancestors. Had they but married women of good wide mouths, such as are sometimes seen, their childrens' would have been of happy proportions.

Steph. Why, so they did, sir, and got great noses instead.

Ran. You lie; they did not do it; but you are the very man for the business. I have in my mind's eye a lass of forty or thereabout—

Steph. Believe me, I shall never marry.

Ran. Marry, why not?

Steph. Oh! sir, I have not that cunning in me that sways the love of the sex. My heart is as naked as water, so that all who run know me to be simple Stephen Wry, son of Solomon Wry, that was. I shall live all my life a bachelor, and die of my woes. Faith, I was thrust out into the world union down, to be the sorrowfulest of men. Good-by, Ransom; I have a hint in my throat that I shall weep presently. God prosper what he will.

(*Exit.*)

Ran. So, so, so. But here comes Kate deep in the dumps.

Enter CATHARINE, *reading the scroll.*

Well, cousin, have you dismissed that rubbish?

Cath. Yes, and found more. Listen to this: (*Reads.*)

> I am the will-o'-the-wisp,
> With wary wing and crisp;
> When the ploughman's work is done,
> And the worm winds her cocoon,
> And out peers the visored moon; —
> When the fleece of stars is bright,
> And the glow-worm spends her light,
> And the owl's in weary plight,
> Then do I come by night.
>
> RANSOM, *thy love.*

Ran. Why, that is very good. I have not seen its like in a twelvemonth.

Cath. Is it not your handwriting?

Ran. I plead guilty to it.

Cath. Art not ashamed?

Ran. There can be no shame to a pleader.

Cath. Truly I think so. What is the meaning of this rhyme?

Ran. Shortly spoke, Will you ride with me to-night?

Cath. Shortly answered, I will not.

Ran. Why, you are shorter than I am. But 'tis dinner-time; let us take care of the hour, and let the next be master of itself. 'Tis certain love is sweetest on a full stomach. (*Exeunt.*)

SCENE III.— *A street in Portland; citizens passing.*

Enter LEVEC.

Levec. Pray, sir, where will this street lead me?
Cit. To the shipping.
Levec. 'Tis very roundabout, is it not?
Cit. No, sir; very direct.
Levec. I should have thought the foxes had made it.
Cit. I see, sir, you are a foreigner. (*Exit.*)
Levec. Is't possible the fashion of the dress
Fashions the value of a man, even here?
I had not thought my native countrymen
Were of that blabbing kind that change their natures
As often as their coats. We see abroad
How each man is a beggar 'fore the world
For tags of merit. Where men varnish o'er
With costly dressing they do but acknowledge
That there are flaws to cover; but there's one,
I am very sure, even in this falling age,
Stands upright on his virtue. Here I'll wait
Upon the flagging till he passes by;
For every day, so I am told, he walks
Upon the quays, and watches 'neath his hand
The nation's living barter. 'Tis most strange
My haunted eyes have not yet gazed upon him;
Yet I half fear to gaze, as one who flies
And o'er his shoulder looks. He's prosperous,
So I am told, and bears his feather well
Among his crowing brothers; yet I think
He is by nature kind, and in his heart
Undressed before his friends. But if the frown
Of hell-bred arrogance and contemptuousness
Hangs on his cheek, and like an officer,
Seems to arrest the world and call it dog,
I'll give his infamy to the bitter world,

Though it should break my heart, and then I'll sit
To the swift painter, for a cast of grief
Shall set the world in tears. No, no, my heart,
Thou canst not hold this stiff and wiry purpose;
Better to be forgotten than forget,
And he was once the dearest friend that heaven
In labor with the earth did e'er beget;
Though in the wit of truth his qualities
Were mixed with an uneven hand, as God
Is said to mix his earthly pensioners.
But soft! he comes. Oh! what a sadness droops
Before him, that he seems to walk o'ercast
Under the shadow.

Enter JUDGE FORD *and* TWO FRIENDS.

First Friend. I am sorry you must part for home so
   soon;
The season's on its flight, the glass goes round,
And merriment's a-tiptoe.
   Ford.   My age is my excuse;
But if you ever sicken, and turn your backs
Upon the idle frolic of the time,
Pray visit me and we will try a hand
Which is the hardier in our country sports,
You, that have swollen your time with balls and feasts,
Where eyes are fuel to the wine, or I,
In the frugality — (LEVEC *passes* FORD *and exit.*)
   Second Friend. What is it?
   Ford. Who was it snatched my hand?
   Cit. He went yonder that touched you.
   Second Friend.   Tut, a beggar.
   First Friend. Look to your wallet, Ford; these gutter
   sparrows
Have fingers light as snow. What! are you pale?
   Ford. It is my native color. Let us make haste
To shake these by-ways from us. If I tremble,
Think nothing of it; 'tis a fault of nature
That flutters in my limbs. Come, faster, faster.
   First Friend. This is most strange. (*Exeunt.*)

SCENE IV.— *The garden of Ford's house.*

Enter RANSOM *and* CATHARINE.

Cath. Oh! you pelt me with love.
Ran.   So will I, Kate,
Until you take the game of kindness up,
And pay me back what I, so prodigal
Of all I am possessed, have given thee.
Nay, I'm possessed of it, for love will not,
Like smiling virtues, coil upon the cheek
At every will and beck; it stamps its form
Upon the heart, and stiffens with rebuke.
The nations had it that were barbarous,
Ere letters watered knowledge, and I think
Warm-blooded beasts and creatures of the field
Most like to men in this. There's not a bird
That swingeth in the hammock of the air
But hath some carol or some matin sweet,
And even the rock-reared whip-poor-will his song.
All this is love, and all the world is love
Save you alone, that, like the stony flint,
Are in yourself most cold, but at a touch
Set others in a very fire of love.
  Cath. Now are you merry.
  Ran.   Nay, I am very sober.
  Cath. If you did love me, sure your words would taste
More of a homeliness and simple sort,
Partaking of the state; for I have noted
How men who are deceivers and who sow
Their vows in every ear, do most conceal
Their fang in ecstasy; of many loves
Ne'er getting once a wife, but o'er the point
Just stepping like a hero carved in stone,
That never downs the foot; they make a pause,
And of the pause a flight; but men whose love
Is seated in their heart to marriage go,
With steepdown visages and sober thoughts,
Holding their vow the very stitch o' the life.
  Ran. Why, so I do.
  Cath.   Then is your life as full
Of stitches as your coat.

Ran.   Why do you put
This show of disaffection upon me?
I am sure I am no weak and dribbling lover,
Just over shoes in passion and no more.
   Cath.   And I am sure, dear cousin (for such you are),
You will not rate my love of that cheap kind
That hangs upon the sleeve of every suitor
Like a canary on a showman's thumb,
And taught to sing
To every fancy that comes wandering by.
   Ran.   But I love you —
   Cath.   Soft! Who comes?

Enter LEVEC.

Sir, what would you have?
   Ran.   Away, you beggar!
   Levec.   Your pardon, friends; 'tis dark, and all my
     eyes
Were inward with my thoughts.
   Ran.   I'll choose my friends in the light. What do
     you want?
   Levec.   A softer speech, young man.
   Ran.   Come, come, you knave,
Get to your gutter!
   Levec.   How now, you stripling!
By heaven, if it were other than a boy
That put such speech upon me —
   Cath.   Pray you, no quarrel.
   Levec.   No quarrel? Why, a man is but a flint,
And being struck, there is no stuff in nature
Can hold the spark.
   Ran.   Out of the grounds, I say!
   Levec.   Nay, I shall pass.
   Ran.   Look to it, I have a knife.
   Cath.   Help! help!
   Levec.   Now by the seven stars, I never thought
To tickle straws with babes. I am unarmed.
Yet with a turn of wrist I've played the death
On many a greater Mars.
   Cath.   Help!

Enter JUDGE FORD.

Ford.   What brawl is this?

Ran.   Why, this dog of a beggar
Comes sneaking —

Ford.   A dagger, nephew?
Out of my sight! You are no blood of mine,
You dastard!

Cath.   You are unjust.

Ford.   What, I unjust!
Learn veneration, daughter. Sir, who are you?

Levec.   Judge Ford, do you not know me?

Ford.   I never saw you, sir.

Levec.   Why, it should be upon your title-leaf
Of memory who I am.   (*Exit* RANSOM.)

Ford.   I never saw you;
But you shall have my ear for any business
You would impart. Here, Catharine, run back
Into the house, for we must speak alone.

Levec.   A moment, stay! I owe apology
To you, good lady. There are times when temper
Takes fiery weapons, and discretion
Goes halting off; know that I am a soldier,
And my rough trade imparts rough usages,
And sways the kindly balance of the mind
Into some frostiness, when smiles should season.
So, under this prologue, give me pardon.

Cath.   It needs it not, sir, for the genial play
Sweeps on beneath the curtain of your brow.
Indeed, I think my cousin more at fault
In this misventure, which is lightly past;
But his excuse lies that his blood is swift,
And in a fit jumps civil ceremony.
He has a better nature that he turns
To his own conning; by a freak of birthing
His dross is o'er his gold.

Levec.   I fear your cousin's
Less perfect than his glass.

Ford.   Will you begone? (*Exit* CATHARINE.)
I pray you, lift your cap; I cannot see you.

Levec.   Be it so; you know me now.

Ford.   If I believe
My senses on this edge of night, you are
That friend Levec.   Why! let me look upon you.
   Levec.   Is this all that you have for me?
   Ford.   By grace,
Am I forgiven?
   Levec.   By grace you were, ere you had injured me.
Though I have taken on a beggar's garb,
My heart it is no beggar.
   Ford.   Spare the word.
I think a trodden and word-beaten pauper
Were better worth than I.   It is a wonder
Fit to be set beside the miracles,
How you can hold my hand and call me friend,
That dealt so foully with you.
   Levec.   Let it lie,
And give me leave to look upon your face.
The very same; by heaven, the years have slipped
And left you nothing worse.
   Ford.   Were I not better,
I were a knave indeed.
   Levec.   Still on that string?
   Ford.   My thoughts go to the tune.   Why do you look
So fixed on me?   Your eyes like swallows sit
Under their eaves, and seem to peer upon me
Like to a gambler bending o'er his cast.
   Levec.   You are the very same, the very same,
Save that your hairs are thinner.
   Ford.   There is a moral
That wisdom builds her nest in scanty locks,
And shuns the curly head.
   Levec.   It is a saying
That springeth chiefer from the branch of custom
Than from the root of truth.   In tender years,
When we are nature's children, nature's law
Shows perfectest; but in maturity
Men get their head and plunge what way they will,
Grow cunning, haughty, proud, and stretch the lines.
Youth knows no boundary 'twixt himself and others,
But manhood climbs upon his fellow's shoulder,
And crows to see himself.   These petty spirits

Grow in false soil; 'tis not in nature writ
That one should be the ass and one the load.
    Ford. No; both are asses.
    Levec.   Has the world prospered with you?
    Ford. Even as you see; these lands round here are
    mine,
Enough besides to keep me from the wet
These many years.
    Levec.   Now you make me unhappy.
In truth, I'm hurt not to be needed by you.
    Ford. That's a fine wish. And have you been in
    France?
    Levec. Yes; slitting wind-pipes; I can swear in
    French,
And fight in English. Well, the wars are done,
And by the leeway of a dozen years,
Though I made not a sail unto that end,
I am grown something rich; firstly, in oaths;
Second, in wounds; and third, in worldly wealth.
    Ford. The last is modest.
    Levec.   As you may say, it is.
Our fortunes meet us in the dark.
    Ford.   And now
Do you not find yourself disposed to ease?
Nay, do not answer. You shall live here with me.
I am a judge, sir, and I give this sentence:
You make my house a prison twenty years.
I am your goaler; come away with me,
And see how prettily I play the host.
    Levec. You are a judge, a goaler, and a host?
Well, I will stay a little time with you,
And then be off.
    Ford. Now by my hand and heart
It shall not be. Come, come, I see your promise
Wavering in your face.
    Levec.   I thank you, Ford.
    Ford. Tut, never mind. Come with me through the
    garden.
Spring has begun her grafting on the trees;
Mine is the fairest orchard in the state,
And now I have an ear to brag into.   (*Exeunt.*)

ACT II.

SCENE I.— *A hall in Ford's house.*

Enter RANSOM *and* STEPHEN.

Ran. Stephen, a word with you.

Steph. You may have two if you wish it.

Ran. I thank you, Stephen; you shall be my treasury; I mean, of words. I have been rubbing my wits to make them bright, and now I am come to tell you a secret.

Steph. O Lord, never do that.

Ran. Indeed I shall, or the birds will tell it to you; for this secret is in the air, in the earth, in the water, and lastly, in the man's face that keeps it. To come short on the enemy, have you noted well this master Levec?

Steph. Very well, very well indeed.

Ran. How does the gloss of new acquaintance wear? Is it gold or sodden stuff?

Steph. I have no touchstone for such metal, Ransom. He is the heart and amidships of all honor.

Ran. O Stephen, the world is young and knaves are old.   •

Steph. So the devil saith.

Ran. What else did he say?

Steph. The devil?

Ran. Yes, Levec.

Steph. Hist! here he comes.

Enter CATHARINE *and* LEVEC, *passing through.*

Ran. I will swear, old proverbs fit new times. Stand back; they are lost in each other's eyes, and will never see us.

Cath. Oh fie, sir, never think so ill of me;
I am not one of those that run about,
Making their ears a sieve for idle talk.
Where do you think, sir, I have been this morning?

Levec. I know not; but 'tis said, maidens like lilies
Hang ever o'er their glass.

Cath.   A face-maker!
I fear you hold me lightly when you say
I gossip and make faces in a glass.

Levec. I'-faith, I did not say it.
Cath. Nay, but you did.
Levec. I cry you mercy; you are what you are,
And no one, I am sure, could wish you else.
Cath. You twist my meanings.
Levec. If I twist them
Into love-knots, who is the worse for it?
Cath. To beg your pardon, sir, your speech is nothing.
If you will come with me into the garden,
I'll gladly try your eyes if they be better.
Levec. And I will gladly follow; but indeed
I wish my eyes more fortune than my tongue.

(*Exeunt* CATHARINE *and* LEVEC.)

Ran. Did you mark that?
Steph. It is but old news. I have noted it many days
that they walk about, as you may say, lodged in one
another. It is old news, I assure you, very old news.
Ran. And did you know it?
Steph. These seven weeks.
Ran. By the stars I will buy me a pistol this day to
shoot thoughts through my brain. Why, this is the very
secret I came to tell you.
Steph. The Lord forbid. Do you think they are in
love?
Ran. Up to the knee, that is certain. Is it not mon-
strous? I am crammed full of rage; I am murderous-
minded.
Steph. He is a very good man, I think.
Ran. A good man! He is the vilest villain on earth.
His father was a villain, his grandfather was a villain,
his great-grandfather was a villain, and his quaintest
ancestors were villains all, which pulls at the roots of
creation. So, all told, he is three times and again a vil-
lain, a coxcomb, a muck-worm, a dung-hill louse, a toad,
a spider, a snake —
Steph. You mean, anything that crawls.
Ran. Will you do me a service, Stephen?
Steph. If it be a thing of honor.
Ran. Tut, 'tis only a penny of kindness that I ask.
Steph. I would it were more, Ransom.
Ran. It lies not in quantity, but it is, as you may say, a

tickle point. I cannot unclose it to others hereabout, whose tongues are all set with hair-springs; but I know you to be very close and crabbed of the most appetizing secrets. Shortly, this Levec has a damned enterprise on foot to smuggle his affections on my Cousin Kate, as you have seen; but I will pull strongly against him, trust me for that; and you shall be my ladder to that end.

Steph. If you nurse any plot, Ransom, keep it in your own breast; I will have none of it. To plot, I take it, is to contrive; and to contrive is a great wickedness, and against the law.

Ran. Stephen, you are right; and now Levec contrives an odious attachment with my cousin. He has committed assault and battery on her affections, which is a jailing offence; if you do not believe it, ask that brat of law, Christopher Keen.

Steph. If it is so, proceed.

Ran. Then tell me, does my cousin return his favors?

Steph. I may say so, in part.

Ran. They contrive to meet here and there, do they not?

Steph. In neither place, I think; but chiefly in the garden.

Ran. And are you not under the bush of their favor at these times? I mean, they suspect you not.

Steph. Where would you bring me?

Ran. To a good inference. If you were of a mind, might you not deliver to me the speeches they drop in your hearing.

Steph. Would you make me a tale-bearer?

Ran. Why, that's a monkey. I would have you but what you are, believe me, only what you are. Hark! was it not a pebble that struck the shutter?

Steph. I heard nothing.

Ran. Is no one beneath the window?

Steph. It is Cade the giant. Have a care of yourself, Ransom; he is flinging a boulder as big as his head.

Ran. But not as thick. Devil take him, he will break the house down.

Steph. I will stop him before he flings another.

Ran. Send him hither, if you can. I will speak more

with you hereafter concerning this matter; believe me,
I will make it smooth to you.   (*Exit* STEPHEN.)
Who would have thought it?   Why I am as blind
As any snow-man that the children build,
Who has a black coal stuck each side his nose
To be his eyes.   My cousin and this fellow!
The devil speed him!   For a dozen weeks
I've stretched my neck to smell their secrecy,
And never till this morning did I find
The tangle out.   I have played eavesdropper
Under her window, and the little jade
Sang only spinster songs; I've crossed her steps
A hundred times, as she has walked alone,
And nothing got by it until this day.
By heaven, my uncle Ford shall know of this,
But first I will have proof; I will rise early
To-morrow morn, and every other morn;
So on, until I find some catch or clue.
'Tis a great punishment to crawl from bed
So early, but I'll patch my sleep at noonday.

Enter CADE.

Cade.   Blessings on you, Ransom.
Ran.   What's in the air?
Cade.   Nothing but holy stars.
Ran.   Where have you left
The other two?   Why are they not abroad?
Cade.   Pray, have you money?
Ran.   Have I money?
Cade.   Yes.
Ran.   Oh what a knave you are!   Let me tell o'er
How many times this week some puffing fellow
Has pulled me by the coat, quoth-a, *good friend*
Will pay the money that you owe in debt?
The inn-keeper, the goodsman, and the tailor,
. The fruiterer, and a thousand other fry,
Till like a vessel rocked in adverse tides
I stick and stay — why, should I tell all this
Word in and out, the day would all be spent
And in a cry for candles.

Cade. But have you not
Some sums in hand?

Ran. Go to, you villain,
You never meet me in the open street,
But that your tongue, that's dripping with good wishes,
To beggary falls at length, like a night prayer
Almost forgot and then spoke trippingly.
Now to be understood and understanding,
If this is all your errand, these few words
Are all my answer, that I have no money
And never shall; but when I have 't, methinks
You shall have none of it.

Cade. No money, say you?

Ran. No, not a penny; my extravagance
Has quit my purse, emptied it, aired it, drained it,
Or, if you'd rather, sucked the marrow of it;
And for the future, 'tis a double star
That marches o'er my heaven; I read it clear
That I must steal or beg. Where's Ratsey? where's
Verrell?

Cade. Deep in the dumps; indeed, they sent me hither
To fill my bag with money.

Ran. Oh damnable bee!

Cade. But since you have it not I'll make return
Into the tavern; but the master of it
He has a doting proverb that cold coin
Is better than warm wishes, and denies
Even the beggar's salt, until he has,
Most miserable wretch! the pay in hand.
You are sure you have no money?

Ran. My purse hath a great mouth and little paunch,
And nothing in 't.

Cade. Good-by, Ransom.

Ran. Oh what a hurry!
As if you were the golden sentinel
That summons up the hours. You were not thus
A moment since. Have you no plans in store?

Cade. Not a pennyworth.

Ran. Why then, to-morrow night,
What time the jarring bird begins to drop

His courtesies in the air, meet me in the wood
That is our trysting place, (you know it well,
Southward the church) and there we'll mix our wits
As choicest liquors are; but for the present
Part this amount between you. (*Gives him money.*)
 Cade.   What! have you money?
Ran. Ay, bushels of it.   (*Exeunt.*)

Scene II. — *Before Ford's house.*

Ransom, *alone.*

Ran. The sun has shot an arrow o'er the hill;
Morning is up, and (curse it) so am I.
Here have I watched and waited o'er this spot,
And paced about it like a minute hand
E'en since the turn of night; and all for what!
Two hours are lost; the fellow is not come,
And with a cough as hollow as a bell,—
Ay, there it goes.— But stay!
What footing yonder comes? The fox is late.
But blessings on the hour; here will I hide.
My twenty eyes under the hawthorn-bush.

      (*Conceals himself.*)

Enter Christopher Keen *and* Levec.

Keen. Is this the place?
Levec. I hold myself much your debtor for this kindness. And I will requite it as I may. But to the business. Stand you here in the shadow and sing me the song I chose out for you, or choose a better yourself. But make dispatch, and I will hold you my friend forever, truly, my friend forever.
Keen. 'Tis nothing; I love to sing. But for the music, shall it be merry or wise?
Levec. Faith, let it be both merry and wise; for merriment of itself is nine parts folly; yet if wisdom be dressed in black she is little regarded. Let me have both in one, and that speedily.

Keen.   I'll do it to the touch.   (*Sings.*)

> Who is this with eyes so blue ?
> Sing ho! so merrily.
> And cheeks that let their blushes through ?
> · Sing it all so merrily.
>
> By the witches there are two;
> Sing ho! so merrily.
> His eyes so grey and hers so blue;
> Take it naught but merrily.
>
> By the hay-cocks, in the night,
> This twain so merrily;
> Gentle people, take no spite
> That the world goes merrily.

Levec.   I am not native to that air; it was born in my
absence.   But I thank you for it.
Keen.   You are critical.   Shall I to it again?
Levec.   If you are speedy.
Keen.   This song shall be for an antidote to the other.
                                            (*Sings.*)

> When winter waves the rushes, O,
> And the huskers weave the corn,
> And farmer lads their fingers blow,
> Think on me, my lady lorn.
> I did sorry fortune wed;
> Fortune laid me here abed;
> At my feet a tumbled stone,
> And over it my letters strown.
>
> When that the spring her violet eyes
> Opens, and makes holiday;
> And all so green my burial lies,
> Think on me, and blight the May.
> I did sorry fortune wed, etc.

Levec.   Enough — 'twill do.
Keen.   Was it not in the mood?
Levec.   Something too merry.   All the world could not
please me to-night.   Now for a last favor, return to your
room and speak never a word of this to any man.
Keen.   I am at your mercy.   (*Exit.*)

Enter CATHARINE, *at the window above.*

Cath.   Sure, it is he.   Is anyone beneath?
Levec.   None but myself.
Cath.   Was't you that sung?
Levec.   Tush, do not thank me for it.
Cath.   Indeed I shall.
Who has but little to be thankful for,
Gives double thanks for that.   Fie, what a night!
I think 'twill rain anon.   Know you the time?
Levec.   Near upon three.
Cath.   Why, you are early risen:
And for myself, I have twice waked to-night,
Troubled with something.   Faith, I cannot tell
If I have anything to trouble me.
It is not well, I think, to have one's life
So early wedded to security.
'Tis as a ship, all fitted up for war,
That never stirs from port, is such a life,
So idle one might paint it.   There's the trouble
That wakes me nights.
Levec.   As, truth, it is not mine.
Cath.   And what is yours?
Levec.   Yourself.
Cath.   Myself?
Levec.   Are you not cause?
Cath.   Why, sir, I never thought
To be the thorn in any person's mind.
Pray, what's the fault?   Where do I misbecome
The nature that I serve?
Levec.   In nothing, sure,
And that's the fair cause of my discontent.
Were you as other women I have seen,
Some being in body gross, and some in mind;
Some whose fair parts had took up evil lodgings;
Some frozen in chastity; some burned in passion;
Some that fall short of sense; some that o'errun it;
Some stained with care; some jaded out with pleasure;
Some that are nursed up in the lap of riches;
Some that are broken-backed with poverty;
Some being wayward willed; others whose tongues

Too much run up and down; some this, some that:
Since 'tis the part of mortals to be frail,
And owe allegiance to their origin,—
But to be few, were you as others are,
I would be now what I have been before.
But when my eyes first lighted on your face,
My lot of love was cast, and ever since
There has it lain.   Oft have I walked with you
Under the waving tresses of the pine,
Listening in silence to your merriment,
While all the time my thoughts, like honey-bees,
Were building golden fancies in my brain.
And so, with good hope and no art at all,
If it can please you e'er to be my wife,
Taking the little that I have to give,
And deep repentance that it is no more,
Sure, I would reckon it the happiest hour,
And high tide of my life.

Cath.   What do I hear?
Oh sir, I am too young, too, too unguided,
And all unworthy of you.   There are faults,
Believe me, there are faults and flaws within me,
More than in others.   I am young and thoughtless,
Untaught in the world's ways, simple, not wise,
Not strong to be your helpmate; and when time
Has ta'en the first bright colors from your love,
I fear, I fear,—

Levee.   Now by my grace, fear nothing.
Cath.   Oh, as you love me, say no more to-night.
Levee.   Nay, love, then I will not.   Think well upon it.
I would not have you hasty.   Now when life
Stands on the shore, ready to be embarked,
It well beseems to look before, and after,
For the first road may never be retraced.
There lies our happiness, if we go right;
There lies our misery, if we go wrong.
Then take the way that most commends itself
To your well being and your happiness,
And for myself, by that I will abide.
So, love, a wise good-night.   *(Exit.)*
Cath.   How quick my breathing is!

This is the trouble that has wakened me,
And which I knew not. Oh love, love, sweet love,
How art thou like the odors of the fields,
Breathed and not seen. The footsteps of the morn
Run hitherward; it is the break of day.
I must within doors, for the night is damp.

(*Exit above.*)

RANSOM *advances.*

Ran. Devil take me if I ever play lover again. Here
is a warning to a sensible man, a timely lighthouse o'er
the rocks of folly. I would rather go my way to a single
grave than take this road to a wedding; ay, and I will,
that's flat. And there is another shall go with me, that's
flat. And for my cousin, she may wed whom she will, if
I choose him. I will have no more of a woman that is
roses to one man and thorns to another, that's flat. And
Christopher! oh the villain! If I do not give him a
sore noddle some night ere he dies, may I turn to stone,
that's flat. And now to my uncle, to breakfast him on
these timely news. He will thank me for them? No.
But though you shut your eyes. good uncle, you must
swallow your physic, and that's flat. (*Exit.*)

SCENE III.—*The garden of Ford's house.*

Enter JUDGE FORD *and* RANSOM.

Ford. Sir, spare this gossip.
Ran. I speak but what I know.
Ford. Come, come, I'll hear no more; 'twere idleness
To ply me further.
Ran. Are you settled in it?
Ford. Most firmly; you are ridden with a folly,
To press such speech upon me.
If you have aught
To say against my friend, say it and done.
Ran. Why, so I have. This morn, being early up —
Ford. So? I think 'tis breakfast-time.
Ran. Will you hear me?
Ford. Scandal is tough food.

Ran.   Being early up,
I heard Levee beneath your daughter's window,
Twisting fine sayings.
    Ford.   What was the hour?
    Ran.   Past four, and somewhat dark.
    Ford.   What did he wear?
    Ran.   A cloak.
    Ford.   Black?
    Ran.   Even as the night
That wrapped him up.
    Ford.   A cloak becomes him well.
    Ran.   Oh! very pretty; your daughter in the window
Seemed even beautifuler.
    Ford.   Now you flatter me.
Didst listen?
    Ran.   Several minutes.
    Ford.   An eavesdropper?
    Ran.   Even so. This very pretty friend of yours
Swore that he loved her well.
    Ford.   And do you doubt
She is deserving of as great a love
As man e'er gave to woman?
    Ran.   Sir, I see
My task is very bootless; yet I wish
I were a better advocate; I might
Stir your suspicion.
    Ford.   That is done already.
    Ran.   I am happy to think so.
    Ford.   Sir, I suspect
Yourself.
    Ran.   Not so.
    Ford.   If you think you carry
The stamp of honesty upon your brows,
When you next pass a standing pool, look in it.
    Ran.   And see an honest man.
    Ford.   Nay, and see
A common tattler, a fellow of more shifts
Than I have breath to tell of.
    Ran.   Let me finish.
    Ford.   No, I am fixed; I see an artifice
In all you say. Pray, learn more cunning, nephew.

When you do slander others you but hold
A lamp to your own folly.
    Ran.   I never in my life
Spoke aught but truth.
    Ford.   Always spoke truth! oh fine!
You fall by aiming high; better to take
A modest station than to fail a greater.
Say you are as the world, in even parts
Falsehood and truth; and now I think the first
Inclines you to put colors on your story,
And slander my good friend. I know him well,
His goodness and his unstained honesty.
There is no man, and but one woman else,
I wear so near my heart.
    Ran.   Is't possible?
You worship a dull idol.
    Ford.   No more of this:
Pray, leave me here; I have some weighty business
Of judgeship to think on. (*Exit Ransom.*) So, he is
    gone.
Oh what a fool I am! Have I no eyes?
No ears? no senses? Oh, my thoughts of late
Have flown too high, and I have nothing noted
Of these affairs that stared me in the face.
I have oft seen a man that bent his eyes
Upon the stars, tread in a mud-puddle.
Oh what a fool! If Catharine and Levec
Keep hours between them, she's undutiful,
And he's unfriendly. For their honor's sake,
I think there's no concern; foul thoughts could find
No entertainment in so fair a man.
But if their mark is marriage — no, by heaven,
He is too old, too old; I will not have it;
"Twere better I were dead. — Yonder he comes.
How shall I bear myself? I'll not be moved
To show a face like dog-days, fair and foul,
All in a minute. I will sift his talk
And sow such words of council in his ear,
Shall souse his lovesickness. I'll droop my lids,
And seem to see him not.
           Enter LEVEC.

Levec.   Lift up your eyes,
And see a prodigy.
   Ford.   So early up!
   Levec.   Earlier than you; some remnant of the night
Lurks in your countenance.
   Ford.   I fear, 'tis sadness.
   Levec. Tell me, what's my humor?
   Ford.   Foul weather mirth.
   Levec. I wander in your meaning. Come, cheer up;
I've seen a pondering crow look grave as you,
But ne'er a man before.
   Ford.   You cannot say
My sadness is not a fair gentleman,
That makes his tongue outstep his finer sense
In merry company, and keeps his sorrow,
As young men do their loves, a thing alone.
And as I think of it, young men and love
Rhymed in my dreams to-night. I' faith, I know
That Catharine is nearing on that age,
Wherein young maidens wont to weave their fancies
About some prop, like orioles on the elms;
And it concerns me much, indeed it is
A freight of worriment, that she should step
Along this edge of love most painfully;
And by and by, if she but look about,
She'll find a road in some man's honest thought
That's worthy to be trod.
   Levec.   Fie on it, friend.
Your fears are feathers; they are parents' fears
That are as quick of wing as parents' hopes,
Startled at naught.
   Ford.   I thank you for the comfort,
And yet, what if she chose, being wayward-willed,
A fellow of no mark; or say, a man
Far past her age, one that were like to make her
A widow in her May.
   Levec.   You live in shadows.
   Ford. Then lead me to the light.
   Levec.   Why, so I will.
Find sunshine in yourself.
   Ford.   Ay, there's the question.

Levec.   Nay, there's the answer.

Ford.   Think not so, my friend;
For at our time of life, the mind is wont
To beat about in darkness, on that limit
Whereto we're all consigned.   There is no right
But takes a cast of wrong; no wrong but grows
More foul by looking at it.

Levec.   The more reason
We should be merry; let the spirit rise
Even though the body fall; let us take mirth
Freely where'er we find it, and cold sorrow
Sparingly when it comes, be comfortable
And mild old men, or death enlists our bodies,
While yet we're ripe to live.

Ford.   Were we all that,
We would be young.   I say I am in trouble
Over my daughter.   You have noticed her?

Levec.   She is right beautiful.

Ford.   Even so, I fear.
Beauty's a candle; every dizzard moth
Flies to it.

Levec. That's injury to the moth, and not to the candle.

Ford.   To answer jest with earnest, I have seen
The candle thus put out.

Levec.   You are my ballast;
Wherein I'm light you're heavy.

Ford.   As you're my friend,
Help me clear up my mind; give me some light.
Say, that my daughter married such a man,
Of twice her age, could even twice her merit,
Prov'n in him, make him suitable to wed
What's past in him? or could her eager fancy
Pull down its flight to accompany old age?

Levec.   I think this is a question for the woman,
The sacrifice being hers.

Ford.   You darken darkness.
Pray, give me some advice.

Levec.   I fear, I cannot.

Enter CATHARINE.

Ford.   Here comes my daughter in the nick of time.
I'll put the question home.   What! Catharine!

Cath. Good-morning, sir.
Ford. Come hither, Kate.
You look the spring : tell me, what is't that puts
Red roses in your cheeks?
    Cath. The wind, I think.
    Levec. The wind has pretty favors.
    Cath. Thank you for that.
    Ford. And what for me?
    Cath. Why, I thank you also.
    Levec. Here's enough for all
    Ford. But put your father first.
    Cath. No sir, my errand first; breakfast is laid,
And I am sent to call you.
    Ford. Faugh! my stomach
Is out of sorts with food.
    Cath. Are you not well?
    Ford. Seldom of late. I see my body grows
Sensitive to the seasons, that with us
Are strangely mixed; the winter's thaw brings in
April in penance, this day soft and mild,
The next a dismal fog coffins the earth,
And opens up the natural gates o' the body
To swarming humors; then the hot July
Burns men and starves the crops; after the which,
September, like a maid with many loves,
Inclines to wet or dry, frosty or hot,
Freezes or sweats the marrow; all which climate,
And weather of sharp corners, rots the flesh,
Keeps our wet noses sniffling of the air,
Our eyes courting the vanes and weathercocks;
Our tongues discoursing if the east be fair,
The moon uncircled, the month upon the wane,
The wind skittish or firm; and thus and thus,
The months all out of tune, and half mankind
At odds between a fan and overcoat.
    Levec. Your blood is growing thin; you should in winter
Go south : you have the means.
    Ford. But not the mind.
Are we so weak? Do not the animals
Crouch in the drifts? Our source is of the same;

Material earth; we are but fair-writ copies
Of grosser underbeings.
   Levec.   But our flesh
Is tender, our fair bodies delicate,
And full of flaws. Therefore I do advise you,
When winter first begins to poke his nose
Out of the north, crawl from your banks of snow
Into a softer climate.
   Ford.   Never, sir.
One-half the season fits us for the other;
Each has its use; summer and winter else
Were out of joint. The snow is wholesome to us
Though it frost-nips our blood; our senses grow
To hardihood and keenness, like fine steel,
Being tempered hot and cold.
   Levec.   You're fixed to put
Yourself beyond recovery. If change is nought,
Where can you find a cure?
   Ford.   Even at my side.
Here is my Catharine, worth a thousand summers.
Come, daughter, are you not agreed to it?
   Cath. To anything you say.
   Ford.   Fie, fie, my love.
You do not mean it.
   Cath.   Truthfully, I do.
I know right well you would not ask me aught
My virtue could not look at steadily.
   Ford. Even so, but what of pleasures? We old men
Are jealous-eyed as cats; wilful and peevish,
Sudden in thought, our whims put on and off,
Like our attire, and when we have affection,
On whom it lights, it seemeth like a curse,
'Tis so imperative and busybody,
So stuck about with thorns; as we should say,
The act of love makes other men our slaves,
That else had been our masters; yet withal,
The love of aged folk shifts easily,
And lights upon the shoulders of a fool,
Much quicker than on wisdom.
Moreover they are childlike and remorseful,
Weep much, and hide their weeping in a scold,

Patter old stories, peep in everything,
Tell falsehoods to the face, and being taxed
Are hurt profoundly, set their tongues like snares
To trip the uninformed, and in a word,
(To make long matter short, short matter long)
Rule with the fondness of a players' king,
So being, their lot fall easy.

Levec.　　　　　　　If this is true,
I'll stop my life at forty.

Ford.　　　　　　　Art so young?

Levec. Passing that age.

Ford.　　　　　Well, hear me to the end.
If I were thus Kate, would you care for me?

Cath. You do me wrong to ask it.

Ford.　　　　　　　Nay, but consider.
Say that a dozen lovers were in suit
For this fair hand I hold, but I, your father,
Would have them not, being niggard of my treasure,
(For you're my treasure, Kate) and like a miser
More fond of cuddling gold than putting it
Into the common market — if love and duty
Beckoned your eyes apart, where would you turn,
To lover or to father?

Cath.　　　　　　Spare my modesty.

Ford. Oh, I shall hold you fast until you answer.

Cath. And breakfast cooling?

Ford.　　　　　Ay, if the earth were cooling
I'd wait an answer.

Levec.　　　Sure 'twould be a cold one.

Ford. Come, sir, you will make a rebel of my daughter.

Cath. Nay, father, he must first make you a ruler.

Ford. See how I'm fleered at, friend. I' faith, she
blushes.
Come Catharine,
Down with your colors, and surrender to me.

Cath. Why, then, I will, in pity that good food
Should thus be wasted. Have you appetite?

Ford. I do assure you, more than ordinary.
This fresh air is a passport to good health.
Come friend, shall we to breakfast?

Levec.　　　　　　I think 'tis time. (*Exeunt.*)

SCENE IV.— *In a wood.*

Enter RANSOM *and* VERRELL.

Ran. Hello! hello!

Ver. What's this? Why are you blowing?

Ran. To warm myself.

Ver. To warm yourself?

Ran. Yes. Am I not next neighbor to you?

Ver. Well, I am not an icicle.

Ran. It needs but a hanging to make you one. Therefore be cheerful. There's justice on earth yet; volumes of it, volumes of it. But tell me, have you not the iciest humor under heaven? Are you not the very north pole of wit, the congealed jest-book of the world?

Ver. What should I say, being an icicle?

Ran. Your prayers, man, your prayers; remember justice, and say your prayers. But indeed, where's Cade?

Ver. He turned back to meet Ratsey. I left him at the stile as we came over, bellowing his own praises, all wrapped up in his own opinion.

Ran. But where's his opinion, man? Tell me that. Is it in his belly or his stomach?

Ver. Bah! you shall split a hair and tell me.

Ran. Why, then, the former; for his brains never grew above his waist. O Verrell!

Ver. What's the matter?

Ran. I was thinking —

Ver. Give me my tablets, ho! Here's a marvel for history to take note of.

Ran. Stop! stop! — But indeed, I was thinking.

Ver. Well, what's the grist?

Ran. Ah! Verrell, if a bullet should strike him in the guts what a scattering of learning would it make!

Ver. You durst not say this to his face.

Ran. Hark ye, good master tree, —

Ver. Stop! fool.— I said, in Cade's face.

Ran. And is it not wooden, Verrell, is it not wooden? There never was such a countenance save on my grandfather's clock; never such a chest save on a century oak; and (bless the mark!) he is gutted like a tenpin.— But here he comes.

Ver. 'Tis some other.

Ran. O fie! I know his step well. (*Music without.*)
Damn my logic; 'tis Christopher.

Ver. What! him that people swear by?

Ran. No, 'tis his brother, the devil. Let us hide here
in the bushes. (*Exeunt.*)

Enter KEEN.

Keen. (*Sings.*)

> Hop along, sister Mary,
> Hop along, sister Mary;
> The wind is a-cold,
> And thy cloak hath no fold;
> Hop along, sister Mary.

Heigho! Out of the wind. What stockish listeners are
these? Good friends, I thank you; but i' faith, you
are the tallest men I ever played before. Oh! God bless
my fortune! — Where am I, where am I? Is this hell,
and are those two devils that come yonder? Nay, they
are robbers, or murderers. God send that they be murderers; I have more than three hundred dollars in my
purse.

Re-enter RANSOM *and* VERRELL.

Mercy, mercy, kind robber; who are you?

Ver. A man.

Ran. Look behind you.

Keen. Oh! I am dead. (VERRELL *strikes him down.*)

Ran. Well struck, Verrell. Thou hadst near made a
bishop of him.

Ver. Are all bishops thus?

Ran. Truly, truly, I fear not. But look at our friend
here, how stiff he is.

Ver. I fear, we have killed him.

Ran. So be it; dead men have their uses. This one,
by six of the clock to-morrow, will be a royal turnpike of
pismires. Death is a correction of nature, and no sin.
But stop up mine ears. Didst ever hear such profound
sighs, such variety of groans? O most piteous! Knock
him once more across the pate, Verrell, and change the
nature of his dreams.

Ver. There's no time to waste. He will wake and see us.

Ran. Peu! his wits are falling yet.

Ver. As you like it; but for me, I am gone.

Ran. Stop! runaway; I have the foreboding of a plot in my brain. Here it is. We will drag this sack of guts into the brushwood here, and load him with sticks and brambles, till. no one would know the difference 'twixt him and his brother the log. Then when our fellows come, we will roll our eyes like full moons, thus, with, *Hem! what a thick black hollow is this!* and, *They say there be ghosts hereabout;* and, *What thing is that yonder?* and the like, and the like. And so, when this dead man comes to his senses —

Ver. But he has none.

Ran. Oh! trust a lawyer to come by what he has not. I say, this learned fiddler will presently fall creaking i' the nose like a tavern-sign. These poor groans are but forerunners to say a greater is coming. Then shall you see their hairs bristle, their eyes start out like rockets, and their cheeks hang down as white as lilies. O, they will run to the edge of the world with the nimbleness of two ghosts, and swear forever after that they saw a dozen. Fear makes the heart heavy and the heels light. Are you with me?

Ver. I fear, he will wake too soon.

Ran. Here, keep the cudgel at hand. Snatch him by that arm; I will take the other. Now, sir. Zounds! what a lump of wood he is!

Ver. Call'st him wood? I think, he is good twenty stone.

Ran. A great bundle of fagots, ill put together. There, lay him there. Throw the brush over him quickly, whilst I watch for Ratsey and Cade.

(RANSOM *retires to a distance.*)

Are you done? I think I hear voices.

Ver. Look for yourself. I have tucked him away like a babe in his crib.

Ran. Verrell, you knave! turn his nose to the air. He is all swathed about with juniper and propped up with a thorn bush. What a pillow for his fat sides! But here they come. Hello, ho!

Enter RATSEY *and* CADE.

Ver. Halt!

Rat. Not with two sound legs.

Ran. Is it you, Cade?

Cade. Ay, by my fist.

Ran. Saw you anything as you came hither?

Cade. Why, trees, fences, and the like.

Ran. But did you not see the devil astride a night-mare?

Cade. Now you are mad.

Ran. Nay, but the spirits are. Saw you it not, Ratsey?

Rat. Away with your fooleries; you cannot put any tricks upon Joseph Ratsey, I can tell you; and if you do not throw down that great cudgel, I will discharge my pistol directly where you stand. If any man be hit, God bless him and give him a happy funeral.

Cade. Why, what's the matter?

Ran. I say, there are spirits abroad.

Ver. Sing, *Heigho! the devil and all.*

Rat. Did you think there were spirits hereabout, Verrell, you would have run into the deep sea ere this for sheer fright; for you fell a-praying but yesternight, when an owl screeched, swearing away an ocean of sins like an eleventh-hour reprobate. I had near split my sides with laughing and cheering on the predicament. 'Twas thus, being midnight, I should say, or near that point. We were on the river-bank, throwing our lines amid-stream. By and by, too-witta-woo! cries an owl, as if he were perched in Verrell's hair. *Zounds!* cries he, his face shaking like a jelly, *what was that? Spirits*, quoth I; whereat he drops to his knees, like a prayer-master and bawls out, *Mercy, mercy, good Lord!* 'twas not I painted the mare white. 'Twas *Ratsey; noy, 'twas Cade;* for he had so much of his wit left. But he prayed on and on, and might have been chattering yet, had I not dropped a live coal on his neck, for hell-fire. I can tell you, it quite out-spluttered his tongue, and put thoughts into his heels. Zounds! Ransom, you should have been by, to see him caper 'cross meadows like Jack-a-lantern; and all the while you might have roasted chestnuts on his

shoulders. And now he has whittled a great cudgel and
thinks to beat in my brains. We shall see, we shall see.

Ver. As I am a truthful Christian man —

Rat. O Verrell!

Ver. Well, then, as I am an untruthful Christian man,
I mean you no ill. I have shaped this handspike only
for ghosts, of whom there are numbers hereabout. Soft!
what is't I hear?

Rat. Poh! there be no spirits on earth, and of late
few in heaven.

Cade. You are too headlong, Ratsey, much too headlong. If a man wakes at six in the morning and snores
again at six of eve, such a man may swear there is no
darkness. But I hold the hour to witness that there is.

Rat. Believ'st in ghosts?

Cade. May my soul 'scape heaven if I do not. Did I
not say to you as we came o'er the stile, *There goes a
ghost?*

Rat. No.

Cade. And did you not say, *Quite true, 'tis a dog?*

Rat. Ay, so I did.

Cade. So — you are finding your memory. You have
an excellent memory, if you will but remember it. Well,
I will swear I was three times struck with hell-whips,
as we came hither; once as we came through the
pasture; again, as we leapt the brook; again, as we
pricked through the thickets; and once again in the
highway. Do you not remember, ·I threatened you for
beating me across the back?

Rat. It may be.

Cade. And did I not cry out with pain a score of
times?

Rat. No.

Cade. Well, I doubt not I howled very softly. I am
a man of stiff courage, and good resolution. I fear
neither man nor ghost; and if one troubles me hereafter
I shall kill it and pin it in my hat like a butterfly.

(*Groans without.*)

Rat. By heaven, what was that?

Ver. Owls, Ratsey.

Cade. O that I were an innocent babe! (*More groans.*)

Rat. Stay if you will; but for me —
Ver. What! frighted at owls!

KEEN *advances.*

Rat. O hell!
Ver. Run for your lives.
Ran. Help, help! I am down.
Cude. Each for himself.
Rat. Take to your heels.
Ran. O the villains! (*Exeunt all but* KEEN.)
Keen. Mercy! mercy! trouble me not, sweet friends.
I'll but go softly home, softly home. Fair gentlemen of
the night, tumble me not for my money. I'll swear by
the clock's tongue, and as true, I have not a penny of
kind in my purse. I am but a poor man, sweet sirs, a
poor, poor man, as barren as the debtor's oath. Gone!
The fiends are gone. May the devil claw at their skirts,
may they be carrion for the law. Damn the law, damn
the law; it protects me not. Faith, 'tis a sweet vulture,
is this law, so the food be killed for its eating. But no
valiant, alack! no fighter. Why, then, who is? Faith,
says the world, Christopher Keen, prentice to the same.
— Says the echo, Who? — Says the world, Christopher
Keen, the sweetest singer out of the hand of heaven.
Prosperous is he, and all the graces run at his heels.—
Quoth the echo, Where is he? — Then says the world,
weeping, Unhappy as Orpheus is he; for he strayed into
the forest when night was in the scales, playing such
witching strains as drew — robbers; for as he tripped
o'er the sheep-path, he was thrust through like a lamb;
in short, he was set upon by numbers.— Says the echo,
Was he valiant? —Says the world, Ay, and dearly did it
cost him. For he was beat across the scalp with flails,
and robbed of a round three hundred dollars, held in
trust for Judge Ford, the eminent. Nor was he merci-
fully slaughtered, but stuck up to dry on a thorn-bush,
with a double acreage on his crown, and the devil's tracks
(that's vengeance) in his heart.— Thus speaks the world
out of her book, whereof I am printer. A likely tale,
is it not? a virtuous tale? So. Now must I howl for
help, and face out the story — be double-faced, in short,

as nature and a club has made me. I wonder if the man
who spins highways has tucked one away in this corner.
Perhaps, there are no wayfarers. Perhaps, I shall never
be heard. But no matter; there's a turnpike in the
clouds. I'll cry to heaven, and trust to my virtue. Help,
help, help! I hear steps to the rescue; now I will hide my
pocket-book deep in my boot.

Re-enter RANSOM *and* VERRELL, *with a torch.*

Ran. Who calls?

Keen. This way, this way.

Ver. Speak softer, man; your voice is everywhere.

Ran. Once again.

Keen. Right on, right on. O gentlemen, as God is
your judge, make haste and save one of his worthiest
creatures. I think I am slain. O help! Look to your
feet; there is a great puddle of blood in the path.

Ran. Give me the light, Verrell; here's foul business.
Softly, softly. Is't you, Christopher?

Keen. O let me die in peace.

Ver. Why, so we would, had you not called us.

Keen. I say, I am ruined forever.

Ran. Tut, man, you cannot live so long.

Keen. Oh, oh, misery has seven lives. Touch me
not.

Ran. Stand off, Verrell, stand off. Have a care of his
heels.— Now sir, leave your sprawlings, and tell us how
you came here.

Keen. God save me, I am robbed, I am ruined. O
Ransom, I fear I am a murderer, and no less. Who
would have thought, when Christopher Keen was a babe,
that he would come to the gallows? My mother has told
me oft I was most gentle when a babe, and nothing note-
worthy, save in a sound flesh and great appetite; for at
ten months I was six pound beyond the grocer's scales.
They say, fat men be good natured, and prone to tickling
sides with laughter, but here I have tickled sides in
shrewd earnest, committed murder, in short; which is
the crime of my most hatred, next to perjury. O, I
shall die and be buried in my sins — O.

Ran. Why, Christopher, you are a finer man than I

had ever thought you. You say, you have murdered these fellows. Have you their money?

Keen. Their money? their money? O Ransom, you do belie me, you tread my honor in the dust. Think you, I would steal a little money, to get in jail for't?

Ran. Nay, Christopher, steal more and get beyond it.

Ver. Come, come, out with the money, divide the money. I promise you, we shall have half of it, or know the reason.

Keen. You mistake me, friends, you mistake me. I have no money, God's will, not even my own. I am the man that was robbed, and no other.

Ran. Zounds! sir, these lies will not stead you: they are too light, too thin for shrewd understandings.

Keen. I have told you the truth, and nothing else.

Ran. Pish! Goat's milk for children. Bring forth the money, or show the reason.

Keen. O Verrell, (is not your name Verrell?) I call you to witness my innocence. The circumstance was thus. I was walking along the highway not above two hours since, very decently, with evil intent against no man; when behold! some six or seven stout fellows came out upon me, chiefly in front; but one that was behind laid me by, and broke a great cudgel across my pate. Some two or three of these villains I am sure I paid back to nature, but by the rest I am pulled down into the gutter, beaten most fiendishly, and robbed of good three hundred dollars that I held in trust for your uncle, the judge. Then I was dragged above a mile into this hollow, and left to die like a common man. So, you have my story. Will you bind a kerchief about my head and bring me home speedily?

Ran. Show me your purse.

Keen. Why, I have none. You may search in my pockets; you may search in my hat; you may search in my breeches; you may search in my pumps; you may search in my throat; and if you find a dollar, a cent, I give it you for the pains.

Ver. Come away, Ransom; the idiot has but stumbled o'er a log and hurt his head; yet he would have us believe the world is in arms against him.

Ran. You are right, Verrell, let us begone. Here, take the light, ho!

Keen. Mercy, mercy! Will you not bring me home?

Ran. Fall into our tracks if you will; and step quickly, for we walk with wings. On, Verrell, on.

(*Exeunt*)

ACT III.

SCENE I.—*A room in Ford's house.*

Enter JUDGE FORD *and* CATHARINE.

Ford. I take it, Christopher has stolen the money.

Cath. You do him a great wrong to think it, and a greater to say it; for you have no proof, nor hope of any. If you were in a session of court and looking nicely into such an affair, I am sure you would never give this wrong a lodging-place in your mind. He has carried many such charges of money, and has ever rendered honest account of all.

Ford. Crime must have a beginning, and by my office, it shall have an end.

Cath. And does it begin in a bruised head, and end in a fever?

Ford. Come, come, these speeches have the flavor of a lawyer's brief.

Cath. Am I not a judge's daughter? and cannot heredity run in the blood of a female?

Ford. Nay, never blur your eyes over law-books, Kate; 'tis the vilest bog of learning that empties into the brain.— But as concerns my clerk, I know not how he came by his sickness, or if he has any.

Cath. Has not the doctor said it?

Ford. Why, he has wagged his head very sagely, and held a great many vials to the light, and stroked the fellow's pulse above fifty times. And all comes to this, that Christopher presently gets on his legs again, and swears the doctor has saved a great man indeed.

Cath. It is much against humanity to charge him with the theft. Were you not yourself very wroth at first,

saying the man should be hanged that committed the
assault? But afterward, when you found all the rest at
one on his innocence, you declared war on reason, and
said himself had stolen the money. I am sure the sum
was not of such value, to buy all this trouble.

Ford. You should know trouble is cheap.

Cath. Truly, it would seem so; and yet you will go a
great distance to pluck nettles.

Ford. Do not set your judgment against mine; you
are all much too wise, much too wise. I fear Levec over-
runs civility to so earnestly protest the knave's innocence.

Cath. He has not spoke of the matter above once, nor
have any of us crossed you in this, as you complain.
Indeed, we know our opinions are like ciphers; they may
be multiplied a thousand times, and get no value.

Ford. O, you will take his part, I warrant you.
Faith, daughter, I have a word to speak with you some
time, concerning this friend of mine. He is an honest
man, as you may say, ay, very honest, but something too
prodigal of his speech. His words are over the brim
at times, much too spendthrift, mark you; and again,
daughter, take wisely only what is wisely given.

Cath. I fear you are out of humor.

Ford. Where have you learned this art of censure?
You are too much in company with Levec, dost hear?

Cath. I would fain hear nothing.

Ford. What did you say? Here comes that pattern of
a rake, my nephew. I have some words for him also.

Enter RANSOM.

Ran. Now, uncle, what's the news?

Ford. Do you know, sir, you are accounted a common
vagabond?

Ran. Now God bless me, is it possible? I had thought
I was the worst vagabond of all, a most uncommon vagabond. I fear some man has slandered me.

Ford. Sir, keep your jests for better company:
perchance they may tickle a wiser man. But here is a
note from some gross fellow that keeps an inn without
the village: he says, you and your custom have near
ruined him, and that you owe fifty dollars to him alone.

Ran. He is a fool at figures; 'tis no less than twice that sum.

Ford. But yesterday, a tailor stopped me in the street and asked me if he should grant you credit.

Ran. Why, he has given me credit these three months.

Ford. Another man told me very angrily, you had broken half the windows of his house.

Ran. And thrown cats in his well?

Ford. He said nothing of it.

Ran. Pah! what a stomach he has!

Cath. You paint yourself blacker than you are.

Ran. What do you think I am?

Cath. To answer that were to speak —

Ran. Beyond praise. I thank you for your good opinion. Sweet speech becomes sweet people; therefore —

Cath. I thank you.

Ran. Therefore I speak well of all people, and am esteemed of all. But why do you change color?

Cath. Out of innocence.

Ran. So? I had thought 'twas admiration.

Ford. Enough of this foppery. I fear you have set up a glass to see yourself that's under duty to your self-pride and consciousness. O time and custom! What a worthless age is this and what worthless tenants. Rank weeds grow in poor soil, for there never was an age when men promised so much and accomplished so little. Why, you shall see a fellow but out of his primer cry hello! to the world, that all men gape at his cunning. At twelve he is so forward in his books and so apt in his wit as to make heaven tremble for her secrets. In another three years he is the style of wonder; affects fine clothes and gross talk, and hath such a fleering and a keen look as cuts the faces of all that behold him. But at twenty this god has lost his wings and become something less than a man. I would not have you like these, nephew, though nature would. If you will put away these wild usurped manners, I'll warrant you a blessing.

Ran. In your will?

Ford. Nay, you had best take my advice to heart.

Ran. And die of heart-burn for a penalty.

Ford. You are smothered up in your own conceit.—I wonder, how does Christopher this morning.

Ran. Even as he pleases; a sick man is a king.

Ford. Does he go about?

Ran. Believe me, these three days. He is the greatest villain but one in the country. I am the other and the greater; but we run in one harness.

Cath. I think you claim better company than you keep.

Ran. You speak religion; quite as true as an angel. I think you are an angel indeed; so put me 'neath the wing of your purity, for I much desire to be better.

Cath. Pray, how much better?

Ran. E'en as good as Christopher, for then I would be three hundred dollars the richer.

Ford. Do you think he stole the money?

Ran. What do you think I have in my pocket? Come cousin, bend a sad brow, and make a guess what I have in my hand.

Cath. I cannot.

Ran. O, I will not be put off.

Cath. Were I in your case—

Ran. You would be a pistol, which God forbid —

(*Pulls out a pistol.*)

Ford. What is the meaning of this?

Ran. Faith, the meaning is lost; it has neither lock nor hammer, and its nose is like my cousin the Jew's. But nathless, 'tis a pistol, though it lacks shrewdness of aim. I keep it in stead for extremities. If I were ever bayed by the law, I would shoot myself most carefully in the vitals. Indeed, I had as lief live as die.

Ford. Sir, I am weary of your ways.

Ran. Are they so difficult? Well, here is choicer company.

Enter CHRISTOPHER KEEN, LEVEC, *and* STEPHEN.

Cath. Good-morning, Christopher.

Keen. Good-morning; good-morning, your honor; and you, Ransom, good-morning.

Ran. Here's dignity with a patch on't.

Ford. I am happy to see you on your feet again; but for a man that has had a fever and two doctors, methinks you are quickly cured.

Keen. Nay, my body cannot be well till my reputation is whole. I am much grieved that your honor doubts my honesty.

Ford. 'Tis to be supposed. Well, sir, I shall hold you to account for the money. If you have stolen it yourself, render it up; if it has been stolen of you, you can bear misfortune with fortitude, being innocent.

Keen. Lord, sir, you will not put the officers on me!

Ford. I shall think on it.

Keen. Stay me up, Stephen, or I faint.

Ford. Tut, tut, do you not blush for your credit?

Ran. Nay, that's past wishing, for his face is a natural blush-color.

Keen. I had thought I was very pale.

Ran. Even so; you show no colors, like a pirate.

Keen. But I cannot be both.

Ran. But you are both; in truth, you're double faced.

Keen. O that any man should have said I was double! Did your honor ever note in me any swerving of virtue?

Ford. Never till now.

Keen. Worse and worse. I'll refer my probity to you, Ransom. Tell your uncle, am I not upright after my fashion?

Ran. Truly, after the fashion of beasts.

Keen. Can you say this, that plucked me from the very talons of robbers, bleeding, and all beaten in between the ears? Do you think I am a man that would commit suicide?

Ran. Not by way of the head, that's certain. Heaven put a lock and key on your little treasure of wit, and I hold you honest in this wise, that you owe but little to nature. But for your misventure, if you have gone fowling for my opinion take it on the wing. You know it is your wont to go wandering about alone, with your head tucked under your wing, and your lips pleading the jury stumps to get from beneath your feet; and so, getting foul of the wood at dark, you were tripped by the heels over a bramble, and went headforemost into a tree

trunk or the like. I have seen you often fall into such
predicaments. Once you were e'en stepping into the
river, but by a fortune saw your own face and fled in a
fright. I have often thought your wit was never quite
recovered. Are you not the man who said the earth was
on her death-bed? I crown him, king of fools.

Keen. O Ransom! your great tongue runs quite
through my ears. What have I done, to pull all this
defamation upon me? 'Tis all abroad in the town how I
am dealt with.

Ford. Who was it told you?

Keen. Faith, your honor, being in the village some
two hours ago, I heard nothing but of my own infamy.
Even as I touched foot among people, one stuttered out,
as if the news were too great for his mouth, *Here comes
Christopher!* and when I thought to sneak away, another
hooks his talons upon my coat, thus, *Is it you, indeed?*
with a great wonder that I was not between the bars.
But a third shuffles up, and wishes my name in his album,
'twixt two members of Congress; *For,* said he, *we must
keep these hot-headed fellows apart* And when I had writ
my name in a good fair hand, *Marry,* quoth he, *now I have
the finest thieves' gallery in the States.* You may imagine I
staggered in his meaning, but I made no questions, for
I was thrust about from one hand to another, much like
a hand ball, or a ferret a-hunting, which indeed I was,
for a hole. By and by a fellow on the edge of the crowd
cries out, *Trouble him not, neighbors;* *he is the honestest
man in fifty miles roundabout.*— *True, true,* said two others
in a breath, *we were by when he was robbed.* *We saw the
thieves.* *We chased them.*— *Nay,* says the other, *you
remember we ran for the officers.*

Ford. Know you their names?

Keen. I inquired straightway. They are two men of
good character, noted for honesty, of excellent 'havior,
and as much modest as virtuous.

Ford: Their names, their names.

Keen. He that is the taller, with a majestical bearing
and a most pleasant and ingenious countenance, his name
is Cade; t'other is Joseph Ratsey.

Ran. Now God save me.

Ford. Do you know them, Ransom?

Ran. Too well for their credit. They are two scandalous fellows, two cut-throats and common pick-pockets, and as great liars as myself.

Keen. Remember that, your honor, remember that. I assure you they are well reported of all men, and loved by many. If you wish to see them, I think they are within calling.

Ford. You said they were in the village.

Keen. Ay, so I did; truly, so I did; but for my honor's sake I persuaded them to return with me, that you might hear their story. I will bring them hither. (*Exit.*)

Ford. What does the knave intend? I have sentenced a score of men, and sweat less.

Levec. Are you sure you are not beating an empty bush? I dare swear, he is an honest man.

Ran. O, his soul is as pure as an icicle. I would as lief dare the devil to a dicing for it.

Levec. I would wager my life on his honesty.

Ran. So; but you durst not risk your purse.

Levec. My purse?

Ran. Ay, your purse; I mean, the money you have in your purse.

Ford. Sir, be still.

Levec. Nay, friend, I have no tremblings for my money. Let it lie here on the table. If Christopher does not confirm himself innocent, I forfeit it with a grace.

Cuth. I beg you, sir, do not bet with him.

Levec. 'Tis nothing, 'tis nothing; I am little the worse if I lose.

Ran. (*Taking up the purse.*) Why, here's a gallant inn, stuffed full of guests. Your leave, sir; let me play the host. I'll turn the key of this chamber, and speak up the tenant; your pardon, sir, do not kill me with your black looks. I am very sensitive. But who's here? An eagle! Why, this is generous; 'tis beyond the level hand of courtesy. I thank you, sir. Ah! what's this? Here come a dozen yellow boys reeling after the first. Where there are drunkards in the attic, there's wine in the cellar. I hold it for a certainty there is pure stuff beneath where such carat is atop. 'Tis wondrous strange, sir, a man

that has been so rich as this should scowl so damnably.
I am quite killed and blasted by your awful nods. Why,
sir, here's a bill with a fortune on its face. I thank you
for it; 'twill round up the account with mine host. And
here is another will buy the cheerfulest face the hostler
has seen in a twelvemonth.

Ford. Art not ashamed?

Ran. What, of my wealth? It is the way of the world.
But step into the street, and you shall see a man sporting
all his wealth and part of another's on his back, and
nothing ashamed of it. Bah!

Enter CHRISTOPHER KEEN, RATSEY *and* CADE.

Ford. What have we here?

Keen. Two honest gentlemen, your honor, caught
abroad in a wicked world. They are the same for whom
I bespoke your honor's audience. This foremost one here
is Cade.

Ran. Oho! is it you, Cade?

Cade. Well, who did you think I was?

Ran. A ghost; look that you do not run away from
yourself.

Rat. What do you mean, Ransom?

Ran. We shall see what we shall see; which is better
than to see more than is to be seen. Am I not right,
master fleet-foot?

Ford. Sir, keep your tattle to yourself. Folly is like a
linnet, sweetest in a cage. — And you, master Cade, methinks I have seen you ere this.

Cade. Your eyes might have been worse employed.

Ford. I am fain to think so. Christopher here has
praised you to be a mountain over other men, both for
modesty, for virtues, and all the kindred qualities of
greatness. I make no doubt you are also truth-telling,
which is more than all.

Cade. There's no doubt on't.

Ford. Then to the question. Do you know aught of
this affair.

Rat. Not all, but the whole.

Keen. I can assure your honor, they are all they say
they are.

Rat. It was thus. Ransom, ourselves, and a lying, cowardly, malmsey, perjured rake named Verrell, we came into the woods on the night wherein this learned and ingenious clerk was robbed and dispatched. What we were saying I have not on file, but of a sudden we were set upon by six or seven villains, whose faces were much bruised and battered, like sots in a session. Whereupon, seeing them, we took to our heels, and narrowly escaped with our lives. But Verrell and Ransom stumbled upon the defendant and brought him away home, as they can tell you. Those who robbed him, your honor, we saw, and also his own corpse in the bushes. If this be not the truth, there is no truth upon earth.

Ford. Say you the same, sir?

Cade. Ay, verily I do. I'll tell you the story. It was thus. Ransom, ourselves, and a lying, cowardly, malmsey, perjured rake named Verrell, we came into the woods on the night wherein this learned and ingenious clerk —

Keen Oh, very well; enough. enough.

Cade. What we were saying I have not on file, but of a sudden we were set upon by six or seven villains, whose faces were much bruised and battered, like sots in a session. Whereupon, seeing them, we took to our heels and narrowly escaped with our lives. But Verrell and Ransom stumbled upon the defendant, and brought him away home, as they can tell you. Those who robbed him, your honor, we saw, and also his own corpse in the bushes. If this be not the truth, there is no truth upon earth.

Ran. Faith, Cade, hang your learning on a peg, and spell your name plain ass the rest of your life.

Cade. What's the matter?

Ford. Were you with these fellows, Ransom?

Ran You, sir, (*To Levec*) you wagered this wallet in good faith, did you not?

Levec. I acknowledge it.

Ran. Why, then, to speak fairly, I was with these fellows, as they say. But Verrell and I came first into the wood by appointment, to hunt up some scent of mischief, and while we stood there, in tumbled Christopher, pattering a villainous little song, and with both eyes buried in the earth. So, in a kind of sport, we knocked him down with a cudgel and dragged him into the bushes.

Ford. Sir!

Ran. Dragged him into the bushes, with the earth for a couch and the sky for a coverlet. Then came Ratsey and Cade here, blustering like an east wind, and in a great fury that we said there were ghosts dwelled thereabout. For us, we held our peace, but Christopher speedily set up such a groaning that both cried out, a ghost! a ghost! —

Rat. A ghost!

Cade. A ghost!

Ran. You may see what a pretty chorus they are; for they cried, a ghost! and fled away swifter than their thoughts. But we, like men of humanity, laid by in the underwood, and after a time brought Christopher home to his kind again.— And now, have I not earned the wallet?

Ford. What say you to this?

Keen. O sir, I beg your pardon and forgiveness.
I will return the money to your honor;
And sooth, I cannot guess what text of evil
The devil set in my heart, to take the money.
But, sir, until your nephew cracked my head,
And broke a cudgel cross my cranium,
Bringing me into fever, fits, and blood,
I was the precedent of honesty.
I think this late dispersion of my senses
Has laid me unto duty to a madness,
A kind of groping and unused blindness,
That, were I not a man of brightest function,
I had not thus so nearly kept the road.
When that the eye of honor is put out,
There's but the moiety of a true man left.

Ford. No more of this.
But let me tell you, sir, since you are mad,
'Twere well I clapped a padlock on my purse.
And for you, Ransom, why is it you fly
Thus in our face, but that your wit being maiden,
Has ta'en in marriage those high-flavored forms

That are the strumpets of an idle mind.
Art not ashamed! Let me not hear of you
Another such a frolic, at your peril.
Give back the purse you hold.
 Levec.   No, not a whit.
'Tis fairly forfeited, and fairly won.
 Ran. And if it were not so, the devil and all
Might beat upon the gates, and never get it. (*Exit.*)
 Ford. I blush for kindred.
 Levec.   Tut, it is no matter.
How often does he win that lays his wager
Upon the crookedness of human kind.
O what a world and wonder wilt be when
Men shall use money and not money men.
      (*Exeunt all but Stephen.*)

    Re-enter RANSOM.

 Ran. So still! Methinks what a thunderclap of sense
should follow such a calm of reason. Here is a piece of
money to unlock your lips, and here is another to clasp
them again, and one more that they may remain clasped.
 Steph. Nay, I cannot take the money.
 Ran. And I can; so the weed thrives at the roots and
the corn withers in the sun.—But to come about to my
point, like a needle — am I not a needle, Stephen?
 Steph. Would you have me say yes or no?
 Ran. You are husband to the gawkiest wit in seven
counties.
 Steph. I think I shall weep presently.
 Ran. What an April visage you wear over your copper
cheeks. Truly, your mother seasoned in April. But
tell me, how does my cousin and master Levec?
 Steph. Very badly, I fear.
 Ran. When did they last meet?
 Steph. A week since, in the garden.
 Ran. Seven days is a long time in lovers' clocks.
Sometimes the coldest men are warmest lovers; and
contra too, or the world's uneven. Did they drop any
vows in your hearing?
 Steph. You may so call it if you wish; *For,* said he,

your wit and beauty, said he, *like the two white pigeons of Venus --*

Ran. The two doves of Venus.

Steph. Ay, the two doves of Venus.

Ran. What said he then?

Steph. Then the bells began, and he said no more. But your cousin ran away in several directions.

Ran. Nay, that's impossible.

Steph. Why, her wits ran one way and her legs another; and when I crossed her a moment after her cheeks were as like to two torches as fire is to fire.

Ran. This was a week ago, you say.

Steph. A good round week, a week with two Sundays.

Ran. By my faith, this fellow has a dry flesh.

Steph. And a dry tongue also. I can tell you, Ransom, he either thinks better of himself, or worse of her. For a week past he has scarce looked upon her, nor upon anyone, but as often as he sees her he runs away with his nose to the ground, as if he were hunting up an old scent; and this morning he beseeched me on what day the stage passed, for a spirit of travel moved within him.

Ran. Ha! mend your tongue.

Steph. I cannot; 'tis the vile truth.

Ran. Are you sure of it?

Steph. As I am living —

Ran. Never mind it. Who walks yonder?

Steph. 'Tis himself, sunning in the orchard.

Ran. As you are my friend, follow me and mark what happens. I will after him and pluck his beard out.

Steph. O Lord, Ransom, never do that.

Ran. May I die like a muck-worm if I do not. Has he not jilted my cousin? Has he not made tracks upon her fair name? Are not his vows flying east and he west? Go to. If you fear to keep me company, hide in the hedge, and you shall see me chop him as fine as a fop's phrase. Come on, come.

Steph. O Ransom, do not so.

Ran. Nay, but I will, and before my heart grows mellow. Follow me, and you shall see a sight to make you wink with both eyes. (*Exeunt.*)

SCENE II. — *In the garden.*

Enter CATHARINE *and* LEVEC, *meeting.*

Levec. Good-morning, Kate.

Cath.   Good-morning, by the sun,
And yet, 'tis evening by your countenance.

Levec. I am right pleased to meet you here apart.
It is my wont, when something's to be told,
To tell it shortly, like the clock its hour.
And yet, I know not, for these many days,
This simple speech has stumbled on my tongue,
And now comes off it very haltingly.

Cath. I hope, 'tis nothing that has come between us.

Levec. Ay, but it is.

Cath.   Can it be fault of mine?

Levec. No, nor of any other, but learn this,
Ill fortune, like a shadow, walks with me,
And everything that's dear to me is cursed.

Cath. Woe me! I thought we were too well fenced
    in,
To think of danger.

Levec.   We are as the sea-gull,
That builds between the breakers and the bourn;
Sometimes 'tis dashed down by the elements,
And sometimes by the blast-blown wave beneath.
So we,
Are by a kind of fate dashed down and whelmed,
That built our nest most sagely up from earth.

Cath. If there has any ill befallen us,
Hide it not from me; I am proof to all.
There's nothing, though the earth turn to a flood,
Can wash my love away.

Levec.   Nor mine, nor mine;
But what if I should say, I must begone,
I must away, and leave you for a time?

Cath. Why, sir, methinks 'twere nothing to weep o'er,
So you returned again.

Levec.   Why, think you so?

Cath. But must you leave?

Levec.   Hear this, and you shall say
I act in good ripe wisdom. It has happened,

E'en since the night I sang beneath your window,
(Whether my love was figured in my face,
Or if a small bird whispered in his ear.)
Your father has looked hot and cold upon me,
Has dropped strange sayings, and a picked care
Perks up his cheek; and though I swear I never
Did think to steal your heart without his own,
Nor to make love in corners, yet, perchance,
I have erred somewhat to the darker side,
In not unfolding this my love to him.
But even as water cannot bide with fire,
Being so contrary in the element,
Sense and discretion cannot live with love.
And something more; it chanced once in the past
He was my debtor for some kindnesses,
And he may say, I come to patch a love
Out of old threads, which, heaven forbid, I do not;
Yet, as suspicion lurks in secrecy,
And darkness doubles all things, there may be
Some ground and footing for his discontent.
You know what I would say — and what to do,
I now am graveled.

    Cath.   And would you desert me?

    Levee.   Nay, say not so; but I have much ado,
My fancy runs so thick in this extreme,
To find some way out of this wilderness,
And this have hit upon; I will excuse
My absence to your father for a time,
Travel, and get my breath in freer air,
And when I shall return, boldly speak out.
I will not long be gone, but in that time
I have a hope his bitter mind will change.
He will think better of me round a corner;
An absent friend's the dearest; and I know
His turning fancy will bring us fair weather.
All shall be sweet for all. Consider this,
And give me answer when and where you may.

                               (*Exit.*)

   Cath. Gone? Is he gone so fast? How am I trimmed
"Twixt love and duty! That my father frowns
Upon this love, I know; but yesterday,

As I did walk with him, quoth he, and coughed,
And strook his chin, *Let not your maiden name*
Play whip to an old handle, and again,
Stowing his hands beneath his coat, as one
That is determined and all unshaked,
There are men, quoth he, *under the screen of love*,
That bob for golden fish. But who is here?

Enter RANSOM.

Ran.   Now, cousin, where's the villain?
Cath.   What do you mean?
Ran.   O my sweet innocence, were your picture ta'en,
With such a young frown growing in the brow,
Mankind — But where's the villain?   Tell me that.
   Cath.   You speak you know not what.
   Ran.   You are you know not what.
   Cath.   Cousin, are you mad?
   Ran.   Fie on't; but where's the rogue?   How like a
      sign
O' the brothel hangs his face over his arm,
Tasking the virtue.   Let me meet with him,
And I will snap his nose off.   Ha! my blood,
Hot with dispatch, brings news of vengeance
From this my heart.   Where is the villain stowed?
I tell you, Kate, he has played foul with you,
Made you the free fan of his sweating mood,
And being cooled, throws you away.   Believe me,
I know it all!   I am your kith and kin,
And while I live you never lack a hand
To make your name good i' the face of the world.
Come, I'll away, and lay the knave aboard.
   Cath.   Stop!   You belie him.
   Ran.   I belie him?
   Cath.   I know you do.
   Ran.   He is as inconstant
As wind in alleys.   Back! you pretty fool;
Did I not see him kiss the tavern maid?
   Cath.   You did not.
   Ran.   Oh, you are right — 'twas you.
   Cath.   Alas! alas!   What is the matter, Ransom?
   Ran.   Did he not plight his faith to you?

Cath.   He did not.

Ran. Ha! mend your speech.

Cath.   ·   And mend your manners, cousin.

Ran. You cannot put me off; he was a blind
To all loose scandal, that did tell me this.

Cath. Who was it.

Ran. A fellow of wit, an infinite freebooter
Into the corners of men's minds, the closets,
Where maidens breach their loves, and in their prayers
Call God and the key-hole fellow to their aid.

Cath. I will not believe it.

Ran.   Believe it or no,
'Tis heaven-protested truth.

Cath.   But I never pray,
Save in the church.

Ran.   Upon a hassock?

Cath.   Nay,
Upon my knees.

Ran.   Why, then, your knees do pray,
And that's the way with many a falsest heart.
I tell you, Kate, he has played double with you,
And half of him is damned. Have I not eyes?
I know it all, trust me, I know it all,
And your denials no more impress make
Than footprints do in water.

Cath.   Who am I,
To be so flouted? Give me way to pass.

Ran. Give me your oath, then, and I'll be content.

Cath. Who'll break her word will break her oath.

Ran.   A maxim
More dead than living; but you look it true.
And so, you do not love him.

Cath.   So I said.

Ran. Why, then, love me will you not?

Cath.   Nay, ask yourself
If you are worthy of it.   (*Exit.*)

Ran.   So, so, so.
A fool, a fool. I think, those who set up
To cleanse their fellows do but daub themselves.
That's flat, that's certain. Cursed are those who ride
In the cockle-boat of passion; sooner or later,

The gale that leaves the steady-tracing bark,
Like as a hawk, with all unbraced wing,
Dashes the painted vaunter in the tides.
But I forget myself. Stephen! Stephen! Come forth.

Enter STEPHEN.

Steph. Is he gone, now?
Ran.   O what a fool thou art!
Steph. Me?
Ran.   Never bring more news to me.
Steph. Lord, is he dead?
Ran.   Were you not looking on?
Steph. Not I; I hid my head between my knees.
Pray heaven, you have not killed him.
Ran.   All is well.
Ask me no questions. I have peppered him
As he deserves. Well, it is dinner time.
Cupid shoots low; I am struck in the stomach, Stephen,
Let us to meals.   (*Exit* STEPHEN.)

Enter RATSEY *and* CADE.

Rat. Here he is.
Cade. Hello! Come here, Ransom.
Ran. Have a care, Cade. 'Tis a rash man that steps
between me and my dinner.
Rat. We are in the mood. Tell me, did you indeed
knock down that scurvy dung-hill lawyer with a club?
Ran. Twice over, I did it.
Rat. Twice the truth is a lie. But never mind. I
would I had his neck 'twixt my thumb and finger;
I would wring his lying tongue from his throat. He
promised us fifty dollars if we would swear we saw him
robbed, which is a good round price for a second-hand
conscience. But when we asked him for it, what do you
think he said?
Ran. Away, vile perjurers! Trouble not me.
Is there not *habeas corpus?* Sue, ye knave.
Is there not law? Is there not equity?
Woo me with law, if thou my love wouldst have.
Why do you stop up my mouth? I have a much prettier
    couplet than that on my tongue's end. It begins
    thus —

Rat. If you speak another line of this, you shall go the road of mortality with half the rhyme hanging in mid air. But shortly, we must have money.

Ran. What is is, and what shall be shall be.

Rat. No mockery, at your peril. Do you know a little old woman that people call Dame Durrell?

Ran. Never meddle with her; she has a tongue like a needle. We met her in the street once, and she named Cade here such villainous terms as made him blench, for fear he was discovered. I tell you, go not near.

Rat. But she has money, Ransom; two bags full for sure. We saw her telling it over by lamplight.

Cade. Ay, that we did.

Ran. The moral is, draw the curtain. Well, what shall you do?

Rat. Your blood is grown tame, if you cannot guess.

Ran. Well, my blood is tame then.

Rat. 'Fore God, that money shall be Joseph Ratsey's.

Ran. 'Fore God, an ill guess. That money shall be Ransom's.

Cade. Are you with us, then?

Ran. If I die not of starvation, I will meet you to-morrow night in the old place; and I swear by all the dark nights in the calendar I will have that money. But 'tis a greater sin to starve than to steal.   (*Exeunt.*)

SCENE III.— *A hall in Ford's house.*

Enter JUDGE FORD, CATHARINE, *and* LEVEC.

Cath. Fie on it, sir.

Ford.   This is most sudden.

Levec. I promise you, 'tis not.

Ford.   So much the worse.
I will not have it, friend, I will not have it.
Why, it is scarce the quarter of a year,
Since we did swear, dost not remember it?
What we did swear. O sir, your memory
Dies quicker than the breath upon a glass,
Quicker than bubbles. You will not dispute it,
You pledged me never to break company;
A spare three months, scantily that; the year

That then was youngster, is scarce middle grown.
Your purpose ripens faster; if it were
A twelvemonth, I might say nature and you,
Were something kin; the grass is strown with snow
All in its season, but your friendship, sir,
Blows cold before its time.

 Levec.   Speak not of friendship.
'Tis laid beneath the frost.

 Ford.   Ay. dead.

 Levec.   My meaning was
That my affection was unshakable.

 Ford.   And mine the same; I hold it in the closet
Next nearest to my heart.

 Levec.   Then hear to me.

 Ford.   Why so I have, Levec, most faithfully,
And as I see all adds to this,
That you are fixed to leave us, how or when
I have not tongue to ask nor ears to hear;
And though you quote a thousand pretty reasons,
Stuck like a plump of blossoms on one bough,
You cannot marry happiness with grief,
Nor make sour discourse sweet.

 Levec.   Sir; I make
Necessity my choice, and so must you.
Pray put aside this dumpish countenance,
As I do mine.

 Ford.   O, I am not as you,
I do not play in masks.

 Cath.   Fie, fie, these tears
Will put your eyes out, father. I promise you,
I take this as a jest.

 Ford.   Oh, here's the humor
That lies in hanging.

 Levec.   Soft! sir, do not weep.
Indeed, had I thought this, I would have come
More carefully on the point. I have said first
What was by nature last, and what was first
I have quite struck out of memory. Bear with me
And give me time to speak. You know right well
That I was ever fitful, wild, mistempered,
Blowing hot and cold at once, ne'er setting foot

Save on a rolling stone. 'Twas thus in youth;
If I did ever settle to a task,
'Twas straightway irksome; if I chose another
The first seemed pleasanter; where'er I stopped
A contrary fit drew me to look beyond,
And heaven was where I was not. You know this,
My shifting ways, my mind of many colors,
Like painters' pallets. Furthermore, to this,
Add my adventures that a trick of fortune
Huddled upon me; for a dozen years
I've ebbed and flowed over the fields of France,
And there I caught the infection of the times,
A smouldering temper and a whirling wit,
That when I sit I have desire to walk,
And when I walk I fret upon the pace,
No faster to my seeming than a spirit,
Carved by the master in a monastery.
This restlessness and wanton temperament
I shamefully confess, but cannot change;
I am not one of those that bend their thoughts,
Like a dark lantern, 'gainst all but themselves.
My inward eye oft tells me I have faults
And social sins; therefore be soft with me.
I now am cloyed with ease; a fit of change
Works in my blood; I need a spice of travel
To flavor life; a little chase of pleasure
Will make retirement sweet; then I'll return,
To be the welcomer for absence sake.
  Ford. Are you determined?
  Levec.   I promise you, I am.
  Ford. I am sorry for't. I have become so grafted
Into your company, your going seems
Like losing of a limb.
  Levec.   A withered one.
  Ford. Nay, do not jest. How long, think you, 'twill be
Ere you return?
  Levec.   A sixmonth.
  Ford.   Too much, by far.
Say half that time shall be the extreme point,
Not to be overrun an hour.
  Levec. So be it.
I shall not set forth under several days.

Cath. Sir, you are like a rabbit.
Levec.   Like a rabbit?
Cath.   Ay.
And we will use you as young wantons use
The rabbit.
Levec.   And how is that?
Cath.   Why, find their course,
And snare them o'er their tracks.
Ford.   Well spoken, daughter.
He ne'er shall leave us but this once; next time
He'll find our home his loop.

                                   (*Exeunt.*)

SCENE IV.— *A street in the town.*

Enter TWO CITIZENS.

First Citizen. Do you not hear a great noise?
Second Citizen. 'Tis Dame Durrell, the bedlam.
First Citizen. Doth she make a speech? Lord, Lord,
neighbor, there is this division 'twixt men and women;
men are moderate in all things, save drink and women;
but women fly to extremes and cantiness. Men cling
and break, cling and break; there are twelve parties and
no government; but women are hotter still and colder
still. The sex, neighbor, owns more opinions than
members; for each woman hath two, one for private
gossip and dissipation of discourse; and one for the sex.
I warrant you, they all hold the same judgment of themselves, infinite goodness, infinite goodness. It matters
not if they all fly to different points, their east and west
of opinion meet on t'other side, the neutral ground of
self-approbation. Hum!
Second Citizen. Let us turn back.
First Citizen. To hear a woman speak! Pah! They
are as like to each other as gutter is to gutter; all flow,
all garbage. To see a woman speak is to see a woman
with four arms, like the wind-mill yonder.
Second Citizen. Nay, 'tis a steeple.
First Citizen. Ay, like a steeple, very like a steeple.
You have oft seen, neighbor, how an orator of good discretion deports himself, with a wave and a gesture, thus

and thus, to notify the stops and periods, the falls and
smooth water of discourse, but always holding to this,
that matter is the flesh of good oratory, and manner but
the flavor of the instant. But look at a woman! How
doth she caper with phrases and dethrone our kingly
English speech; ay, so justle extremities, so make earth
of heaven, and heaven of earth, and, to be private, so
make hell of both, that the words sing i' the ear. But
what creature comes yonder?

Enter DAME DURRELL, *at a distance, a crowd following.*

Second Citizen. 'Tis Dame Durrell, as I told you.

First Citizen. What does she say?

Second Citizen. She says, she has been robbed.

First Citizen. Truly a woman, very like a woman. If
your good honest citizen has been robbed, does he
publish the thief about the streets? Pah! But your
woman! O your woman! What does she say now?

Second Citizen. Listen, listen; she comes this way.

First Citizen. Is it possible.

Second Citizen. Look how her skirts are fouled.

D. Dur. Robbed! robbed! robbed!

Second Citizen. Poor soul. Good-morning, dame.

D. Dur. Are you the sheriff?

Second Citizen. The sheriff, ma'am?

D. Dur. Give me my money. 'Twas he that did it.
Get me my money. I saw him in the face, in the face,
mind ye. His mask fell off in candle light. All gold, all
gold. 'Twas Ransom, the judge's father. He and three
others have got my money. Mercy! mercy! Load 'em
with chains, hang 'em. Give me my money.

Third Citizen. Come away, woman; you're mad.

D. Dur. Gold, gold; all got by stitching. 'Twas a
sunlight to a poor soul. Gone, gone. Are you not the
sheriff, sir? Give me my money.

First Citizen. Sure, she has lost her wits.

Fourth Citizen. Ay, that's certain.

D. Dur. O! O! O!

Fifth Citizen. What's to be done?

First Citizen. Lead her away, some of you.

Fifth Citizen. Do it yourself. She lives three miles

out from the village, and it rained all yesternight. I
will swear, mud and water are a foot deep all the way.

D. Dur. My money, my money. Where's the sheriff?

First Citizen. Peace, peace; he shall put you in the
madhouse.

D. Dur. Will none of you give me my money?
Robbed! robbed! Bring me to Parson Bradley. Have
mercy on a poor soul.

Second Citizen. 'Tis a great shame she has lost her
money.

D. Dur. O! O! Parson Bradley shall give me my
money. Bring me away. I shall have my money yet.
Bring me to Parson Bradley. Gold, gold. He shall load
'em with gyves. Give me my money.

Enter RATSEY *and several others.*

Rat. What's here, what's here?

D. Dur. Are you the sheriff?

Rat. Out of the way, woman.   (*Strikes her.*)

Several. Hold off! hold off!

Rat. What dung-hill creature is this? Pah! how she
smells!

Second Citizen. Do you know where Ransom is? She
says he has stolen her money.

D. Dur. Robbed! robbed! robbed!

Rat. What a pretty tale is this! She has lost a penny
in the mud, and calls every man she meets a robber.
Look up, you jade. Was it not I that stole your money?

D. Dur. My money, my money. Chain him, load him
with gyves. He stole my money. · Never tap your fore-
head; I'm not mad. You stole the money. Thief, thief,
thief!

Rat. Stop your tongue, Jezebel; you're as mad as
Jack-a-lantern. Take my word for it, she never had
enough money to buy her coffin. Look at the tatters
hanging over her heels; look at her hands. I'm cursed,
she has been grubbing in the muck for her money. Bring
her away to the madhouse.   (*Exit.*)

First Citizen. That's it, that's it.

Second Citizen. Have you eyes, and cannot you see
she has been foully dealt with? I will wager my soul

Ransom and his crew have meddled with her. Is that
not Judge Ford yonder?

Fourth Citizen. Ay, 'tis he.

First Citizen. He shall know of this. Mark me, good
wife. Here comes Judge Ford, who will make all your
odds even. When he passes, call to him, cry him for
justice.

   Enter JUDGE FORD *and* CATHARINE.

D. Dur. Justice, your honor.

Second Citizen. Louder, louder.

D. Dur. Justice, justice, justice.

Ford. Who calls to me?

Third Citizen.   This poor crazy hag.
Her brain's uncradled; she goes to and fro,
Knotting her hands, peering in holes and crannies,
And saying 'tis for money she has lost.

Ford. Is mad, you say? 'Twere best she were con-
  signed
Into the jail, waiting inquiry.
One cannot tell what mischief may start up
Out of the embers of dark lunacy.

Second Citizen. Nay, she's civil.

Cath.   'Tis Dame Durrell, father,
A poor old woman, well disposed and mild;
The flickering of a candle is more safe
Than life to her poor body.

Ford.   Know'st her, then?

Cath. Right well, and never did I know her thus.
Look up, good mother; nay, look in my face.
How came you here?

D. Dur. My money, my money. Give me my money.
I'll go my ways.

Ford. She is distracted.

First Citizen.   There are many like her,
Go cross-roads in their speech, but never yet
Have I seen one so aimless and distempered,
So dubious and wide-winnowed in her speech,
Stuck like a weather-cock to tell the winds.
She even says her money has been stolen,
Raves about robbers, knives, and painted faces,

Calls for the sheriff, the parson, and the judge,
But most of all her money, being a woman.
 Ford. I'll speak to her. Gossip, who stole your
money?
 D. Dur. Fairies, sir.
 Ford.   True, true, what was their color?
 D. Dur. As black as hell.
 Ford.   'Tis certain, she is mad.
Come daughter, let us begone.
 Cath.   Nay, I am loth.
Surely, she has some wrong.
 Second Citizen.   You speak it well.
Judge Ford, be not so hasty; stay a moment.
Look at her limbs; they're jaded out with travel,
Her feet wilt under her; I venture it,
She has plodded through the mire upon the roads
Three miles or more since midnight; now 'tis morning.
How she found out her steps i' the darkness hardly
Falls short of miracle, unless her madness
Hovered her sinking life and kept it warm.
I make no doubt she has been nabbed and plundered
By these wild fellows that infest the town,
And love to play pranks upon travellers,
When they are hugged up in their overcoats
On stormy nights. Your honor, 'tis a pity
This poor frail creature should be blown about
By youngsters and mere ruffians. Shall't be said
Men are unkinder to decrepit age
Than flaws and north winds are? Even now, I think,
Were it not for fright, she could a story tell
Would blast the ears of those have done her wrong,
And make their tongues, like coals, burn i' the mouth
For shame, did not her fear set up a ghost
In your unpitiful eyes and clenched lips,
To make her wits run headlong.
 Ford.   What's this to me?
 Second Citizen. Nothing to you, perchance.
 Ford.   Fleer not at me.
 Second Citizen. Mark me, Judge Ford; she has thrice
  spoken
Your nephew's name, labeled him with the crime,
And as I think, most justly.

Ford.   Dare you say this?
Second Citizen. Ay, dare it and say it, too. There's
  not a man
That lives within the town, but his opinion
Claps hands with mine.   There were ever hereabout
A sort of ruffians, fallen out with fortune,
Ready to turn their hand to any business
That had a smack of wildness; but their body
Lacked legs, until your nephew came among us,
And now they kick their heels up in such frolics,
As cannot be endured.   The lazy law
Plays blindman's buff, and gets a general laughter
That 'tis so old and weak; and not being stopped,
Their course has run the broader; men and women,
Being out of nights, are laid by in dark places,
Their beards cropped or their heels tripped up and tied,
Their pocketbooks unloaded at a port
They were not bound for, and such matters done
As need no telling, nay, as are not told of,
For shame and fear o' the pestilence of laughter,
So tickled is misfortune with a brother.
All these are known, and now this poor old woman,
That scrimped her food to lay by a few dollars,
Is swept as clean of them as is her cupboard;
I tell you, sir, 'tis not to be endured,
And shall not, on my honor as a man.
    Ford.   O you vile slanderer, who put you forward
To use your stabbing tongue against my nephew?
Who played you down, you ruffian?
    Second Citizen.   Call'st me a ruffian?
    Ford.   You shall hear of this.
    First Citizen.   Fie, fie, fie, no quarrel.
    Ford.   You pack of wolves, I'll throw a torch among
    you,
Shall set you scurrying.   What! slander my nephew!
I'll set him 'gainst the field.   There's not among you
A man, but if a little sickly candle
Were held up to his deeds, would be as black
As now he's seeming white.   I know you, sir,
And you, and you.— O what a mire of thieves
For a young man to fall into!   O well!

Go to, go to. O very well, good neighbors.
You'll hear of this, mark me, you'll hear of this.
My nephew has strong friends and willing ones,
And I am of them. O you backbiters!
Go home and gnaw yourselves, there's food for you.
Ah, well! ha. Well, I'll not say more of it.
But if my vent were open, I know something
Would scorch you damnably. I have it down,
All jotted in a book. O you cursed neighbors!
The devil's your next door tenant; lay in with him,
And tilt at virtue. So; come, daughter, come.
Pah! how the place smells with the people in it.

(*Exeunt* JUDGE FORD *and* CATHARINE.)

Third Citizen. O fine! Who would have thought it?
Fourth Citizen. You cannot say it was I.
Third Citizen. Nor I.
Fifth Citizen. Nor I.
Fourth Citizen. I am not here, mark ye. (*Exit.*)
Fifth Citizen. Nor I.
Third Citizen. Nor I. (*Exeunt several.*)
Second Citizen. It would seem they had all swallowed hot irons.
First Citizen. Neighbor, 'tis late o' day. You have leaped over ears in quicksand; as for me, I shall leave my tracks in it. (*Exit.*)
Second Citizen. Go, go, you knaves. I do not fear the law, I.
D. Dur. Ay, thou'lt make laws; thou'lt thou God Almighty, and make laws. Ay, thou'lt make laws.
Sixth Citizen. What's to be done?
Second Citizen. She is nigh done to death already. Pray you, friend, help me to bring her away, and leave the rest to me. Here's matter for the sheriff.

(*Exeunt.*)

SCENE V.—*A tavern.*

Enter BOY.

Boy. Master, master, hurry you. Ho! master, master.

Enter HOST.

Host. I say, you rogue. _

Boy. There are two fellows on great tall horses in the yard, a-sitting in the rain and cursing the hostler. They say, you're a villain; they say—

Host. Take their bridles, you rogue. (*Exit Boy.*) Hark! here they come.

Enter RANSOM *and* VERRELL.

Good morrow, friends; your healths, your precious healths.

Ran. Damn you, sir, will nothing but a cannon wake you?

Host. Bless my ears, I thought you were two thunderstorms tramping this way. Shall you have some broth, some hot stuff or other; and then, a taste of fowl, some bacon, some eggs? Never say nay; I can place your appetite by the dial. Let me see, let me see. 'Tis noon; nay 'tis passing noon; nay, the clock is clapping hands at twelve. Lay your equipment here, and here. And now, shall you have a hot broth, and a rum in water?

Ran. What you like, and let it be liberal.

Ver. Remember, old parrot, we're sufficient.

Ran. And look you — ho! sir — lock the door and leave us to ourselves; and when the meal is ready, rap on the panel ere you enter.

Host. I'll warrant you, I'll warrant you. (*Exit.*)

Ver. Look to it, Ransom, has he shot the lock?

Ran. Ay, we're jailed.

Ver. Do not say it jestingly. An' we were jailed indeed, you would never see the humor of four solid walls.

Ran. Have you the money fast?

Ver. The half of it is here beneath my coat. I would we had ta'en it all.

Ran. O you glutton!

Ver. Nay, no glutton; but I am sure you gave Ratsey the fuller pouch. Look, what a lean rag is ours! There's no meat between the ribs, and no stuffing in the belly. Let me undo the cords, and divide it. If there be an odd piece, 'tis mine.

Ran. No, I shall have it.

Ver. Devil take you, Ransom, have I not tugged it through mud and water these three miles?

Ran. And have I not tugged both you and your baggage? O Lord, you are the sleepiest rascal that ever took horse at midnight. Every three rods would you fall wagging your head like a tree-top, and thrice you pulled me by the coat and swore the ditches had legs —

Ver. Even so; my jade was knee deep and more.

Ran. And wheeled your horse this way and that, like a blind man in the game; and ran pell-mell into the fences whenever a dog barked; and swore you saw the north star in the southwest, when it was but a firefly on your nose; and — Zounds! man, what an ass you are!

Ver. Peace, peace, you shall have the coin.

Ran. So will I, or break a dagger over your pate.

Ver. Oho! you are merry. Look, I stop up the mouth of the bag with my hand. Now I pluck it away. See there, and there; golden words, golden words. I would all orators spoke such pretty language.

Ran. Bah! your eyes dance a hornpipe.

Ver. Well, a jig never chased sweeter music. Look there, there. That's a piece of money that is like a preacher's angel, neither man, nor woman, but better than either. Weigh it on your finger, Ransom. Is't not proper? What an odd face it has! 'Twas stamped these fifty years ago. Ay, more than that. It would sweeten o'er the face of an alderman, I'll warrant you; it is the key to all doors.

Ran. Do it up in your sleeve quickly. I hear steps.

Ver. O what a clinking it makes! (*Knocking.*) Whistle, Ransom, I beg of you. Sing me a song; sing it loud as you may, and hide this clattering.

(*Sings.*)

> Come over the stile to me, love,
> Come over the stile—

As you love me Ransom, sing, sing.

Host. (*Without.*) Hello!

Ver. (*Sings.*)

> Come over the stile to me, love,
> Come over—

Host. (*Without.*) Hello! hello!

Ver. Help me, Ransom. O what a damnable clinking!

Ran. Come in, come in. What a battering you make.

Enter HOST *and* SUSAN, *bearing dishes, etc.*

Host. Here's wine for you, sirs, of a good ripe age.
Taste it, Ransom; you are an excellent tippler, and as fine
a judge as your uncle.

Ran. A good mettle, a right good mettle.

Host. You shall have more presently. (*Exit.*)

Ran. Susan, your health.

Susan. Pray you, sir, look to your own.

Ran. So I do, sweeting. Now I shall kiss —

Susan. You dare not.

Ran. The bottle; methinks 'tis sweeter than a shrew.

Susan. Have your ways, sir. (*Exit.*)

Ran. O Verrell, there's a woman indeed. You may beat
the bush the world round, and ne'er find a better.

Ver. I think I will peep at the gold again.

Ran. Most sodden wretch!

Ver. Thirty pieces at a count.

Ran. A rare creature, by my faith.

Ver. The topmost is an eagle.

Ran. Has she not eyes like ovens? I burn, I burn.

Ver. The next is its half value.

Ran. Never, sir, she is the better of any three.

Ver. Soft! here comes the host. (*Sings.*)

> Come over the stile to me, love,
> Come over the stile, I pray.

Re-enter HOST *and* SUSAN.

Host. You shall have a fowl of rare flesh presently.
Here's mutton. (*Exit.*)

Ran. And here's a silly sheep.

Susan. Fie on your courtesy.

Ran. I shall sing you a song, Susan. Come, Verrell,
you shall sing a song, and make over the sentiment to me.

Ver. I shall sing for no one, mark that.

Ran. Look, Susan, this fellow is bewitched of his
senses. He supposes he has a mint of money in his
sleeve that he stole from Dame Durrell, and being bloated
with the thought, he will not sing.

Ver. Did I say I would not?

Ran. Yes, you denied it.

Ver. Faugh! denied a song. Listen to me. (*Sings.*)

> Come over the stile to me, love,
> Come over the stile, I pray;
> Your daddy nods in the old arm-chair,
> And we'll play trip and away.
>
> Come trip and away with me, love;
> (I played a spring on the green.)
> We'll see such sights the world thorough.
> As haply never were seen.

Ran. Faith, a pretty couplet.

Susan. What said the maiden?

Ran. Do you hear, sir? Sing me Susan's answer.

Ver.   (*Sings.*)

> Then quoth my love over the stile,
> This hot blood never will hold;
> Who plays at trip and away when young,
> Will trip and away when old.

Susan. Well answered, O! well answered. (*Exit.*)

Ran. Take that to the devil with you.
                    (*Flings a glass at Verrell.*)

Ver. O God! Ransom; will you murder me?

Ran. Come back to your mess, fool. You jump about like a grasshopper.

Ver. But what have I done? tell me, what have I done?

Ran. Thou art an ass. I could send this bowl after you with a good will.

Ver. And if you do, I will let sunlight into your bowels with this rapier.   (*Seizes an old sword.*)

Ran. Pah! you cannot swing it with both hands.

Ver. I warrant you, I can. Was it not borne in the Revolution?

Ran. Faugh!

Ver. You may ask the landlord. He has as fine a pedigree as any horse hereabout; and a wholesome remembrance of his grandfather. This way he comes.

Re-enter HOST.

Tira-lira. O, sir, this is a very curious weapon.

Host. A weapon? O yes! This was my grandfather's sword, gentlemen, and a braver soldier ne'er mounted horse. I promise you, he was the *finis* of many a stout Britishman; not one of these cold water fighters, but a soldier that drank the bottom from his bowl, and was blessed with a marvelous red eye-ball. You will see, Ransom, this blade is most horribly hacked.

Ran. It could not have been done better with a chisel.

Host. You flatter me.

Ver. Are you sure he fought in the Revolution?

Host. Marry, I am. Was he not my grandfather?

Ran. But where is the sheath?

Host. Right here, under your nose.

Ran. Nay, that cannot be the sheath.

Host. Why, sir, I tell you, sir, why, why,—

Ran. Bah! bah! bah! I daresay this grandfather of yours never drew sword at all, for all brave men were used to throw away their scabbards on going into battle.

Host. Was it the fashion?

Ran. Believe me, not so. It was a law in those days.

Host. But was it 'gainst the law to pick up the scabbard after the victory? Tell me that.

Ran. Very good, sir; it was not.

Host. There I have you on the hip. Ha! ha! I assure you, gentlemen, 'tis in history. I received a ticket once for proving it; for, mark you, if he is the grandfather, mark you, I am the grandson. I think no man may dispute that; and if he does, I have a ticket to show for't.

Ran. Prithee, where was he killed?

Host. Killed?

Ran. It was the law, you fool. They must all be killed, or go to prison for't. I will wager, your grandfather was shot.

Host. Ay, truly, truly. Where do you think he was shot?

Ran. In the back.

Host. O! O! Never, sir. I mean, in what battle?

Ran. Brandywine; 'tis a frequent cause of apoplexy. Your heady liquors keep ill company with your light wines.

Host. Now you bandy with me; — 'twas the battle of

South Carolina, and a bloodier was never fought.— But hark! I hear shouts. There are more guests at hand. Your excuse, your excuse. (*Exit.*)

Ver. Listen, Ransom. What clatter is that at the doors?

Ran. A compound clatter, both hand and foot.

Re-enter SUSAN, *running.*

Susan. Fly, fly, fly.

Ran. So I will, just into your face, and steal a kiss. O! it burns in my lips, your cheek is so red. A handkerchief! a handkerchief! Let me wipe my lips.

Susan. For your lives, get upon your horses. There are a dozen officers beating at the doors. Fly, fly.

Ver. This way, Ransom. We are betrayed.

Ran. Slink away, you coward! I will never stir from these footprints. Pass me the rapier! out with the rapier. No, keep it yourself; I will stab 'em with a fiddlestick. My virgin, by your leave. (*Kisses her.*)

Susan. Here they come.

Ver. And here I go. (*Exit.*)

Susan. After him, Ransom; come, come.

Ran. Wilt kiss me in the hall?

Susan. Quick, quick.

Ran. So, so; 'tis darker there. You will be a firefly indeed; you will stick out of darkness like a star. Keep your fingers from my coat; I follow you in chains.

(*Exeunt.*)

Enter presently, bursting the door, HOST *and several* OFFICERS.

First Officer. This way, this way.

Host. God 'a mercy, you shall pay for this. You shall not break my windows, burst my doors, invade my premises, pursue my customers —

First Officer. Stop your mouth, sir.

Second Officer. Speak quick; where are they?

Host. I am both to speak and be still, am I? We shall see, we shall see. Two doors thrown down, the panels cracked, the hinges snapped short, both being in good repair, stable, new painted —

First Officer. Search everywhere. They are but lately
gone; the nest is hot. (*Exeunt several.*) Now, sir, come
with us.

Host. What have I done?

First Officer. Given aid to thieves.

Host. Thieves?

First Officer. Come away, and you shall see.

Enter an OFFICER.

What news?

Third Officer. They are gone. They were off on their
horses like the last wink of sleep.

First Officer. Get us a mount, and quickly. They are
both hard riders, and will run cross-country through the
fields. Make haste, make haste.

Host. Lord save us, has the devil turned sheriff?

(*Exeunt.*)

ACT IV.

SCENE I.— *A highway.*

Enter RANSOM.

Ran. I wonder where is Verrell. They all promised
To meet me here by ten; now 'tis high noon;
Ay, past that time; the shadow I've been watching
Has once diminished, and begins to creep
Into the east. Have the fools left the town?
That's their confession. O, this timeless frolic
Has dipped us all in trouble. If they go
For good and ever, they will take my guilt
Upon their heels. The law has such a lookout
For common runaways, it cannot see
One who's at home. They have not the spirit
To keep them here. No, I may be the one
That's coward by remaining. What in one
Is cowardice, in another is sheer bravery.
I think each man is made after himself,
Without a pattern; so 'tis vain in all,
The preacher and the lawyer and the judge,

To reckon in a word; they might as well
Say every plant grows like on every soil.
Well, what is best for me? Shall I go with them,
Or stay for Catharine? Women are traps,
Burglars are caught in. Fie, this was no robbery,
Though my soul names it so. We call crime great
Only by penalty. If this old woman,
This mangy, hoarding miser, had the wit
To keep her mouth shut, I would pay her back
What we have taken; there was plenty left.
Where thieves are pitiful law should have pity;
But that is not the case. We took enough
To drink and have a bout on; 'twas a lark,
Wherein our fancies got a-soaring madly.
Well, shall I stay here, like a robin charmed   ·
With danger? Ho! here is my uncle; now
He walks for health; 'tis an odd time at noonday,
But strange diseases have strange remedies.

Enter JUDGE FORD.

Good-morning, uncle.
Ford.   O Ransom! Ransom! Ransom!
Ran. What is the matter? Can you not be pleasant,
As I was?
Ford. O that I ne'er had a nephew!
Ran. O that I ne'er had an uncle!
Ford. Ransom, you stand in most gross need of one.
Ran. I think I do.
Ford.   This lightness sits ill on you,
Like weeds on heirs; you cannot hide from me
Distress and sorrow.
Ran.   No, I never tried to,
I cannot hide good nature.
Ford.   Why should I
Be cursed with relatives? O Ransom! Ransom!
You are my kin, my ward, my sister's child;
Blessed be that she is dead. Those are thrice happy,
That die before their children come to manhood;
They have the pleasure of their pretty youth,
And tenderness of budding nature, but
Time kills the flower of their expectation.

Then the world chides both guardian and parent,
As if a teacher could make a person over.
Youth is the excuse for those heroic failings;
But then, what's in will out. That is the law
Of malice, which does make relations share
Your evil name.
  Ran. Now what have I done?
  Ford. You are no better than a thief, even if
You took her money in a frolic.
  Ran.   Yes.
  Ford. You keep bad company; that's evidence
Against the pureness of your mind. I would
Be your excuse, but every gossip knows
That you are close with Cade and Verrell; then
What can I do? I have the shame of kindred,
And that's enough, without the charge of favor.
My enemies do talk among themselves,
How kin in blood is kin in mind; but people
At large hate murmured accusations,
And take all muttering for scandal: thus
I gain by whispered hatred; but let me
Sell justice for a minute, to my sorrow,
To my love for you Ransom, there's a thing
All men can see and reason.
  Ran.   But are you sure
That they will reason?
  Ford.   Some hint at it now.
  Ran. A hint forcruns a quarrel; every tattler
Insinuates till he finds all the others
Are wise as he; then they fall to discussion,
The proof of reason, next to quarreling,
And after that to parties. If you have
A party on your side, the question's lost
And made the shuttlecock of patriotism.
O, get a party and play the devil, uncle.
Your graced opinions cannot stand alone,
But half a dozen crawling knaves can give them
The argument of numbers. Let them reason.
There is no surer way they can go wrong,
And that's the justice I love. What is this reason?
The preacher's inspiration, and the poor's

Resignment to their fate, the rich man's hate,
A scurvy politician's name for trickery,
The lawyer's and the attorney's argument,
The prisoner's defence, the state's sure proof;
Some say it comes by study; others think
'Tis bred by nature; but 'tis no such thing;
'Tis all fish, uncle.

  Ford.   Well, what will you do?

  Ran. I'll turn fishmonger, and I'll catch my fry
Out of men's mouths.

  Ford.   You talk most shameless nonsense.

  Ran. Hum! why should I not? I am much ashamed
Of my poor maggoty ware.

  Ford.   You are bound
To come to nothing by your lightness, Ransom.
The wind that blows a paper kite is not
More varying than our fortune; nor are you
Less light than that. You have begun a way
That in this world will not have end; look to it.
Heaven has spent all its mercy; my own share
Had given out long ago, but I kept on
For love of my dead sister; none should say
I did not do my duty to my kindred,
And none that I did not do it to justice.
O! 'tis a bitter choice 'twixt love and law;
But 'tis your fault; you might have come among us,
With a name as bright as sunlight; but instead
You take up with three rowdy fellows who
Came here before you. Four of you together
Have been so boisterous in this sober town,
The people are disgusted; you are seen
In company of women, that you bring
From the foul city; and you waylay travellers
For sport and pocket; in short, are a nuisance,
That I must clear away. Who are those coming?
I shall not be seen here.

  Ran.   Where? up the road?

  Ford. Yes, yonder.

  Ran.   Those?

  Ford.   You have the younger eyes.

  Ran. So I have, uncle.

Ford.   Well, who are they, quickly?
Ran. O, they are better company that have come
To talk religion to me.
Ford.   They are Cade,
Ratsey and Verrell; they hang down their heads
Like poppies, for I know them by their walk.
I do renounce you, Ransom, still and forever,
For keeping mates with these. Go your own way,
And cursed be gratitude.
Ran.   You are no uncle.
Ford. Tell them not, it is I.
Ran.   No, I will say
'Tis some old silly clod-hopper. (*Exit* JUDGE FORD.)

    Enter CADE, RATSEY, *and* VERRELL.

         How dare you
Come by the road?
Ver.   Because it was the nearest.
Ran. Thieving's not your profession; you had rather
Be jailed than run. O, you are all so lazy!
Ver. Yes, they said so.
Ran.   They are both liars, Verrell.
Ver. Notorious; but I told them 'twas as safe
For thieves to walk at noonday. All the sheriffs
Take heavy dinners.
Ran.   O, if you were rich,
You would have wit enough for a fop.
Ver.   Thank you.
Cade. What's to be thankful for? I wish you two
Would think us some way out.
Ran.   So, let us reform.
Rat. In a reformatory?
Ran.   Yes, let us give
Ourselves to justice; those who flee from it,
Endure more than it can inflict. I'm weary
Of constant watching against constant harm.
The last four days I've undergone more torments
Than bars and prisons have. 'Tis a relief
To know our place and station, to be fixed
'Gainst the inconstancies of life, and better
To be confined than always dreading it.

We are like poor and little birds that hop
Merrily round, to look at, but are really
Keeping away from hawks and shrikes.   I have
Money enough to bribe our wardens, if
They treat us vilely; we may learn a trade
That will support us honestly, or at least
May get the knack of honest knavery.
What do you say to standing trial?
   Ver.   Hum!
Let us consider.
   Cade.   God!
   Rat.   Cade is a-praying.
   Cade.   Thunder!
   Rat.   There's more of it.   I would not think
To see a man so changed.
   Ran.   All miracles
Are wrought in minutes.
   Rat.   He was a great sinner.
But now — Ho!   (*Cade starts off.*)   Where now, Cade?
     Are we not good
Enough to be your company?
   Cade.   You are —
   Ver.   O, he commends us.   But whereto so fast?
   Cade.   To no damned jail, i' faith.
   Ran.   Give me your reason.
   Rat.   Ay, he was always reasonable, the best
Among us blockheads.   But what's to be done?
   Cade.   Why, go to Portland, and wait there a while
Till the whole thing blows over.
   Ver.   This is like
A revelation, Ransom.
   Ran.   Ay, it sounds well.
   Rat.   Like an old clock striking familiar wisdom,
A dear friend at our elbow; I ne'er thought
Cade had such wit; but we will follow him.
   Ran.   Yes, to the gallows, if need be.
   Cade.   Come on.
   Ran.   Consider what time it is.   We will make ready
To start to-night.
   Ver.   The watch-dog knows us better
Than does his master; let us go this minute.

There are short paths that lead through woods and caverns
More dark than night.

Ran.　　　　　　Nay, I have pressing business.

Rat.　To say good-by to Kate.　Ha! ha!

Ran.　To get drunk, fool.

Ver.　　　　　The wise man's own indulgence;
Better than sleep or any drowsy drug
To crack my care.

Ran.　　　　　I have nothing to take care of.
Officers must look out for their own heads.

Cade.　To the haunt, fellows.

Ran.　　　　　　　　　　　Come away.
　　　　　　　　　　　　　　　(*Exeunt.*)

SCENE II. — *The garden of Ford's house.*

Enter LEVEC.

Levec.　O misery! my heart is buried here,
My body like a ghost does wander forth.

Enter CHRISTOPHER KEEN *and* STEPHEN.

Whither so fast?

Steph.　　　To get the horses ready.

Levec.　Is it so late?

Keen.　　　　　　Near midnight.

Levec.　I would have said 'twas noonday, or the like.
How sorrow puts the minutes underfoot!
Our passions are the glasses of our eyes,
And double what we look at.　Are we mirthful,
The world is foppish with us; are we splenitive,
Then everything is sour; are we in love,
Then all the earth is bridal.　The color of mind
Paints every being likest to our fancy.
Who's up within?

Keen.　　　The judge and Catharine.
I think he means to take the ride with you.

Levec.　It is a wanton kindness; the road is easy,
Having such company as home-bred thoughts.
It is three miles or more?

Steph.　　　　　O, more than that.

Levec. By heaven, he shall not do it.
'Tis perilous for old and feeble bodies
To take the wafture of the wet night air.
Whither art going?
 Steph.   For the horses, sir.
 Levec. Stop! stop! O let me think! Nay, stay with
 me.
I shall not go to-night.
 Keen.   Why, this is well.
 Levec. What did I say? Come, come, are you ready?
 Steph. Ready, sir?
 Levec.   Yes, with the horses.
Is there yet time?
 Steph.   Double what is needed.
 Levec. I would not miss the stage for twenty worlds.
         (*Exit* STEPHEN.)
Now, Christopher, I have some words for you,
That I was telling over to myself,
Like beads, when you broke in upon my mutterings.
 Keen. There is no harm, I hope.
 Levec.   No, no, no.
Perhaps you have some slight regard for me.
 Keen. Much more than I can tell.
 Levec.   Soft! (*The bells toll.*)
The Lord have mercy on us; what was that?
 Keen. The bells a-tolling.
 Levec.   So it was. Who's dead?
 Keen. Dame Durrell.
 Levec.   I had thought it was myself.
Well, it has happened two or three times,
I have shown you some little kindnesses;
And though I do not clap my sometime favors
Down in a note-book to be answered back,
Nor stand in expectation of such answer,
Since they are given from an open heart,
Save when bad fortune or a circumstance
Blocks up our ways; — Come, sir, you have my meaning.
 Keen. If there is anything within my power
Can bring you benefit, 'tis yours at once
Free as the common air.
 Levec.   Thanks, and more thanks.

You are kind, right kind. Taking of some men
Is pleasanter than giving. If 'tis true
You hold yourself in some slight bond to me,
There is a certain service you might do me,
Would wipe the page and more. I ride to-night
To Portland, then to Boston; the next stage
Lands me at York, a miserable city,
Where dollars mix with dirt; half the men die
Of lean starvation, and the other half
Of swinging a great belly. Pitch as you will
Death wins the toss; that's woeful.

 Keen.   And then.
 Levec.   Canst count the seventh day?
 Keen.   A primer boy could do that.
 Levec.   Seven days from this
Finds me at — where?
 Keen.   Did you question me?

     Enter JUDGE FORD *and* CATHARINE.

 Levec.   Break up our talk; here comes graced com-
  pany.
 Ford.   Is it you, Levec? This darkness is hard-
featured.
 Levec.   'Tis I, indeed.
 Ford.   By favor of the night
We have stumbled on your council. Shall we stay?
 Levec.   Be well assured. Methinks, 'tis a warm night
To be so bolted in an overcoat.
 Cath.   The ride is long, sir, you will need your own.
 Levec.   Thank you, not I. You are not going with
me?
 Ford.   Thank you, I shall.
 Levec.   Nay, friend, there is no need.
 Ford.   Nay, friend, there is.
 Cath.   My father sings as shrewdly as a parrot.
 Ford.   You are a prettier bird; teach me your notes.
 Levec.   That is very true.
 Ford.   O ho! Kate, do you hear that?
He keeps his tongue primed very wittily,
And beauty holds the match.
 Cath.   I saw no wit.

Ford. I'll warrant. Well, where's Stephen?
Cath.   It is too early.
Ford. Why girl, 'tis midnight; if you get not in,
You will not put your eyes out till the stars.

Re-enter STEPHEN.

Steph. All is ready.
Ford.   Are both horses in?
The roads are heavy; it were best be so.
Steph. Ay, sir, both.
Ford.   Then come on, Levec,—   .
There is an hour yet 'twixt our sorry parting.
Levec. Though I have said good-by to all ere this,
Once more,
May your health prosper, Christopher, and yours.
                            (*To* STEPHEN.)
Kate, by your leave. (*Kissing her.*) There goes more
    kindness with it
Than I can tell; and my lips take away
More sweetness than a thousand musk roses,
One other such a parting were sufficient
To break my life.
Cath.   And one such other greeting
I hope, enough to mend it.
Levec.   And all the rest is hope.
                      (*Exeunt severally.*)

SCENE III.— *A cross-road.*

Enter RATSEY, VERRELL *and* CADE, *with* RANSOM *drunk.*

Ran. Come out, you rogue.
Rat. Stop your bawling; you're drunk.
Ran. Kiss your heel, you knave. 'Tis not I that am
drunk; 'tis the world. O Lord, my bowels are very
empty. I have eaten nothing but pepper and salt these
seven days. I mean, liquor. Does any man contrary
me? None. Write me down, the world. Ay, that's it.
And then, 'twas born in a jig and it danced on its birth-
day. Verrell, a bee in your ear. What sleek-guts is
that, strutting in the road?

Cade. Mind your tongue.

Ran. Soft! What dog barked?

Cade. I will stop up your mouth with mud, like an ants' nest, if you speak again. The whole county will hear you.

Ran. Verrell, Verrell, fetch me two cannon, and a quart of hot shot. If the devil ask the reason, tell him 'tis for his brother's funeral. Tell him that.

Ver. Come on, come on.

Ran. Not an inch, as I am a fool. I will stick my knife into that giant, or beg mercy of a gallows. Come on, round robin; I know you. You robbed Dame Durrell; you put a gag in her mouth. Come on to Portland, come on. If you're not walking to prison, you're running. Verrell, my cannon, and make a coffin for Cade.

Rat. If you will not come along, we will leave you here in the gutter, that we will.

Ver. Lookout, lookout.

Ran. You'll leave me, will you? Take that.

(*Passes at* RATSEY *with his knife, and falls.*)

Rat. O God, was ever a man so near death, and no prayers said? O you murderer! Lie there and rot. Go not near, Verrell; he will kill you.

Ran. Kill dogs and witches. Is it not night?

Ver. Ay, and a double darkness to you. What is that?

Ran. Help me, help me! Yonder comes a man with a torch.

Rat. Run! 'Tis the officers.

Ver. O what a light! Away, away!

(*Exeunt all but* RANSOM.)

Ran. Help, help, help, help! Let the nags trot; 'tis only the moon. Verrell, Verrell! O ho, my saint! Devil take mosquitoes; what a pest-house they keep. If I catch small-pox, I am a man to be pitied. I wonder, could a horse make so cold a jest on so hot a night. Ha! my parents, say'st thou? My father was a percheron, and my mother was a Morgan mare. Ha! ha! Now, I have proof positive. That was the mightiest horse laugh ever laughed in the face of heaven. God

send me a sweet peck of provinder. But indeed, I
deserve not God's blessing. I will crawl into the bushes,
or I am a scoundrel.

     JUDGE FORD *and* LEVEC *appear in the distance.*

Ha! have I eyes? Yonder's old woolen-tongue and
t'other fellow. By my soul, they come this way. Lie
close, and watch.

  Ford. Nay, Stephen, hold the horses by the head;
The roan is skittish. We will walk a pace.
I would have words with you.
  Levec.   And for myself,
I have no stomach for it.
  Ford.   Wilt still play
On the short strings?
  Levec.   By heaven, I cannot help it.
  Ford. Nay, but you must.
  Levec.   If any man has reason
To call life death 'tis I.
  Ford.   Look where you step.
The hill grows steep. Upon these country roads,
One must walk up or down, or else stand still.
  Levec. Is it so?
  Ford.   A fine place for wind-mills.
Look, yonder's the village.
  Levec.   I can see it faintly.
  Ford. That is the church that crows upon the summit.
  Levec. Methinks the blue cape of the sky falls on it.
  Ford. 'Tis providently placed, so that the parson
Can preach into the sails o' the wind-mill next.
  Levec. Are you so heretic?
  Ford.   Nay, but the people
Slide from the mountain tops into the city,
And only the gloved fops in summer time
Make it their perch.
  Levec.   What is the reason of it?
  Ford. Heaven! what is here?
  Ran. (*Rising.*) Wilt tread on me? Take that.
         (*Stabs* JUDGE FORD, *and rushes past.*)
  Ford. Murder, murder!
  Levec.   Ho, Stephen! A light, a light!
Where are you hurt?

Ford.   I am more stabbed with sorrow
Than with ungentle steel.   Was it my nephew?
   Levec.   Woe me, I know not.   This way; a light, a
light!
   Ford.   Touch me upon the breast.
   Levec.   O, this is blood.
   Ford.   Is my watch in my pocket?
   Levec.   I can feel it.
   Ford.   Then 'tis my watch is beating, not my heart.
Certain, my life is out.   Who would have thought
My frozen blood would melt so readily?
Didst see the fellow's face?
   Levec.   A light!   Make haste.
   Steph.   (*Without.*)   Ay, ay.
   Levec.   Where is the dumb devil stowed?
Lean on my arm, and do not speak again.
It makes the blood flow faster.

     Enter STEPHEN *with a light.*

   Steph.   Lord, sir, take the lamp.
I am all dizzy headed.   Who is dead?
   Ford.   My nephew, 'twas my nephew.   Give me your
   ear.
Levec, you have been much on battlefields,
How does a man feel that is dying of wounds?
   Levec.   O, speak not so.
   Ford.   I tell you, 'tis a lie.
What are these visions, at the point of death,
That stuff men's eyes with horrors?   Nothing, I say.
A lie, a lie, a lie.   Are you there?
   Levec.   Right at your elbow.   I've a vial here
Will bring your strength up; it is on your lips.
   Ford.   Fie, fie, there's death in doses.   (*Dies.*)
   Levec.   Hold the light close.
O what an hour!   Look, here the knife ran through,
And pierced into the heart.   Ay, he is dead.
O, muffle up the lamp; I dare not look
Into his face.
   Steph.   By grace, what's to be done?
   Levec.   Lend me a hand to lay him on the grass,
Out of the mud; and when the stage comes by,

I will make chase after the murderer.
He ran this way, and vanished like a breath
Into this thicket here. No, heaven forbid
That I should leave his body, though 'tis dumb;
But I will raise the town, and set the nose
Of law upon the scent. Here, take him up,
The sward is fresher on the other side.

(*Exeunt, bearing the body.*)

ACT V.

SCENE I. — *On a highway.*

Enter RANSOM, VERRELL, RATSEY, *and* CADE.

Ran.   What time is it?
Ver.   Neither night nor day.
Ran.   Then let us rest a while upon this bank.
Rat.   Right in the gap of travel?
Ran.   I care not.
I am so footsore, weak, and travel-stained,
So malcontent with life and weary of it,
The miles so many and the paces short,
Twixt here and safety, though it were my ruin,
I would stand still, like does charmed with a torch,
Right on the brink of danger.
Cade.   Stand there then.
For me, I'll take the covert of the wood.
Ran.   And lie beneath a brake-bush? That were
    heaven,
Were it not for griping hunger. Have you food?
Ver.   O, plenty of cold thoughts.
Ran.   Nor you?
Cade.   Not a crust.
Ran.   Nor you, Ratsey?
Rat.   It was you that carried it.
Ran.   And I have lost it; I could fall down and die
Of thirst and hunger.
Rat.   There is a farmhouse near,
And you have money.
Cade.   More than all together.

Ran.   Here, take it; get us something and make haste.
Rat.   Not I.
Cade.   Do it yourself.
Ver.   Let us cast lots,
And whom it falls on, let him take the money,
And get us food.   The rest will leap the wall,
And lie in ambush till he comes again.
Rat.   That's well.   See, I pluck up a blade of grass.
Stand back; to which of us the flaw directs it,
Let him call it fortune's finger.
Ver.   Throw it high.
Rat.   Mark how it falls.
Cade.   Ransom!
Rat.   Ay, it was you.
Ran.   'Tis foul, you stood me i' the eye of the wind.
Cade.   Go to, I did not.
Rat.   By my soul, 'twas fair.
Ran.   You know right well, it was not.   'Tis a mean-
     ness
Bitterer than wormwood.
Cade.   What a craven are you!
Do a man's part.   'Twas fortune threw the grass
Upon you.
Ran.   And you are my evil fortune.
Rat.   You shall repent it if you do not go.
Ran.   O Verrell! take my place.
Ver.   Not I.
Ran.   But I am feeble; all my nerves are quivering
Like bowstrings; there are cankers on my feet,
That I can scarce keep footing; my poor spirits,
That were so tipsy but an hour ago,
Are fall'n down flat; the knots that bound my limbs
Together are untied; 'tis not in nature
To take another step.   You are my friend,
Then fill my place for me, and do this errand,
I will repay it you a thousand times.
Ver.   The lot fell fairly; you must do it yourself.
Ran.   Your heart is made of dust.
Ver.   Look how he snarls,
Just like a painted lion on a show-bill.
Cade.   Ay, and as harmless.

Ran.   My spirits are washed out.
But you shall have a hint of what they are.
   Cade. Do you threaten us?
   Ran.   The words stick in my throat.
Or I would tell you what —
   Rat.   Come, if you spit
Your spleen on us, you shall repent of it.
   Ran. On you!
   Rat.   We are better than you are.
   Ran.   You!
   Cade. Come, we are starving.
   Ran.   I get the food this once;
Another time my sides shall fall together,
Like to an empty bag, ere I will stir.   *(Exit.)*
   Cade. Think you he means us harm?
   Rat.   I cannot tell.
   Ver. Believe me, he has lost all resolution.
Did you not note him when he joined with us?
   Rat. Somewhat in haste.
   Cade.   And all his color out.
   Ver. Ay, more than that; saw you how wild he looked,
As if his count'nance had soaked up despair?
You will remember, when you two stood talking
Midway the road; — upon a sandy bank
Where blackberries grew; well, I was culling them,
And there I saw him first, skulking along
Almost upon all fours, much like a bird
Shot in the wing; — well, he ran up to me,
And beckoned me into the thorn bushes,
Ne'er minding where they stabbed him; and, believe me,
His eyes hung on his cheeks for very fright;
And there he told me —
   Rat.   What?
   Ver.   You will not tell?
   Rat. Come, what did he say?
   Ver.   Why, when we left him,
Mired in the road, last night, he lay a while,
All motion having fallen with him: by and by,
There came two men, his uncle and another;
(And what the reason was that fetched them out,
When nothing but the stink-cats are abroad,

I mean, being midnight, there was madness in it.)
Well, when they tread upon him, so he says,
Being so pestered by mosquitoes that
He was at cracking heat, and high in blood,
Like the quicksilver in thermometers, —
    Rat. Stop not for that.
    Cade.   Tell it plainly.
    Rat. Go on, go on.
    Ver.   Well, being so boiling angry,
He starts up in a fit and rubs his dagger
Between his ribs.
    Cade.   Whose ribs?
    Ver.   Why, why, why —
    Rat. One tongue at a time.
    Ver.   Why, his uncle's.
    Rat. Did he tell you this?
    Ver.   All of it and more.
And made me promise by a thousand oaths
Never to breathe a word on't.
    Rat.   You have told it
Without once breathing, so no vows are broken.
    Ver. There spoke a friend.
    Cade.   But did they see his face,
When he ripped up th' old devil with his knife?
    Ver. Why, so he says.
    Rat.   Then mischief is at large.
    Cade. But how could he be seen? The night was
dark.
    Ver. Alas! I know not.
    Cade.   Are you sure of this?
    Ver. Death is not more certain.
    Rat.   And he has brought
The plague among us.
    Cade.   So he has.
    Rat.   In this forfeit
We stand with him. Look you. it comes to pass,
There will be hue and cry, racing and chasing,
To find the murderer, and we who stand
Right in the trade and highway of suspicion;
(For, look you, 'twill be said those who have stolen
And had the spot rubbed in, will also murder,

Since they are reckless where they drive.) it comes
We shall be run down by the officers,
And clapped in jail; while for a little theft
We might slink by the sentinel of law,
And ne'er be thought of.

Cade. But we did no murder.

Rat. I tell you, we are rivals in the crime.

Cade. S'blood! we are not.

Rat. O you addle-head!

Ver. 'Tis certain, he will bear us no good will.

Cade. Not he.

Rat. Marked you what he said to us,
Just as he parted?

Ver. He was as mad as fire.

Rat. He said, beware of Portland; when he came
there
He washed his hands of friendship.

Cade. So he did.

Rat. And looked a volume of the law at once.

Cade. His purposes are dark.

Rat. Yet you may read them
By the uplightings of his countenance.
How often has he twitted us of crimes,
And blown the fire anew!

Cade. Ay, more than that.
Has he not said, 'twere best throw up our hands,
And go to prison? And last night in drink
He threatened to betray us to the law.

Ver. Let us take to our heels, and leave him here
Grounded upon his malice.

Rat. That were bootless,
His tongue being loose upon us.

Cade. 'Twere best to stop it.

Rat. Cade!

Cade. What is it?
(RATSEY *motions him apart.*)

Ver. I have ears also.

Rat. Stand back, and keep your own thoughts company.
(RATSEY *and* CADE *converse together.*)

Ver. Why, what is this? O tell me what you mutter!

Rat. Prayers for Ransom.

Ver.   You do not mean him ill?
Cade.   Not I.
Rat.   Nor I.
Ver.   Then why this hanging brow?
For heaven's sake, friends, do him no injury.
Rat.   Soft! here he comes.

Re-enter RANSOM.

Ran.   Here, take the basket; there is food enough.
O, I am faint.   I tell you, here is food.
If you are hungry, eat; my breath is lodged,
And I must rest.   Here, Cade, and will you pay me
With silence and hot looks?
Cade.   Take that, and that!
(*Stabs Ransom.*)
Now you are paid.
Ran.   O, wondrous dark!
Ver.   What have you done?
Rat.   Be still, and lend a hand
To throw him in the gutter.
Ver.   Fly, fly, fly.

Enter several OFFICERS.

First Officer.   Ho! here they are.
Second Officer.   Stop, villains.
Third Officer.   Stand! I say.
Rat.   What would you have with us?
Second Officer.   Who is this here
Lies on his face?   Wake, wake, I say.
First Officer.   This is Ransom.
Second Officer.   And murdered in the breast.   Water!
get water!
First Officer.   No more; his spirit is laid.   Look how
   he bleeds.
His face is white as paper.   O, you villains!
Which of you has done this?
Third Officer.   They cannot speak.
First Officer.   This body can.   Come, put the irons on
   them.
And bear this hacked corpse to the farmhouse yonder.
For you, sirs, 'tis a wonder but your life

Is stretched to snapping; you are gallows marked.
We here are witness to this bloody time.
What lawyer now can lay the paint on crime?

(Exeunt.)

SCENE II.— In the garden.

Enter CHRISTOPHER KEEN and two NEIGHBORS.

First Neighbor. But have you heard the news?
Keen.   Touching myself?
First Neighbor. You well may call it so, touching
  yourself,
And striking others. To be short with you —
Second Neighbor. Since, by the will of God, we all are
mortal.
First Neighbor. Our bodies being mortal.
Second Neighbor.   And heaven, which is
The ocean of our being, heaven is pitiful
To those who fall not in the ripe of nature,
But by a gust or oddness of affairs
Blown from their stem; — the Lord has mercy on them,
And so have men.
Keen. O, sir, 'tis good religion, but poor truth.
First Neighbor. To take the road of speech —
Second Neighbor.   Ay, mark him now.
First Neighbor. You here can bear me out.
Second Neighbor.   Both can and will.
Keen. Pray, tell the news, and do not run about
Taking each other's dust.
Second Neighbor.   We stopped to tell you.
Keen. Well, then, my ears are open; tell it me.
First Neighbor. Did Judge Ford sleep here yesternight?
Keen. He did not.
First Neighbor. Well, he is dead.
Keen.   Dead! Now you jest with me.
First Neighbor. I tell you, he was stabbed.
Second Neighbor.   Right in the highway.
Keen. Woe is me! he owes me money.
First Neighbor.   The more the pity.
Keen. The more the more pity. But who told you
this?

First Neighbor. Now you shall hear. It seems the
 judge's man
Was with him, and another, at the cross-roads,
Waiting the stage. Well, as they walked about,
Up starts a fellow like a flame in straw,
And cut the judge a gash across the breast,
Making the blood to weep out at the wound;
And so, being dead, it seems this Stephen is sent
To give you word; we passed him on the road,
And came first to the mark.
 Keen.   What was his favor?
 First Neighbor. O sir, most strange; his mouth pursed
 like a wallet,
Wherein from both eyes trickled silver tears.
 Keen. He is the man. How shall I break this story?
 First Neighbor. He will be here anon.
 Keen.   Then he shall do it.
He has his wages for such work as this:
I am for law. Bless me, here is Kate.

    Enter CATHARINE.

 Cath. Good-morrow, sirs.
 Second Neighbor.   The same to you.
 Cath. I would not thus have broken in upon you,
But for anxiety, that keeps no hours.
 First Neighbor. As, truth, our business does. Give
 you good-day,
And hopes of many a better.
 Cath.   Is it constraint
Hurries you hence?
 First Neighbor. Believe me and — good-day.
       (*Exeunt* NEIGHBORS.)
 Cath. O Christopher, I have been searching for you.
Know you my father's whereabouts.
 Keen.   Your father?
 Cath. Yes, have you seen him?
 Keen.   He has not returned.
 Cath. Alas! I feared it.
 Keen.   What is there to fear?
Has he not often, on a spur of business
That took him unawares, left us in haste,
And nothing of his destination known?

Cath. But where is Stephen?
Keen.   He will come betimes,
I warrant you; the sun has hardly set
His brief upon the clouds; 'tis morning still.
   Cath. I fear some mishap has befallen them.
   Keen. Pish! pish! it cannot be.
   Cath.   Why do you turn
Your count'nance from me, like a weather-vane?
   Keen. Did I so?
   Cath.   Your words are all oblique.
O, if you have intelligence of harm
That has befallen my father, tell it me.
You cannot rob me of my comfort; 'tis
All burned to ashes now.
  Keen.   O fie and nonsense!
I warrant you, your father is as safe
In life and limb as we are; otherwise·
We would have heard of it. The news of ill
Are blown about in the community
As with a wind. There's nothing that befalls,
Of import bloody, wild, and marvelous,
But every tongue turns carrier.
   Cath.   O, such fears
Run through my body, I am robbed of thought.
Who is it walks this way?
   Keen.   Stephen, ah! Stephen.

            Enter STEPHEN.

   Cath. O what a blackness is between his brows!
As God is merciful, what has happened?
   Steph. Heaven save us all and give us comfort, if it
may.
   Cath. Where is my father?
   Steph. Bless me, 'twere best done shortly. He is dead.
   Cath. Dead! O my body!
   Keen. She has somewhat fainted. Get some water,
ho! Nay, 'tis but weakness. What a fool thou art!
   Cath. Where am I? what is done?
   Steph. The Lord have mercy on us. Come away
Into your room.
   Cath.   Nay, touch me not. O Stephen,
Can this be true?

Steph.   I will tell you all.
But come within the house, out of the wet.
What sieves my eyes are! Let me hold your hand.
  Cath. As you will have it; I am sick to death.
O what a morning! I could wish a tempest
Would put the sun out, that I might die with it.
                    (*Exeunt* CATHARINE *and* STEPHEN)
  Keen. O Lord, what a heaviness has befallen us! I
think I was born under fighting stars, so contrary to my
desert goes my fortune. No sooner does a man owe me
a six-month's wages, but he must needs walk o' nights
and be murdered. S'blood, was ever a man so pestered,
so galled, and so harnessed to other men's misfortune?
A twelvemonth's wages, and the man dead! Let me
think. The man is dead; ergo, he is not alive. This
man owned certain goods, chattels, properties, and divers
lands, and buildings thereon. But the aforesaid man is
dead; ergo, he forfeits to his heirs the aforesaid rights
and ownerships; ergo, I shall clap an attachment on the
aforesaid goods, chattels, and properties, to-morrow at
the furthest. 'Tis a good thought; I will record it in my
note-book. Thus, item; for two years' faithful and fruit-
ful services, etc. etc. That is well. My fortune is
marble, but my wit is steel. I have a shrewd tongue,
that's certain. But bless me, I shall scarce venture out
at night hereafter. I think all calamities, like summer
showers, fall in the dark.

                    Enter LEVEC.

But here comes a thunder-storm, and by day. Are you
back so soon?
  Levec. I am twenty winters older in a day.
  Keen. I am sorry for it.
  Levec.   You well may say so.
Has Stephen come?
  Keen.   Some minutes ere yourself.
And with such doleful news as made the light
Fall from these eyelids.
  Levec.   Is all known to all?
  Keen. To both of us.
  Levec.   How did the news affect her?

Keen. Very sadly; she fell backward upon Stephen,
Like one tree lodged in other.
Levec.   'Tis a pity,
But much a weakness of my own inclining.
And yet the man that has no tears within him,
Like a dry well, shows filthily at bottom.
Keen. Men are stiff mould.
Levec.   . Ay, some, but he was not;
I mean, Judge Ford; against this sottish world
He was a star in midnight, very lonely.
'Twere heaven on earth when men that copy him
Pass current in the world.
Keen.   Much to be wept for.

Re-enter CATHARINE *and* STEPHEN.

Cath. I heard your voice within.
Levec.   I am come back
To my firm center. Would I ne'er had parted.
Cath. Is it the truth then? Is my father dead?
Levec. I cannot say you nay.
Cath.   It cannot harm me,
For I have touched the quick of sorrow now.
Levec. Would I could say the like. The sting of
   death,
Goes not so deep as my contrition does.
Cath. Say not so.
Keen.   We cannot dodge our fate.
Levec. No more of this.
Steph.   .   Hark! what's the noise?
Levec. Methinks it is a sweet and comely voice
Comes rapping at the portal of mine ears.
Cath. No, sir, 'tis harsh and loud. Let us step back.
A chill runs in my blood.
Steph.   Look there, look there.

Enter CADE, RATSEY, *and* VERRELL, *with* OFFICERS *and*
   CITIZENS *following.*

Keen. Why are they chained up so? what's the offence?
First Officer. They have murdered Ransom.
First Citizen.   At four o'clock the morning.
Second Citizen. Look! yon tall fellow was the man
that did it.

Cade.   And I would do it again, curse on you all.

Second Officer.   Not with this love-knot on your wrists,
you rogue.

Cade.   You are a cur; a curse on officers!
They are much worse than those they hang upon.
I tell you what, I will bite off your ear —

Second Officer.   Stop up his mouth.

All.   Away to prison with him!
                    (*Exeunt* CADE, *etc, etc.*)

Levec.   The air breathes murder.   Come within the
     house.
We ne'er will part again.

Cath.   I know your meaning,
And sir, I gladly do lean half my sorrow,
And half my faults upon you.

Levec.   O that I
Might prove a worthier underprop to virtue!
But stay, these words fall lightly from a tongue,
That should be charged with heaviness and grief.
And yet, my honor is known to myself,
What matter if the world goes blind to it?

                              (*Exeunt.*)